This book is dedicated to you (yes, you!)
my wonderful readers across the world who
have faithfully followed the Benedict boys,
their soulfinders and their friends through
the ups and downs of their relationships.

Thank you for joining
me for the adventure.

Chapter 1

Sunlight poured through the chapel windows, spilling in colour-flecked ponds a little way from my seat. I was tempted to slip off my shoes and splash in the sunbeams.

Summer, I told myself, *remember where you are; people would think you were crazy.* A run of notes on the organ drew my attention back to the wedding that was soon to start. *No more daydreams.*

King's College Chapel, Cambridge, had never looked so beautiful. Blue and scarlet flowers formed exuberant explosions by the altar. I was sitting alone near the reading lectern, looking on as the seats filled up with friends and family. Despite the groom being from the States and the bride's relatives scattered across the globe, there was a large congregation gathering. I had never seen so many extravagantly dressed people in one place. The bride's friends amongst the theatrical costume and design world had produced an amusing one-upmanship on who could be the most outrageous. So far I gave the prize to a woman wearing a hat that looked like it was a rocket on take-off.

Following the hat's imagined path upwards, I admired the world-famous ceiling, chiselled pale stone in fans of the lightest lacework. That is what a sonnet sequence by Shakespeare would look like if transfigured into an object. A favourite line of poetry floated into my mind: *Like as the waves make towards the pebbl'd shore, So do our minutes hasten to their end . . .*

Pay attention, Summer! Stop being such a nerd. I checked the order of service again, making sure that I had the reading correct. The choice wasn't Sonnet 60 but 116, of course: *Let me not to the marriage of true minds.* The bride and groom had asked me to read under the mistaken belief I was less likely to make a mess of it than either of my best friends. It was true that Misty was prone to blurting out uncomfortable truths thanks to her savant gift, and Angel was easily distracted, but I wasn't sure what I had done to earn the reputation of being the calm public speaker. Most days I felt I was walking a tightrope, only a misstep from disaster.

My gaze met the brass eyes of the eagle that supported a huge Bible on outstretched wings. *You are going to make a hash of the reading,* its expression said, *you'll fumble a word or lose your place.*

I glared back; I shouldn't let an ancient old bird intimidate me. I was a Whelan, which meant 'little wolf' in Irish, so I could eat such carrion for breakfast, hah!

My spirits rose as Angel strode up the aisle looking deceptively cherubic in an amazing peach chiffon dress and matching wedge-soled sandals, strawberry blonde hair shining in a shoulder-length bob. Her arrival caused more than a few heads to turn. That was no surprise because, ever since she had begun her music career, her picture had become familiar in the music press and gossip columns. Not that this had changed her one iota, thankfully.

Angel collapsed into the seat next to me.

'Oh, Summer, I should've listened to you. My feet are killing me already,' she groaned. 'They looked so awesome in the shop though, I couldn't resist.'

I tucked a strand of Angel's hair behind her ear as it kept getting stuck to her lip gloss. 'I thought you were supposed to be an usher.' There was a whole squadron of ushers as nephews too old to be pageboys had been roped in, as well as friends.

Angel snorted with laughter. 'I did ush but I got the sack from Margot as apparently I was distracting Marcus.'

'Distracting him how?'

Angel wiggled her brows.

'Couldn't you restrain yourself, Campbell?' My tone was mock-severe. 'We are at a wedding.'

Angel clasped her hands to her chest. 'I know. And what could be more romantic than watching a Benedict brother finally tie the knot with his gorgeous soulfinder? Of course I had to kiss mine, just to remind him.'

I smiled, pleased but also a little envious of my friend's happiness. After some serious relationship problems when they had first discovered their connection, Angel and Marcus had entered on a smoother phase—though with their character mix they were never far from fireworks. Both were savants, like many of us at the wedding, which meant we had a gift of extra-sensory perception. The powers varied with each individual. In addition to telepathy, which we could all do, Angel could manipulate water and Marcus had a direct connection to people's moods through his music. My gift was quite different in that I could read thoughts; I could also shadow someone through the unique signature of their mind and even take over if I had the stronger will. I hadn't yet met anyone who could do the same. Many savants were rightly suspicious of those of us who could get inside heads so it wasn't something I felt I could discuss with others.

Angel nudged me. 'Summer, look, the headliners have arrived!'

I turned. The seven Benedict brothers had just entered escorting their mother and father to their seats. 'That's some boy band. I thought at a wedding the bride was the main attraction?'

'Not to a girl with a pulse. Don't they look perfect?' The groom had insisted that he couldn't choose between his siblings so they were all his best men. It was going to be a squeeze in the front row. They were dressed in contemporary style suits in various shades of navy blue and grey.

Angel wriggled in her seat. 'If I weren't already linked to the hottest guy on the planet, I think I might just throw myself at them in hopeless adoration.'

'I think Diamond, Tarryn, Margot, Crystal, Phoenix, and Sky might object,' I said, listing the Benedict soulfinders on my fingers. 'I'd hate to see the bride get blood on her gown as she bops you on the nose.'

Angel chuckled. 'Oh well, it would have to be Victor then.'

My gaze moved to the third of the brothers, the most guarded of them. Victor's dark hair was longer than his brothers' but swept back from his forehead for this formal occasion. A new departure for him was a neat beard outlining his jaw—it suited him. His three-piece was silver grey, tie almost night-sky blue. Misty, Angel, and I considered him an enigma and often speculated about him. We all admitted that we got a pleasurable tingle down the spine when talking about him, as he was a winning combination of being dangerous and very easy on the eye. Working for the FBI on savant liaison, his job called for him to play his cards close to his chest, but there was something unknowable about him. He was the most powerful mind-controller that I had ever met, though he kept his skill on a short leash. Like I did. Birds of a feather, Victor and I, but he didn't flock together with me or anyone as far as I could tell.

'Not sure about the beard—hmm, yeah, maybe. I'll just have to get used to it. He doesn't look very happy, does he?' said Angel, also studying Victor.

'Would you be? All your brothers have their happy ending

with their soulfinders and you are left as the only one alone.'
I also knew a little how that isolation felt, now that my best
friends were paired up, Angel with Marcus and Misty with
Alex. 'This wedding must be a kind of torture to anyone
without a soulfinder.'

Angel shot me a shrewd look. 'Is he going to be OK, do you
think? He got a tough break when Crystal told him where his
soulfinder is—behind bars in Afghanistan.'

No one should be unhappy at this wedding. I dipped into
my gift for a second, looking for a way to cheer him up. Victor
shielded his mind from most people, keeping his energy levels
low, but I had never told him I could get past that blockade.
He concentrated on stopping people reading him but my
power lay in getting inside undetected, like parachuting at
night behind enemy lines. I hadn't yet met anyone I couldn't
read.

'Oh.' What I found was chilling—an expanse of grey seas
under stormy skies. 'Oh. He's in a very dark place.'

Angel turned to me, blue eyes wide. 'Oh my God, you can
see inside Victor? No, that's impossible!'

It was always embarrassing to admit to my skills. I didn't
want to sound like a Peeping Tom. 'I'm only reading general
impressions, not digging into secrets.'

'Dark? What way dark?'

I gently disengaged, not wanting Victor to know I had
visited. He would hate that, and perhaps I shouldn't have
snooped, even with the best intentions. 'Like a storm about
to break.'

The organ struck up 'The Arrival of the Queen of Sheba',
the signal that the bride was ready. The congregation rose to
their feet.

'Tell me more later,' whispered Angel.

I rubbed my bare upper arms. 'No more to tell. I won't pry

any deeper without permission, you know that. Just let's be really nice to him today, OK?'

'Be nice to Victor? For me, that means keeping out of his way. He thinks I'm a liability.' Angel tapped her shoe against mine. 'He thinks you're an asset though. You talk to him.'

I couldn't reply as Crystal had appeared at the far end of the aisle on the arm of her favourite brother, Peter, surrounded by her attendants. Their father had died a few years ago and the Brooks were holding the wedding in his old college as a way of making him feel close to the family at this special time.

'Oh my! That's how I want to look when I get married,' sighed Angel as Crystal stepped properly into view.

She was wearing a tall column of a dress, white silk in soft pleats across a bodice with halter-neck strap, skirts falling from a clasp on her hip and a swirling train. Her spiralling dark blonde hair was caught up with a light veil streaming down her back. She looked both classic and modern at the same time, like a beautiful Greek goddess statue come to life. Her bouquet was a spiky clutch of exotic flowers in red and blue— no mild roses and orange blossom for her.

'So that's what she'd been keeping a secret,' I said, admiring her handiwork. She had made her own gown and designed the ones for the bridesmaids and pages. They followed in a little fleet, smallest to tallest. The littlest girl was in a ballerina-style blue dress and the colours of the rest went through the spectrum to a muted frost-grey worn by the older attendants, Misty, Phoenix and Sky. The three of them looked elegant in strapless gowns echoing the column shape of the bride's.

Angel bobbed on her toes to peer past me. 'Xav is going to swallow his tongue.'

I switched my attention to the row of Benedicts. Xav was staring ahead at the altar, expression revealing how daunted he felt, but on a nudge from Zed next to him, he turned. His look of awe and wonder was so beautiful it brought tears to my eyes. I wasn't embarrassed by giving in to sentiment: if I couldn't go all marshmallow when a very good friend got married, when could I?

'And that's how I'd like my soulfinder to look at me,' I murmured.

Angel squeezed my hand in sympathy and dipped into telepathy. *He will*, she promised.

After a perfect service and sumptuous meal served in a marquee on the lawns by the banks of the Cam, the reception began to relax from formal to fun. Peter gave a lovely heartfelt speech about how special Crystal was to the Brook family, and how proud they all were of her. Predictably, Xav had us all laughing the moment he started talking. Crystal also insisted that they break with tradition and allow the bride a few words, and she gave as good as she got from Xav. The best men's speech was a stand-up routine as Xav's reputation was gently destroyed then put lovingly back together by his brothers. Only Victor didn't take part in the banter, reserving the role as proposer of the toast to the bridesmaids for himself.

I couldn't completely relax. Victor's mood had grown even darker; it hovered at the edge of my consciousness even when I wasn't trying to sense him.

Then the band set up on the stage at the far end of the dance floor. This was no ordinary set of jobbing musicians hired for the occasion. Weeks before the wedding, Angel and Marcus had begun arguing which of their two groups would have the honour of playing at the reception until finally Margot, soulfinder of Xav's brother, Will, had cut through with an order that they both would be playing, but with rock star legend, Kurt Voss, on lead vocals. Sky was backing them on keyboard and saxophone, Zed on drums. This impromptu band were amazing—helped no doubt by the special chemistry that sizzled through the music when Marcus was using his gift. If three of them hadn't already had recording contracts, the group—styling themselves The Soulseekers in honour of Crystal's gift—would have had a dazzling future in front of them.

'Just make sure none of this gets on YouTube, people,' said Kurt as he played a cover of 'Hey, Soul Sister' at Xav's request.

Refilling my glass, I wandered around the edge of the dance floor looking for Victor. I found him by the exit watching his brothers and parents dance with their soulfinders. Savant gifts come with a price attached: at the same time as you are conceived, someone elsewhere in the world also receives the matching half of your power. Mostly that combination is amazing, like Misty with Alex, her truth-telling matched with his persuasive power, each shaping and augmenting the other. Yet there is also a darker side. You might never find your partner, or find them and discover that their gift has turned sour. That happened to Alex's mother and . . . I didn't let myself finish the thought.

'Hey, Victor.' I stood at his side, not pushing. He wouldn't like that.

He turned towards me, mood lightening a little. 'Summer. You doing OK?' He nodded at the dancing couples. Diamond, Crystal's sister, was swaying dreamily in the arms of Trace, the oldest of the Benedict brothers. Was that a little baby bump revealed by her sky-blue silk dress? When were they going to tell us about that?

I blinked away some tears. Ridiculous to get all choked up about the prospect of a next generation of the Benedicts. 'I'm fine, thanks. You have to be happy for them, don't you?'

'It's good to see my brothers so well matched. I won't worry about any of them again.'

'Of course you will. You may be third in age but you have big brother mentality encoded in your DNA.'

He smiled. 'How about you? I don't know much about your background. Do you have brothers and sisters? You seem very responsible for seventeen.'

That wasn't a role I had ever been able to duck. 'I have an older brother.' I didn't like talking about my family but I could hardly persuade Victor to confide in me if I refused to answer the most straightforward questions.

'A savant?'

'Yes, he is, but Winter isn't well.'

'Is it serious?'

'You could say.' I could tell he was waiting for me to expand. 'It's mental, his illness. He hears things, echoes of voices that have once spoken in a place—part of his gift that he never learned to control. It gets so noisy in his head, he's not very good at telling reality apart from all those ghost speakers. It's like he has no filter.'

Victor lightly pressed my arm then let go. 'I'm sorry. I think we both know that savants with mental illnesses really have the hardest time.'

'Thank you. It's difficult for me to talk about. I wish I could help him but he has a particular problem with me.'

'Because you can see inside.'

'Yes. He knows I can see how little control he has over the voices he hears and that shames him. It shouldn't, but it does.'

Victor nodded as if he knew what that was like. 'Tough for your parents too.'

If only he knew. 'So, are you OK?' Having given something of myself I felt I had a right to ask.

'You're sweet, you know, Summer? I'm all right—or will be.' He looked down into the beer he had forgotten he was drinking. 'Let's toast ourselves: to the misunderstood.' He raised his glass.

Goosebumps pricked my bare skin at the hint that he could read me as well as I could read him. With a bright smile, I chinked my fizzy elderflower against his tumbler. Our job today was to pretend we were OK.

'To the misunderstood.'

Chapter 2

'I've left the caterers in the kitchen, Miss Whelan. Have you got everything you need?' Mrs Bainbridge, our housekeeper, hovered by the front door, shopping bag slung over her shoulder. She knew it was going to be a difficult evening for me.

'Yes, thank you. I'll be fine.' I smoothed down the black dress I'd chosen for entertaining my father's clients. 'We've used this company before, haven't we? If I remember rightly, they're good.'

'Very efficient. Your guests are due at seven-thirty. I've already set out the drinks tray and nibbles in the drawing room. Coffee and mints are on the sideboard in the dining room. I've shown the chef and she'll tell the wait staff.'

'Good. I'll make sure it all runs smoothly.'

Mrs Bainbridge patted the car keys in her pocket nervously. 'I could stay.'

Part of me wanted to plead with her to do so. 'No, it's fine. You've promised your daughter you'd visit her tonight with the groceries. You don't become a grandmother every day. You go.'

'But your mother—'

'I'll . . .' I'll do what? 'I'll make sure she keeps calm.'

'I left her with a stack of magazines and the remote within reach. She should be settled for the night. I just hope it isn't one of her evenings when she thinks she should join you.'

'Well, if she does, then she does. Please, don't worry.'

Mrs Bainbridge knew all about our family problems, being a savant herself, skilled in dampening down emotions. I don't think I would have survived if Dad hadn't found her three years ago. He paid her well for her silence but I knew her care for me went beyond a financial transaction. 'Oh, pet, I wish I could do more to help.' She gave me a quick hug, a little awkward as we were a formal family and my dad disapproved of me treating the housekeeper as a surrogate mother.

'You do more than enough. Really, you do.'

'See you on Monday then.'

'Yes.'

With a sinking feeling, I watched her hurry off to her car parked around the side of the house. Dad didn't like her battered old Ford out where people could see it in case they mistook it for one of our cars. Gainsborough Gardens near Hampstead Heath, a pretty road of late Victorian detached villas with large gardens and mature trees, was the kind of street that worried about appearances; if you had anything less than a Mercedes you were breaking the unwritten code of conduct. I was sorely tempted to invite Angel to park her psychedelic tour bus on our forecourt.

I ducked into the kitchen to check on preparations. All seemed in hand. I glanced at my bracelet watch. Dad was cutting it fine if he was going to get back before his guests started arriving. I sent him a quick text but there was no reply. He was probably stuck in traffic. I breathed through the bubble of panic in my chest. Nothing I could do. He would expect me to offer drinks and make his guests feel at home. I had presided over his client evenings for three years now; I knew what was required.

My phone chimed with a message from Angel.

Free evening at last. Marcus and I are going to cinema. Do you want to come? You can pick the film.

I would much prefer to go eat popcorn with my friends but duty called. *Sorry. Dinner party.*

Bad luck. Love you. Hugs. xxx

I was fortunate that my friends put up with me placing home demands before them. I was aware that they knew something was not right but so far I'd managed to keep them out of the worst of it. My family was toxic and I had to limit the spread of the pollution.

Have fun. x

I put the phone on charge so I wouldn't be tempted to carry on messaging all evening. Dad had made it clear that wasn't the behaviour he expected from me. His family came from two traditional families, Irish on his dad's side and Pakistani on his mother's. He had been raised the old-fashioned way to expect daughterly obedience and showed no sign of moving with the times. He always added that if I wanted him to pay my phone bills then I had to play by his rules.

Sometimes I just wanted to walk out the door and not come back. I could see myself doing it, disappearing down a starlit road, leaving the goose-feather bed and following the raggle-taggle gypsies of the Scottish folk song.

Work through the panic. It's not that bad tonight. Don't go off the deep end just because you can't do what you want all the time.

The desperation subsided, locked back behind the cage door in my chest.

Back to the business at hand. Look in on Mother.

I took the stairs to the first floor where she had a sitting room, and tapped on the door.

'Yes?'

Checking my shields were in place, I entered.

'Summer.' Mother didn't smile but beckoned me closer. She had her feet up on the daybed, and was wearing an ankle-length red caftan and layers of clicking beads. With her long black hair and dramatic dark eyebrows—a feature she had given me—she looked more like a character from fiction, an Indian princess or fortune teller. That fitted with her background, a mixture of Irish and Breton. Many of her forebears had travelled with European circuses, using their talents in the most overt way possible without detection. Her room was decorated in oxblood red, walls covered in framed photos of Edwardian fairground characters, clutter everywhere from potted ferns and a screen made up of old postcards varnished to the surface. She had asked the designer for Bohemian but I always found the result oppressive and as far from true Bohemian freedom as you could get.

I leant over Mother and gave her a brief kiss on the cheek. She caught my wrist in her bony grip, fingers like sticks. Hadn't she been eating properly? I'd have to check with Mrs Bainbridge that Mother wasn't hiding her food somehow like she had in the past.

'How are you tonight, Mother?'

'Bored.' Her nails stroked my wrist feeling for the pulse point. I tried to keep my heartbeat smooth but adrenaline was coursing through my veins at her answer. Bored meant trouble.

'You've got your magazines—and there's bound to be something on television.' I kept my voice light.

'Nothing I want to watch. You sit with me, Summer. Tell me what you've been doing. I hardly see you these days.'

I licked my lips. 'I've been reading in preparation for the new school year next week.'

She let go. 'Studying—always studying. What about the things that really matter? Friends—boyfriends?'

I had to keep those things away from her. 'No one special. Just a few friends from school, but I told you—we're not close.'

'You should bring them home—let me meet them.'

Like that was going to happen, not in a million years. 'I'll see.'

'I'm so empty here. Your father doesn't let me meet anyone new.'

For their own safety. 'Can I get you anything?'

'Let me have a little taste.' She rubbed my arm again. 'Lift your shield for a moment. I can't feel anything unless you let me in.'

Oh God. 'That's not a good idea, Mother. You know what it does to us both.'

She tugged at her beads fretfully, a prisoner testing her chains. 'I'm not an addict. Your father's wrong.'

No, he was right. She was hooked on absorbing the emotions of other people, getting high on their feelings to the extent that she had deadened her own. When she latched on, she could suck feelings out of you, leaving you weakened; on rare occasions the damage was permanent leaving the victim empty, the emotion never returning. People like my mother were the vampires of the savant world, as much as it hurt me to admit it. Dad had explained that she couldn't help it, that we had to protect her and not give in to her addiction even if it seemed the easier path. If we didn't stick to a firm line she would have to be sent away— to where he never specified—but somehow I always knew he would consider it would be my fault if we reached that point. I had been born to help him cope, he said.

'Mother, you don't need my emotions. I have to go. Mrs Bainbridge told you about the guests?'

She waved that away with her scarlet-tipped nails. 'Yes, yes, boring bankers and stockbrokers, not an interesting feeling among them, just greed, which gives me indigestion.' She gave me an assessing look. 'You're thinking of wearing that? The colour does nothing for you.'

There it was again, the constant chipping away at my self-esteem. It had taken me years to see what she was doing. She wanted me to be upset so she could feel it. 'I like it.'

15

'You look tired.'

Yes, I was tired—soul-deep tired of managing her needs. 'I'll be fine. See you tomorrow.'

She shrugged and picked up one of her glossy magazines. 'Maybe.'

'No, really, tomorrow. Please.'

The doorbell rang.

She looked up with a distant smile. 'Hadn't you better run and answer that?'

Not sure it was safe to leave her, I hurried to the door.

'Mr and Mrs Anderson, sorry to keep you waiting.' I stepped back to let the couple in.

'We met your father parking the car. He said to tell you he'd be with us in a moment,' said Mr Anderson, a jovial colleague of Dad's from the City. I was never sure what any of them did beyond knowing that my dad's gift with numbers made him a legend in investment circles. Willowy Mrs Anderson, however, was much more of a known quantity as she also happened to be my English teacher.

Mrs Anderson, may I take your coat?'

'Thank you, Summer. Looking forward to the new term?'

'Yes, very much. I've read all the Virginia Woolf novels you recommended.'

She laughed. 'All? I rather meant the class to pick one or two, but I suppose I should've expected you to be several steps ahead. Don't forget, if you want to apply for Oxbridge you've got to do that immediately when we get back.'

I hung her jacket on a wooden hanger and placed it in the large hall cupboard. 'Oh, I'm not sure I'll put in for that.' Dad had said he wasn't in favour of me going to university, at least not one out of London.

'It would be a criminal waste of your brain if you don't apply.'

16

'Dad isn't sure the time is right.' I led them into the lounge where the drinks were waiting.

'You mean he wants you to take a year out?' Mrs Anderson wandered the room, brushing her fingers over the floral arrangements on the side table. A petal fell off a lily so she stopped. 'It's a good idea for those who need to grow up a little before taking on more studying, but I wouldn't put you in that category.'

'What category is that?' asked my father, coming in from the garage. He shook hands with Mr Anderson and kissed Mrs Anderson on the cheek.

'That of exceptionally talented young lady. We were just talking about what college Summer is going to apply to, Aidan.'

My dad gave me a strained smile. 'Summer hasn't made up her mind yet what she wants to do.'

I had but he didn't agree with my decision. The only thing I hadn't made up my mind about was whether I was going to defy him.

'Is everything under control with the caterers, Summer?' he asked, giving me the hint that he wanted me out of the room and the subject changed.

'I'll just go and see.' Brittle with anger at his life-limiting attitude, I left the room and hid in the kitchen while the rest of Dad's guests arrived. I scrolled through my telephone messages as an excuse for my presence in this hive of activity, vegetables draining at the huge double sink, croutons frying on the gas burner, parmesan being grated on a wooden board. Part of me knew that I would have to make a break from home—I wasn't stupid or so feeble that I couldn't see how Dad was manipulating me—but the prospect was terrifying. He would blame me for anything that went wrong afterwards with Mother or Winter; he'd say I had abandoned him, punish me by cutting me off, probably hoping I'd crawl back. Withdrawal of money wasn't the issue—I'd take a student loan, work part-time like others did—but did I really want to lose my family as the cost of going to read literature for three years somewhere beautiful and, more importantly, away from here? I could fold, do what he wanted and take a course at University College London—they had a great English literature department—but then I'd be expected to live at home so my life wouldn't change. The burden would still rest on my shoulders. Once upon a time Dad used to carry the responsibility but, as soon as I reached ten he considered me old enough and had passed it over with the excuse that he had to earn our living. I'm not sure he even realized what he had done: made me into my mother's carer and, far too often, gaoler. His life was a mess and a disappointment to him. Being linked to an off-kilter soulfinder was like living with a fairy-tale curse that you couldn't break. I felt sorry for him, I really did, but I also felt a little bit sorry for myself that I was their daughter.

The chef was shooting me 'what are you doing in here?' looks. I think she thought I doubted her abilities. 'You can tell your father we are ready to serve, if convenient with him,' she said snippily. 'I need to keep the doorway clear for the serving staff.'

Doing a U-turn on my earlier resolve, I switched the phone to silent and slipped it into my pocket. It spoiled the line of my dress but right then I needed to feel as though my friends were only a text away. 'I'll let him know.'

The eight guests were chatting happily in the drawing room unaware of the threat over their heads and the stormy emotions choking the throat of their young hostess. I didn't need my power to read their thoughts: envy of my father's success, puzzlement as to why they never got to meet the mysterious Mrs Whelan—I caught Mrs Anderson picturing a *Jane Eyre* scenario which wasn't far from the truth—and eagerness to get down to the financial talk, which was why most of them were here.

'Dinner is ready if you'd like to go through now,' I announced.

'Thank you, Summer.' My dad patted me on the shoulder in a show of fatherly appreciation. 'For those of you who haven't met her yet, this is my little ray of sunshine, my daughter, Summer.'

I said a shy hello to the strangers.

'She's charming,' said one lady banker. 'Have you any other children, Aidan?'

'A son, but he's away at university,' lied my father. Winter was actually living a precarious existence in a newly built flat in East London where there were no old voices to haunt him.

'Does he take after you—is he a wizard at numbers?' asked another.

No, he was a wizard at attracting other dropouts and danger. But, of course, I didn't say that.

'Unfortunately not.' My dad gave a false laugh. 'But each to his own, eh? At least my children won't have to worry too much about the first down payment on a house round here, thanks to their old man.' He deftly shifted the subject to the perennial favourite of rising property prices.

I followed the guests into the dining room. The pink roses in the bowls down the centre looked pretty but restrained; I felt a pang of regret that they couldn't be the exotic blooms that had featured in Crystal's bouquet. By some quirk, I had been the one to catch it when she had tossed it into the crowd. Not seeing any prospect of me being next to be married, I had taken that as a sign that Crystal hoped I would press the flowers and send them to her when she returned from her honeymoon on Zanzibar. She knew I'd think of that kind of detail. Besides, Uriel and Tarryn were due to be married in

Colorado this autumn, so we already knew who would be next.

'And what do you do, Summer?' the lady at my side asked me. Mrs Dupont, I reminded myself, CEO of an internet firm specializing in medical equipment.

'I'm still at school and entering my last year.'

'Oh? You look so grown-up and sophisticated I would have put you down as twenty at least.' She laughed a little at her mistake. 'Not that you look old, I must tell you, but because you have an air of a much older person about you, a young Audrey Hepburn, but I can't be the first person to tell you that. My own daughter is about your age and has gone the spikes-in-the-earlobes-and-too-much-eye-liner route. She wants to go to art school.'

Good for her daughter. 'We each pick our own path, I guess.'

'I was a bit of a rebel myself so can hardly complain, difficult though that is to imagine now.' Her eyes twinkled as if she hoped I'd see the revolutionary still lurking inside the business suit. 'It's not until we have to think of someone else that we settle down, is it?'

'You're probably right.'

'Lovely soup. I do like a cold soup at this time of year.'

As I was about to make a suitable reply, the door from the hallway opened and my mother came in, a gash of red in the cool white room. I froze with horror, mind spinning uselessly looking for a way out.

'Oh, darlings, I didn't know we had guests,' she said with a confident waft of her arms, a prima donna entering for her aria. 'No, no, please don't get up. I'll find my own chair.' She pulled one standing by the side of the room next to me, edging me out of the hostess position. 'Aidan, introduce me.' She took my glass and filled it with wine from the bottle sitting in a cooler.

The guests' eyes were round with shock at the interruption. Mrs Anderson was the first to rouse herself.

'Mrs Whelan, lovely to meet you at long last. I'm Moira Anderson. I teach your daughter at St Winifred's. She's my top English student by quite some margin.'

'She is?' My mother eyed the teacher, seeing someone who wasn't a boring banker but a rather more intriguing emotional creature interested in the arts.

'Summer,' growled my father as if this was somehow my fault. 'Ladies and gentleman, I'm very sorry for this interruption. As you can see, my wife is not entirely well at the moment and should be resting.'

'Oh, Aidan, you old fool, I'm perfectly well this evening.' Her green eyes shot sparks at my father.

'Summer, take your mother back upstairs.'

I swallowed. His words were an order to use my gift to take over my mother's will and force her from the room. This was the dark part of my power that I never liked to employ. It involved becoming one with the subject and was horrible for both of us. I tried reason first. 'Please, Mother, it's best if you rest tonight.'

She looked at me as if I were a beetle she was considering crushing. She had long since ceased to love me; she only had room for loving her addiction. 'I'm the adult here, Summer. You don't get to tell me what to do.'

My father's expression radiated white-hot fury and Mother would soon start dining on it if I didn't stop her. She would get unbearably high and he would lose control. I'm not sure what he would do if I refused to solve this embarrassment for him; Mother hadn't confronted him while he had business clients for years, so he had ceased to expect it.

'You mustn't worry for our sakes, Aidan,' said Mrs Anderson, letting him know that they would understand the tricky position he was in. The other guests, less involved with our family, did not look so forgiving. One or two were glancing at their Swiss-made watches.

'Mother, come with me please.' This time I slipped the leash on my gift and merged with her mind. I already knew her brain signature so was not shocked as I had been the first time by the strong appetites raging there. It was a nightmarish place but I knew I was strong enough to control her rather than let her control me. 'Let's go.'

Docile now, expression in her eyes fading to dreamy calm, she took my hand and followed me like a lamb from the room. I hated this. I took her up to her bedroom.

'You are feeling very tired. You want to go to sleep.'

'That's right. I want to go to sleep,' she repeated, slipping under the duvet still wearing her clothes. I took off her shoes and necklaces so she would be more comfortable. I curled the beads like a nest of serpents on the side table.

'Goodnight. I'll see you in the morning.'

'Goodnight, Summer.' Her eyes fluttered closed. Once sleep engulfed her, quieting the sharp pangs of her desires, I disengaged. Light-headed after the buffeting from her addiction, I gripped the bedhead. Emerging from her mind always left me like this: sickened, drained, somehow tainted. I needed a shower to wash it away. Dad could manage his guests himself for the rest of the evening. This gaoler was going off duty.

Chapter 3

The doorbell rang, a distant trill downstairs, deadened by the duvet and pillow over my head. Checking my alarm clock, I saw it was only six-thirty. I wasn't expecting anyone and no staff were in today so it was most probably a delivery. Dad's guests had left at midnight, meaning he was unlikely to be awake to answer; I had to get there before my mother took it into her head to go down. I slid out of bed and pulled on a silk kimono my great-grandmother had once sent me from Singapore, a bold golden dragon on the back. I often imagined it as my protector.

The bell rang again, this time more insistently.

'All right, I'm coming!' I called, a little annoyed at the impatience. What did the company expect if they tried to deliver parcels so early in the day? I ran down the stairs, silk flying like a superhero cloak behind me, to open the door.

'Why didn't you answer my texts or telepathy?' Angel burst out the moment she saw me.

Angel, Marcus, Misty and Alex were all standing on the doorstep.

'What?' I ran my fingers through my hair. I really hadn't got my brain in gear yet. 'I was asleep.'

'But I've been texting you for the last hour!'

'I . . . I think I put it on silent last night, for the dinner party, and didn't remember to change it back.'

'But you never forget to do that kind of thing!'

Marcus, a tall blond god of a rock star, pulled Angel back a little. 'Give Summer a moment. Not being in contact twenty-four seven isn't a crime.'

My thoughts began to click into place. Angel and Misty were both radiating extreme distress, the boys were disturbed and worried. 'Oh God, has someone died?'

'Can we come in?' asked Alex, his soft South African accent soothing us. He was pushing a little with his persuasive gift to put us all on a more even keel.

I glanced behind me. My mother's appearances were never predictable and these were the four people in the world I most wanted to protect. 'Is there somewhere else we can go?'

Misty grabbed my hand. 'No time. We've got to fill you in now and you have to come with us. I know you told us never to visit you at home but this is an emergency.'

If Misty was telling me this then it was the truth. I couldn't leave them standing on the doorstep. 'Let's go into the kitchen.' Mother hardly ever went in there. 'I'll get dressed. If anyone comes in, can you . . . can you say you're the caterers tidying up from last night? Not you, Misty, obviously, I know you can't lie, but the rest of you?'

They exchanged a puzzled look. I could hear a few stray thoughts as to whether I was ashamed of them. That was so far from the truth it was darkly funny.

'Yes, we'll do that. Don't worry,' said Angel, stepping inside.

'We'll make coffee, or tea if you prefer,' offered Marcus.

'Tea for me. Keep opening cupboards until you find what you need.'

Leaving them standing by the long kitchen counter that had already been scrupulously cleaned by the crew last night, I dashed back upstairs. My mother, with her usual nose for trouble, came out of her bedroom. She looked as hungover as I did, the usual after-effect of me taking control of her.

'I heard the doorbell. Who is it?' she asked.

'Cleaning crew.' I watched with a sick feeling to see which way she would go.

She sniffed the air. 'What kind?' She meant what emotions were available for her to sip. The intense feelings coming from my friends would be a feast for her if she followed the trail to the kitchen.

'A couple of Ukrainians, you won't understand them. They look bored and I think they are chatting about visa problems.' Nothing was more tedious than discussions of governmental bureaucracy.

'Oh.' Her fingernails did a little scratchy drum roll on the doorframe. 'You owe me, Summer, for what you did to me last night.'

'Yes, I know, I'm sorry, but you know what Dad is like.'

'You don't have to obey him. You could rebel.' Her eyes brightened as she scented the possibility of a new kind of emotion from me.

'Yes, I could, but right now I need to get dressed so I can open the outside storeroom for them. They want the floor polisher.' *Be boring, be boring*, I told myself.

'You have to pay me back later.'

'I don't think I can do that.'

'You obey your father but not me? I'm your mother!'

Who wanted to suck my emotions dry. I couldn't afford a long argument with her which would increase the risk the others would come looking for me or, worse, cause me to lose control and drop my shields, giving her the flood of feeling she craved. I took a deep breath. 'I know you're my mother. Let me just get the cleaners working and I'll come up and talk it through with you. I'll bring you some breakfast at the same time.'

She hovered, undecided.

'I think there are waffles.'

25

'All right then. With butter, not maple syrup.'

'Yes, I remember.'

With immense relief, I watched her return to her room, disaster averted once more. I grabbed some clothes from my wardrobe, had a quick wash and I was ready to go back down. My heart was racing, not only because I was worried my mother would change her mind, but also because whatever news had brought them to my door was bound to be bad.

My friends were seated around a small table in the window looking out at the swimming pool in the garden.

'You have a lovely house,' said Alex, pushing out a fifth chair for me.

I was shaking a little as I sat. 'Thank you.' I could tell they were all wondering why I never invited them here before. I'd spent a lot of time at Misty and Angel's homes, neither of which had a pool or all this space. It wasn't the house I was ashamed of though. 'You'd better fill me in.'

'It's Victor,' said Angel. 'He's gone AWOL.'

Of course it was. As soon as she said his name, I knew what was coming. 'He's gone to his soulfinder.'

'We think so. But that's not the main problem. When I say AWOL, I mean it literally: absent without leave. He is a senior agent in the FBI and considered by the American government a top security risk.'

'They've kept him from going before now by saying he would endanger more than his own life if he is captured by one of the rebel groups operating in the area,' explained Misty. 'They promised to help him through their diplomatic contacts but that never materialized. There's too much going on in Afghanistan to worry about one private matter.'

'We think he just snapped and decided to go alone,' said Alex.

'You sensed it, didn't you, at the wedding?' asked Angel. 'A storm about to break, you said.'

26

'I suppose I did, but I had no idea—'

'Of course you didn't,' said Marcus, putting an arm around his soulfinder. 'We should've seen the clues for ourselves.'

'He'd grown a beard,' I murmured.

'And Uriel told me that Victor's been doing an intensive Dari language course. He said it was the language used by most Afghans.'

'Yes, yes it is. There are lots of local languages but most people can speak it.' My Pakistani relatives had explained that to me when I had asked about their western neighbour. I had been trying to find out as much as I could since learning where Victor's soulfinder lived, hoping I'd be able to help him. I'd never visited these cousins but they came by to see Dad on trips to London and were quite eloquent about the difficulties of travelling in the region. The north was more stable but the south was a cauldron of conflicts.

'The Benedicts all thought that it was a sensible preparation, that Victor had a well thought-out plan in hand with the help of his employer, but now he's off, with no official sanction and without telling anyone,' continued Misty.

'In fact, Trace says that some of the Feds want to arrest him. They think he's gone rogue,' said Alex. 'He's in deep trouble when they catch up with him.'

'But he wouldn't care about that, would he, if it meant he found his soulfinder? I wouldn't,' said Marcus, who until a few months ago had not even heard of the concept. Angel had converted him to its importance in the life of a savant.

I cradled the mug of tea, letting the warmth seep into my palms. 'How far has he got?'

'No one knows. You wouldn't expect him to leave a trail, would you? This is Victor Benedict we're talking about, not Hansel and Gretel,' said Alex.

The news was serious but that still didn't explain why they

were here and not just sending me texts. 'I'm really sorry to hear all this. Karla and Saul must be going crazy with worry.' I had always liked the Benedict parents and had sometimes wished I could be adopted by them. I took a sip then pushed the mug away. 'I've got to make breakfast for my mother. Anyone else want waffles?'

Angel grabbed my sleeve. 'There's no time for cooking. You've got to come with us. The Benedicts need you.'

'I'm sorry, but I really have to do this. You don't understand. My mother isn't . . . isn't quite right in her head and I have to keep her calm.' That was as much as I ever would tell them about it.

'Then let us do the cooking while you listen,' said Misty, moving towards the stove.

Alex headed her off. 'You stay with Summer and explain what we want from her and I'll make the waffles. It's safer that way.'

She grinned at him. Her inept moments were legend. 'Aw, looks, brains and he can cook! Does it get any better?'

He shook his head at her as he put on an apron. 'Watch it, or you won't get any.'

'There's batter in the fridge and a waffle iron in the pan drawer. Mother eats hers with butter.' I sat back down. 'OK, explain.'

Marcus got up to help Alex, leaving me with my two friends.

'It's my fault,' said Angel. 'But I thought you wouldn't mind when you knew how serious it is. The Benedicts asked Crystal to try and find him—you know how she can locate things through her soulseeker power?'

I nodded.

'Victor disappears from her radar when he puts up a strong shield. Everyone had gathered at Misty's house to Skype her; Marcus and I had gone round there after the film, so we listened in. Crystal was really upset she couldn't sense Victor and it was really hard to do any detecting from Tanzania as she had to jump from Xav to Victor and the link was really frail, ending in a blank wall. She and Xav are threatening to cut short their honeymoon. They've only been there a few days and none of us want that. So I kinda blurted out that you could mind-shadow Victor without him knowing.'

I could see where this was going. 'But not over great distances—not like Crystal.'

'Yes, but we know roughly where he is, don't we? Crystal has given him some more clues over the last few months to help him narrow his search. She repeated what she told him to us and Uriel is piecing the information together. We think it likely we can work out where Victor planned to start. There are only a few savants registered in Afghanistan so we think the network there is quite small. We just have to hope his soulfinder is known to them. Find her and we find Victor.'

The sweet smell of waffles wafted our way but I didn't even feel hungry. 'Are you seriously suggesting that I go after him?'

'Not on your own, of course,' said Angel. 'But the Benedicts are putting together a team to reach him before the Feds catch up with him or, worse, some anti-western elements among the locals realize they've got a very interesting person on their hands. The Benedicts want you to pinpoint him so they can go in and get him out, hopefully with his soulfinder, and have him back in America before too much harm is done to his reputation.'

I put my head in my hands. My life couldn't absorb a sudden rash plan to run off to Afghanistan. I had my fragile home, school next week, my safety to consider. Dad would never agree in a million years. My friends had to be caught up in the frenzy of worry not to see just how unlikely it was that I could throw myself into the mix.

'We can help smooth the way,' said Misty, brushing her fingers over my bent back. 'Alex will persuade your parents it's a good idea. He can talk to your school—get permission for you to go on an educational trip for a week.'

'You don't know what you are talking about.' I was never usually this blunt but my distress was extreme. 'Mind-shadowing isn't like telepathy; it works over a much shorter range. I have to be within sensing distance of the person—that's a few miles at most. Afghanistan borders five or six countries, he could enter from hundreds of different directions. The only viable strategy is to get ahead of him and wait in the place you think he's heading for. This won't take less than a week, maybe a lot longer, and it could be really dangerous.' I said this knowing I was just being sensible, but somehow they all made me feel like I was being mean. The Benedicts had risked so much for the savant community and I was shying away from helping them in this crisis because I was . . . what? Scared stiff? Even as I spoke my doubts, I knew that I wouldn't be able to back away from this. But how, realistically, could I go with the responsibilities of home resting on me? It would be like removing too many Jenga bricks and having the tower fall if I went away.

Misty wasn't following my inner debate though, so took my words at face value. I could feel her cooling, withdrawing a little in disappointment. 'I suppose it is a huge ask, and I hadn't understood that it might be dangerous for you. No, of course, you shouldn't go. Why should you? I mean, Victor isn't a relation or anything.'

Angel looked disgusted at my prevarication. She was more a jump-right-in kind of person. If she thought she could help, she would be on the first plane to Kabul. Her bravery made

30

me feel worse. 'He's a friend, Summer. He's always been there for us and other savants. Just two years ago he took down the biggest international network of criminal savants pretty much on his own, and freed Phoenix from the Seer in the process. I'm sure since then he's done many other good things that he hasn't told us about. He doesn't have to be a relative to be worth saving.'

'He was there for me when Alex's uncle tried to kill me,' said Misty.

'And me, when the anti-savant gang snatched me,' added Angel.

My bottom lip began to quiver and tears filled my eyes. They were going to hate me if I refused to go. I squeezed my elbows, putting a cramp on my emotions. 'You don't understand.'

'Then help us understand.' Angel folded her arms and cocked her head to one side, echoing my position, challenging me.

I had never wanted to admit to the truth about my family. I was so deeply ashamed of my parentage, even though Dad had always stressed my mother couldn't help herself. 'I have to be here to look after my mother.'

Misty frowned. 'If it's money you need for a nurse, Yves and Phoenix can see to that. You know they've got the funds.'

'Is she, like, near to the end or something?' asked Angel, now worried for me.

'No, it's more of a long-lasting problem.' I laced my fingers together and pressed them to my lips, trying to keep the words inside. Was I finally going to tell them? Would they treat me with more suspicion once they knew the truth? Everyone who had that vampire strain of savant gift in their family met with fear and loathing from others; no one wanted to pass that on to their children. No, I didn't want them to know.

31

'Then what's the obstacle to going away for a while?' Angel asked reasonably.

Alex carried a plate of waffles to the table and placed it between us. 'Dig in. I've got a tray for your mother. Do you want me to carry it up to her?'

I leapt to my feet. 'I'll take it. Don't wait for me. Eat them while they're hot.' I hurried out of the room, carrying more than just the tray as I now had a whole new load of self-disgust to add to the pile.

'Summer, thank you, they look lovely.' My mother poked at the waffles. 'You've never done them like this before. The sliced strawberry on the side is very pretty.'

I hadn't noticed that Alex had improvised a few touches to make the meal more appetizing for what he assumed was a normal invalid. 'I hope you enjoy them.'

'What about my coffee?' She nibbled the strawberry leaving a red stain on her lips.

'Coming right up.' I tried to muster a smile but something was cracking inside. From the glitter in her eyes I could sense she knew. I had to get out. 'Won't be a minute.'

I ran back downstairs hoping there would be some left in the cafetière my friends had made but it was down to the dregs. Not saying anything I dashed to the sink to fill the kettle, aware that they were all watching me.

'Summer, you seem really tense,' said Misty softly.

'Wow, that's astute of you,' I said bitterly. Oh no, now I was being horrible to my best friends, exactly opposite to how I wanted to behave. I slammed the kettle on the electric pad and flipped the switch. I then whisked the coffee press from the table and washed it out under too strong a jet of water. Spray hit me in the chest.

'Damn it all!' I slammed the tap to the off position.

Their silence was worse than if they had tried answering

back. Marcus got up and took the cafetière from my hand, taking over the coffee-making. Angel passed me a tea towel to soak up the water.

Misty was holding Alex's hand tightly. I could tell they were whispering telepathically together and with a little effort I could have listened in but I had a rule not to intrude. 'Summer, why won't you tell us the truth about what's going on here?' she asked.

I held up a forefinger. 'Don't—don't you dare let loose your power on me. I have the right to my privacy. I wouldn't forgive you if you did that.'

Alex bristled in her defence. 'Hey, Summer, give her a break. You know she finds it hard to hold on when upset—and you're upsetting her.'

'You'd better go then.' It wasn't what I wanted really—they were my only refuge in the madness of my life—but it was the safest way. I probably should have realized that I couldn't keep my friends away from my toxic family permanently, that something like this would happen. It would be safer if I just didn't let them so close again. The future suddenly looked a whole lot bleaker.

'So you want us to tell the Benedicts that you're turning them down flat?' asked Angel. 'You're not even going to listen to what their plans are? You know they wouldn't put you in danger.'

'This isn't about them.' I remained by myself, back to the sink, while my friends stood together with their soulfinders. I loved them but I also hated them for making me feel so alone.

'But they need you. You're the only one who can help. Even Crystal can't shadow him if Victor's blocking, which he is.' I could tell that Angel just couldn't get my intransigence on this point. 'How will you feel if something really terrible happens to him?'

About as bad as I felt right now. 'There must be someone else who can do what I can do?'

'There really isn't,' said Alex. 'They've checked and double-checked. No one wanted to come to you for this if it could be avoided.'

'I never had you down as a coward,' said Angel. 'I don't believe you are. So why are you acting like one?'

Just as she posed the question, my mother entered the kitchen.

'Ukrainians, are they?' Mother asked, raising one coal-black eyebrow.

'Mother, go back upstairs now!' I tried to exert my gift but my own shields were crumbling and I couldn't muster the power.

'Oh, Summer, you're really upset!' she crooned, coming to my side and clasping me around the upper arm. 'Shall I get rid of the nasty people for you?' Her power was worming inside, past the defences I'd maintained for years. The atmosphere in the room seemed to dip to freezing.

'Just go away!' Tears were pouring down my cheeks unchecked. I felt like I was being peeled apart like an orange segmented.

'What's she doing?' whispered Misty. 'Get away from Summer.' She stepped forward but Alex pushed her behind him.

'Keep back.'

'Summer, shove her off! Don't let her do that to you!' called Angel.

'Careful. I've seen something like this before,' Alex told her. 'Marcus, Summer's mother has to be an emotion leech, a vampire savant. You mustn't let her touch you or Angel. Once she latches on it is extremely hard to break the connection.'

Seeing my friends' expressions of horror released new

34

outpourings of shame inside me, a bubbling fountain of misery. For years I'd locked it all away, now it was flowing out. My mother was shivering in ecstasy, not having absorbed so much in years.

'What can we do?' Angel grabbed a broom from the corner, primed to take drastic action.

Alex waved to get my mother's attention, like a bullfighter trying to distract the bull from a downed matador. 'Mrs Whelan, Mrs Whelan?' He was layering all his persuasive powers into his voice. 'Please, let your daughter go. Can't you see that you're hurting her?'

But my mother was locked on and unreachable in this state, even to a powerful savant like Alex. I was emptying, my world going grey. I felt like Lear stumbling on the blasted heath, dispossessed of all that once had been mine, friends, hope, love. I began to sag. Not long now and I'd lose consciousness. I remembered that path from childhood.

'Daddy,' I whispered.

I must have sent the appeal telepathically because I heard a crash overhead as my father leapt out of bed. Mother's absorption doubled as she knew her time was limited. Then Dad burst into the kitchen in his pyjamas, took one look at the situation, and chopped at the point where my mother held my arm. The brief contact numbed her grip and she let go. I sank to the floor, in too dark a place to do anything else. My mother was now giggling and grinning, the most horrid phase of her addiction.

'See, Aidan, see, you can't stop me. I have to live!' She danced around the kitchen holding all the lovely emotion to her chest. 'Oh, I could run a marathon, climb Everest on Summer's donation. You wouldn't think that our boring daughter had all that feeling in her, would you? You've trained her well to hide it.'

'Get out!' snarled my father at my friends, who had huddled in a corner away from my mother. 'Leave!'

'But Summer—!' protested Angel.

'I'll look after my daughter, thank you. It's no business of yours. Out!'

'Just go,' I whispered, blocking out their telepathic questions.

Abashed, my friends filed out of the kitchen. I heard the door slam behind them and their voices fading as they walked down the drive.

'I told you never to have guests in the house!' My father rounded on me.

'I know.'

'Maeve, go upstairs. You've had your meal; go digest away from us.' My father stood between me and my mother, waiting to see which way she would take.

With a wild laugh, she spun out of the kitchen and up the stairs. I could hear her singing, skipping, still high as a kite. The crash wouldn't come for an hour or so.

My father seemed to crumple as soon as she left. He sat beside me and pulled me onto his lap, cradling me in his arms. He didn't need to say anything. He was angry with me, yes, but I also knew he was furious at himself, at my mother, at life that had dealt us such a bad hand. 'It'll pass,' he whispered. 'This too will pass.'

Chapter 4

On my father's orders, I spent the rest of the day on strict bed rest. I didn't have any energy to do anything else. Even the pile of books on the bedside table didn't get opened, Virginia Woolf's loosely linked sentences far too difficult to grasp when my own brain felt like wisps of fog. I lay looking up at the ceiling, ignoring the vibrations from my phone as my friends tried to contact me. In the end I switched it off.

The shadows from the silver birch tree outside my window flittered across the carpet like a cloud of black moths. The swishing noise of the leaves soothed in a mindless fashion, transporting me back to days spent on a Cornish beach, lying with skin against hot sand, sea breaking gently at my toes. I'd developed these places in my memory as a defence against the ugliness I glimpsed in others. So many people carried terrible things in their heads, either bad intentions or the wounds left by the cruelty they had experienced. Sometimes the burden of being a savant with mind skills like mine was too overwhelming and I had to check out of reality for a while.

The doorbell rang and I heard my dad answer. A little later he came up to my room with a light lunch on a tray for me.

'I'll give your friends marks for persistence,' he said, placing the tray on the covers next to me, a lock of his dark hair dropping over his forehead.

'What did you say?'

'That you thanked them for their concern but that you didn't want to see them. Am I right?'

'Yes.'

'You should never have brought them here, Summer.'

'It wasn't arranged. They just called round. There's a problem with one of the savant families and they wanted me to help.'

'But now they know.' He sat on the edge of the bed and smoothed the duvet, straightening out the Indian elephants that marched across the counterpane.

'Yes.'

'Will they tell anyone?'

'I didn't get a chance to ask them to keep it a secret, and you remember what Misty's power is, don't you?'

My father looked much older today in the light of the August afternoon. Handsome and blue-eyed, he had once stood tall and strong. Recently, his shoulders had begun to slump and deep grooves were notched in his cheeks and between his brows. 'So who will they tell?'

'I don't know. The Benedicts maybe?'

He groaned. One of Dad's worst fears was that he would no longer be able to maintain this charade that his family was a success. He had 'solved' the problem of Winter by brushing him under the carpet, but my mother was too dangerous to be dealt with like that. They were soulfinders and, despite everything, there was an unbreakable link between them. Each day, like Sisyphus in the Greek legend, he had to submit to having his punishment renewed.

'I ask too much of you, don't I?' he murmured.

'Who else do you have to ask?'

He squeezed my hand, both of us silenced by the labyrinth in which we were trapped. My thoughts now about running away to university—for that was what it was when looked at

38

straight—appeared horribly selfish. My thoughts circled back to Victor. I couldn't get my dream but that was no reason why he couldn't have his. 'Is there any way you could spare me for a couple of weeks?'

He cleared his throat. 'How do you mean?'

'The reason my friends called by, it's serious. Victor Benedict has disappeared and I'm probably the only one who can locate him.'

'Disappeared to where?'

'Afghanistan. He's looking for his soulfinder.'

He gave me a sour smile. 'Maybe he'll be lucky enough not to find her. That stuff: it's not all it's cracked up to be.'

'For some of us.'

'Yes, for some of us.'

'It's not really just about him. If things go wrong, it would be a disaster for all savants as he's our main channel to the law enforcement agencies. They help us co-exist with non-savants in peace; keep our presence quiet; we don't want them to start thinking of us as a threat.'

'Summer—'

'I can help find him. It'll mean missing the beginning of term but I'm ahead in my subjects so that should be OK.'

'Don't be absurd, Summer. I'm not letting you go off to Afghanistan.'

'Because you're worried about my safety or your own here?' It was a low dig perhaps, but I wasn't feeling very charitable right now.

'I'm worried for you, of course.'

'Dad, you've got a mind reader as a daughter.'

'I can't do this without you.' He gestured angrily to the house, meaning our life, our existence in this quiet spot of respectable Hampstead. In his mind, I couldn't leave him to cope on his own for the simple reason that he wouldn't.

My heart sank. I knew him well enough to guess what I had to say to get this concession from him but it meant sacrificing a dream that had kept me going for the last few years. 'Dad, how about we strike a deal? I'll apply to a London college for next year if you let me go for a few weeks?'

His eyes sparked. My dad hadn't made it in business just by a savant gift for numbers. He knew how to bargain. He looked over my shoulder at the pastel picture of a desert oasis that I had over my bed, Middle Eastern robed figures allowing their horses to drink, Lawrence of Arabia style, another of my escape dreams. 'I'm not sure, Summer. Not because I don't think you should help but because I know that there are still large areas that are no-go for civilians. I don't want to send my daughter into a war zone.'

And so it begins. I hugged my knees. 'They're sending a team and at least one of them has a gift for sensing danger. They will be as eager as you to keep me away from actual risk, trust me.'

'I do trust you. You're the only person that I can count on one hundred per cent.' He hung his head for a moment, letting the weight of family responsibility bear down on us both.

I tried to wriggle free of it. 'You could ask Mrs Bainbridge if she can stay for a few weeks. She'll be pleased to have the extra money for her daughter and son-in-law.'

He smiled. 'And Baby Jason. You know he's already started moving things with his mind? That's one child who won't stay in his crib for long.'

I waited. 'So you'll let me go?'

He gave a put-upon sigh. 'I'll consider it. I know the Benedicts by reputation; they're good people. If you go, I'll lay down a few limits on what you can and can't do.'

'So you'll be OK with Mother while I'm away?'

He shrugged, the martyr again. 'We'll have to be.'

'We'll start over again when I get back.'

Dad nodded but he looked uneasier than ever. 'It won't be the same. I need you to understand that.'

'How do you mean?'

'Now the truth about your mother is out.'

'What difference will that make?'

'You know there are rules, don't you? In the savant community, I mean.'

'Rules about what?'

'About people with your mother's condition. Maybe I should call them traditions. It was decided long ago that those with her ability should not be allowed to reproduce. They not only drain their victims of emotion, but mentally weaken those they leave behind, sometimes permanently, so their powers never recover. In darker periods of history, whole savant enclaves killed themselves over that gift when it ran riot among them. To spare others this misery, they agreed to breed the gift out of the savant DNA.'

A nugget of resentment formed in my chest. 'No, I'd not heard that. I knew savants like Mother weren't liked but I didn't know it went as far as a rule.'

'A stupid rule—impossible to police as it went against human nature. But technically you and Winter wouldn't be here if we'd stuck to it. That's one of the reasons I've always impressed on you that your mother's problem should be kept quiet. It'll go on record now somewhere and there'll be consequences.'

'What kind?'

'Unless the policy changes, they won't want you to have children either as you'll be regarded as a carrier. Your condition will be noted on the Savant Net soulfinder search engine and marked as ineligible.'

I'd never thought seriously about having a family, but to be told I wasn't worthy to have one felt like a punch to the throat. 'That's unfair.'

Dad wasn't meeting my eyes. 'It's not for every relationship, just savant ones. If you had children with a non-savant, the chances that a recessive gene comes through would be tiny, but with your soulfinder, whoever that might be, then no. He wouldn't thank you if you produced a vampire child. He might think the risk too high.'

'But you didn't.'

'No, I took the gamble.'

'And do you regret it?'

'To be honest with you? Some days, yes. Winter is so ill—and you're often so unhappy. I think I've just bred more misery.'

I didn't want my life to be dismissed like that. 'But so can any parent. There are genetic mutations of all sorts that we might pass on.'

'It's all a question of reasonable risks. I took an unreasonable one and am paying for it. But the real trouble is, so are you.'

The next morning I woke up with a fresh resolve. My future had taken shape for the next few years. Dad had agreed to the bargain late the night before, even drawing up and making me sign a contract saying I'd apply to colleges in London in return for this three-week holiday.

Holiday: that was a sick joke.

I switched on my phone and scrolled through the million messages my friends had sent me. I didn't delete them but neither did I reply immediately. The confrontation with my mother had shown that I couldn't have friends like that; as my dad put it, the risk was unreasonable. At least Mother had attacked *me*. If she had gone for one of them, I never would have forgiven myself. Without making a song and dance about it, I would quietly detach myself from their lives. Angel and Marcus had each other and their careers; Alex and Misty were very happy in Cambridge, spending all their free time together. They wouldn't notice a gap if I just faded out. It would be gradual. No one would be hurt. It wasn't just to keep them safe. I wouldn't live among savants if I couldn't really be one of them. It hurt too much. They were past the stage of handing out a bell and getting me to toll it on my approach like a medieval leper, but the situation held certain similarities. I needed to get used to living among ordinary people to whom none of this meant anything.

I put a lot of thought into a short reply. *Thanks for your messages. I'm fine now. See you soon.*

The next step was to find out where the Benedicts were assembling their rescue party, the last thing I'd do for the savant community. I sent a text to Sky, soulfinder to the youngest of Victor's brothers, and got one back immediately.

So relieved to hear from you. Misty told us all what happened. If you need to talk just call. I had experience of an emotion leech in Vegas a few years back. Victor locked up that guy along with the rest of his family of criminals but I still remember what an attack feels like.

Great: so the secret was out already. But how could Sky know what I felt like? A single attack from a stranger was hardly the same as years of such assault from someone much closer to you. Just as well Sky wasn't here or, with her gift, she would see my emotional aura pulsing red. She meant to be kind but that made it worse. *Thank you for your concern but I'm fine.* Did she hear the bitterness? They were all used to me being scrupulously polite so probably not.

Her reply came back immediately. *No, you're not. Zed tells me that you need a big hug right now so I'm sending one with this message. I think the Benedicts are planning to contact your dad to see what the Savant Net can do to help. You're not to worry about Victor. We'll sort that out with our own resources.*

The Savant Net, an informal governing body of our kind, would want to control us, according to Dad. That was the modern name given to the same old community who had once decided that my kind couldn't reproduce. *Best not contact my dad. I don't think he will want anyone interfering. Back to my question: I'm going to help find Victor so where is the team gathering?*

There was a pause at Sky's end, then the reply came through. *If you're sure? They're at an army base on Salisbury plain. They'll come and fetch you.*

Dad wouldn't want anyone else to come to the house. *Just give me the address and I'll make my own way.*

The Benedicts must all have thought me incredibly stubborn but I insisted on this point after a few more text exchanges.

Packing was difficult as I had no idea what I was facing. Kabul was going through a building boom according to the internet; I'd swiped through photos of shopping centres and hotels, so city clothes would do there. Out in the countryside the conditions would be much more basic. And, of course, the rule was to dress modestly everywhere. I hated not to be prepared for anything but my wardrobe didn't have the ideal outfits. Adding the necessary toiletries, I laid out my choices neatly on the bed. My friends teased me that I always had the perfect item on hand no matter the situation—tweezers, nail file, paracetamol, I was the one expected to produce it from my handbag. This didn't happen without careful thought. Finally, I was reasonably happy with my selections and packed them in a small pink case, the kind that could go in the overhead locker so we didn't need to check in baggage.

Dad arrived with a letter. 'This gives permission for you to leave the country with the Benedicts, just in case someone asks.'

'I've never been asked for anything like that before.'

'Times change, Summer. The border guards look very closely at anyone heading off for a known hotspot. The Benedicts will handle any visa issues but still, it might help clear the way.' He handed me a second slip of paper. 'These are the names and addresses of my family in Pakistan. They're the closest in the event of an emergency and will understand the savant angle when locals might not.'

'Good thinking.'

'I'd drive you to Salisbury but I daren't leave your mother, not today.'

'I understand. I'm fine with getting the train.'

'I know. You are ferociously competent.' He gathered me to him and kissed the top of my head. 'Look after my girl.'

'I will. I'll be back soon.'

'I've transferred some more money into your account. Stock up on good reading for your subjects on your tablet, my treat.'

'Thank you for thinking of that.'

'I'll look forward to your safe return.'

The taxi took me out to the army base situated five miles out of Salisbury. In the journey escaping the city ring road, I'd only had a glimpse of the famous cathedral with its needle-sharp spire, before we were out in the rolling countryside. That wasn't a cliché—the hills really did roll here like a swelling sea of grass. Lines from Thomas Hardy sailed through my brain. It was easy to imagine his characters roaming this landscape, desperate Tess and equally desperate Jude. Neither made cheerful role models so I tried to put myself on more positive tracks. Hardy's poetry—sublime. On a far hill a tractor was ploughing a field, turning pale stubble over into rich brown earth. *Only a man harrowing clods In a slow silent walk With an old horse that stumbles and nods Half asleep as they stalk . . . Yet this will go onward the same.* Hardy hadn't been quite right about that, had he? When was the last time I'd seen a horse and plough outside a costume drama?

Maybe in Afghanistan I'd see one.

'Here you are, love. Are you sure this is the right place? You don't mean the family quarters down the road?' The taxi driver looked dubiously at the sentries on guard and then at me in my flowery sundress and white cardigan.

'Yes, this is it. How much do I owe you?'

He read off the meter and I handed over the fare plus tip. 'Have a good day now.'

I wasn't sure that was on the cards. 'And you.'

I pushed open the door and slid out, pulling my case with me. I extended the handle and wheeled it over to the soldiers at the gate. Both were watching me, faces blank with professional calm, but I could hear echoes of their thoughts and caught their amusement at the image of me towing a pink case towards them. *Tough, boys, you won't make me feel embarrassed. I happen to like pink.*

'Hi. I'm expected,' I said briskly to the one standing by the sentry box on the right-hand side of the gate.

'Really?' He actually chuckled. 'You aren't on my list, Miss Expected.'

I rolled my eyes at his lame joke. 'It's Summer Whelan.'

The amusement faded as he found my name on the computer screen. 'Oh, you're one of them.' He silently added *the freaks*, the thought leaking out to me like the smell of a passing rubbish collection lorry.

'Yes, I'm one of them.' Curious to find out how much the sentry knew and not feeling too respectful of his personal space right then, I pushed a little deeper. He was aware that he was guarding very hush-hush operations, the blackest of black ops. He'd seen enough unexplained stuff going down—things hovering without support in the air—to believe it was freaky to say the least. His training had taught him it was best not to know too much.

'I have to search your case.' He gestured to a table inside the sentry box.

I hadn't anticipated this but should have done. This was a top-security facility; I couldn't just waltz in here with a case like I would a hotel. There was no X-ray machine so he meant I had to open it for him.

'OK.' Determined not to be ashamed, I lifted it onto the table and opened the zip. My OCD tendencies were out there for him to see in the neatly rolled clothes, jewellery case and separate make-up and wash bags. He dug down between the layers but fortunately didn't ask me to unpack everything. He then did the same to my handbag before turning back to me.

'Arms out, miss.'

I imagined what came next would be a humiliating pat down but fortunately he had a wand-like thing for that search and I didn't cause a bleep.

'That's all in order. Go down the drive and report to the first building on your right.' He rolled back the gate to let me pass. I could feel his eyes on my back as I walked along the side of the road, wheels of my case making a too-loud rumble in the silence. I felt ridiculous now and out of my depth. I'd not given much thought to the fact that our rendezvous was a military camp. This meant it was an official operation. I'd anticipated we'd just get on a flight and go look for Victor. And I'd bought a pink case rather than my rucksack. My mother's attack must have messed up my reasoning process. I would never normally make such a crass error.

Word from the front gate must have been passed to the Benedicts that I was on my way because Saul, Victor's father, was waiting for me in the reception building. A tall man of Native American heritage, he always carried himself with quiet dignity, reminding me of a character striding out of the forest in a Fenimore Cooper novel. I'd never before seen him wearing army fatigues though—the effect was disconcerting.

'Summer.' He folded me into a warm hug. 'Thank you so much for coming.'

'I'm sorry I couldn't say yes straight off. I know I disappointed you all.'

'You never disappoint. We understand your situation.'

They really didn't, but it was nice to hear that. 'So who else is here?'

Saul signed me in and presented me with a pass. 'Let's walk. Leave your case here. I'll see it is put in your room later.' We stepped out into the sunshine, taking an asphalt path between lawns towards what looked like a sports stadium. I could feel the heat on the back of my neck as I'd put my hair in a ponytail. I was grateful for my sunglasses; there was quite a glare in the noonday light bouncing off the light grey surface of the path.

'You can imagine that all of my sons want to go pull Victor out of this mess,' said Saul, 'but I've put my foot down. We're taking only a small team of essential personnel.'

'Oh, OK.'

'Before we heard that you had changed your mind about coming I'd already made some other arrangements.'

'You mean, you don't need me?' Could I null and void my agreement with Dad? I felt a twist of hope, but also, I had to admit, a glimmer of disappointment now I'd psyched myself up for the trip.

'We definitely need you. But we need more than just a mind-shadower. We need a team who can get in and out without causing a rift in diplomatic relations. We have to have people with special forces experience, which is why we are here. Victor's got quite a few friends in high places.'

'I thought the FBI wanted to arrest him?'

Saul gave a wry smile. 'He's also got enemies. Not all the Feds are after him, just the ones who don't like dealing with savants.'

I could imagine that that was a line that stretched round the block. Savants are more often feared than trusted and there were quite a few of us who preferred to use our powers for criminal gain. 'So tell me about the team.'

'From my family, just Trace and Will are going. They both have skills we need. Will and I can run a security perimeter around any place we stay as we share the ability to sense danger approaching.'

'You're coming?' I had to admit I was surprised.

'You sound like my sons. Of course, I'm coming. Victor's my boy. I'm the one who gets to kick his ass for thinking he had to do this alone.'

Hard to imagine anyone telling off Victor but I suppose his father was the most likely candidate.

'Trace will be able to piece together the tracking once we find something of Victor's out there. Between you two, you should be able to hone in on his location.'

'And the others?'

'I've called in all my favours and got the Robinsons.'

'Should I have heard of them? I take it they aren't the Swiss family version?'

Saul laughed. 'No, and it would be rather disappointing if you knew about them. They're undercover specialists. They work for the military of friendly countries on an ad hoc basis, doing the most difficult tasks, hostage extraction and personal protection.'

I wrinkled my nose in distaste. 'They're mercenaries?'

'Don't let them hear you call them that. Think more along the lines of a special unit working on behalf of the savant world. They're our SAS if you like.'

Technically they were still mercenaries though. If they got paid for it and weren't under a flag, that's what the dictionary would label them. 'How many of them are there?'

'There's Lucas Robinson, he's the commanding officer. His gift is to anticipate, makes him hell of a tactician in a fight. His lieutenant is his younger brother Scott, the navigator. That boy is like a walking human GPS, I've never seen anything like it.'

'Boy?'

'You got me there. He's mid-twenties but anyone under thirty is a boy to me.'

I sensed there was an 'and'. 'That's it? Just the two?'

'No, they've got a third on their team, their logistics expert and youngest brother, Hal, but you should know up front that he's not a savant.'

'How does that work?'

'Their parents aren't savants either. Lucas and Scott are aberrations. Hal knows about their gifts though, so you don't need to hide who you are around him.'

'Does that happen often? Non-savants producing savants?'

'Sometimes. The gene can hide for a while in the line. Usually if you look back there's a grandparent or two with a gift.'

I didn't want to think about genetic inheritance right then. I repeated the names to make sure I had them straight. 'Lucas, Scott and Hal Robinson.'

'Correct. Be nice to Hal, won't you? He must find us all rather . . . peculiar.'

We had arrived at the sports field and I saw that it wasn't set out for track events but as an obstacle course. Five men were running the circuit, all dressed in fatigues. Will and Trace were neck and neck on a climbing wall with two men I didn't recognize. Out front was a slim-built younger man currently making short work of a rope over a muddy ditch. I looked down at my sandals and dress.

'I think I might have miscalculated the nature of our mission.'

Saul chuckled. 'Don't worry, sweetheart, they are just doing this as a break from the planning while we waited for you to arrive.'

'They're doing this for fun?'

One of the strangers had just fallen into the mud thanks to a nudge from Will, causing much hilarity among the other competitors.

'Yep.'

'It takes all sorts, I suppose.'

Saul called to them telepathically and they all changed direction to jog over in our direction, the one at the front taking a second to pick up on the clues from the others. That had to be the non-savant brother. When they reached us, Trace and Will both gave me a brief kiss, excusing themselves because of their sweaty state. Part of me wondered if their hesitancy to get any closer was really due to the news about my mother. A leper bell clanged mockingly in my head. Then Saul turned to the Robinsons.

'Here she is. Summer is one of the best mind readers I know, giving even Victor a run for his money.'

The three brothers stood in a line, mud splattered, faces flushed. The older two had the battered look of guys that played rugby; one had had his nose broken, possibly more than once. The younger one was on the same track, though he still had a lean, wolfish build. Tall, taller and tallest, I nicknamed them, wondering if the height went in age order, making Lucas the towering one nearest me. It would be interesting to see how they washed up; they all looked pretty impressive even with all the mud. I held out my hand.

'Nice to meet you.'

Lucas suddenly put out a palm, not to take mine but to stop his brother. 'Don't say it, Hal.'

The lean wolf snorted. 'Seriously, Luc? You're thinking of taking Snow White here into a war zone? You have to be crazy, sir.' This last was directed at Saul.

'Summer is very competent,' Saul said calmly.

'You really don't want to say the next thing either,' muttered Lucas, his gift for anticipation in overdrive.

'Competent in what? Getting matching manis and pedis? She looks like she can't last two minutes away from somewhere to plug in her hairdryer.'

If I hadn't just had to sell my future to be here I would have dug deep and found some poise to answer him. Withering politeness is what I normally fall back on when insulted. Feeling wide open and vulnerable I did the only thing I could think of: I turned and walked away. From the sound of elbow in stomach and 'oof' from Hal I guessed the idiot's brothers were telling him what they thought of his company manners.

'Summer, wait!' Will jogged to catch up with me. 'I'll take you to your quarters while Dad sorts that out. We're sorry: the Robinsons aren't used to working with civilians. They're making a huge concession taking on this mission with us along for the ride.'

'Good for them.' Hal Robinson was just a rude squaddie; I could rise above unearned scorn, not let it touch me. Just because I coordinated the polish on my nails and toenails with my outfit, so what? 'But I don't have to stay to listen.'

Will's friendly expression shifted to shock. 'You're walking out on us?'

'No. I'm going to my room to check my manicure and reapply my make-up.'

Catching the sarcasm, Will grinned. 'Atta girl. The only way to beat tough guys like Hal Robinson is meet them head on.'

'Meet them? You misunderstand. I'm way ahead. He is merely trailing in my Chanel-scented wake.'

Will gave me a quick one-armed hug. 'Adorable. He doesn't stand a chance against such a class act.'

I laughed, feeling much more like my old self.

Chapter 5

Accommodation was Spartan—that much I had anticipated correctly. Will showed me into a small room with white walls, a single bed, and sheets folded neatly on the top for me to make up. A tiny ensuite had been crammed into one corner, 'the VIP treatment' Will assured me. I got the impression the boys were all bunking down together.

'What next?' I asked.

'Planning meeting after dinner.' He placed my case on the bed, manfully restraining himself from any derogatory comments about the colour.

'How's Margot?' I asked, dropping my handbag on the bedside table and kicking off my sandals.

Will's rugged face broke into a grin. 'Great, thanks. Gifted has just headed off for Italy else she'd be here. I guess right now she's scrambling to get everything set up for the performance tonight. The guys tease her but they know their tour would fall apart if she wasn't doing the thinking for them.'

'Kurt giving her a hard time?'

'As only an older brother can.' Will's expression sobered. 'You know, we're really grateful to you coming to help Victor like this.'

I stuck my head into the shower room: clean but smelling of harsh soap. I was glad I'd packed my own. 'Please don't thank me. Your dad has said all that's necessary.'

Will folded his arms, not ready to go quite yet. 'And you?

You're OK? Is there anything I can do?' He always tried to put himself between danger and those he was protecting. 'You took a beating the other day, Misty said.'

Thank you, friend, for being so indiscrete. 'It was nothing new so I'm OK.'

Will paused, dipping into his gift for a moment. 'I can't sense any lingering danger so I guess I have to believe you.'

I gave him a brittle smile. 'Hadn't you better go shower or something?'

He glanced down, only now remembering his muddy state. 'You're right. See you at six in the mess hall. Just follow the signs.'

As soon as he left, I remembered that I hadn't asked him what the dress code was for supper. Getting that kind of thing right mattered more to me than it did my friends. From what I had read, some mess halls could be formal if they were for officer class, others were like canteens. It didn't seem important enough to reach out with telepathy and interrupt Will's shower so I played safe with a dark blue shirtdress. I washed out the one I had been wearing with my travel detergent—the Benedict hugs had got it a little muddy—and left it on a hanger by the open window. I was on the ground floor but it seemed highly unlikely anyone was going to climb in and steal my purse in the middle of a top security army base.

Summer, just listen to yourself, I upbraided myself. *You are so . . . so uptight*. I thumped my forehead in frustration. I wished sometimes I could be more spontaneous, less worried about everything. Angel and Misty had told me so many times I needed to chill.

Thinking of them, I knew it was time to text my friends to let them know what I was doing.

Hey guys, just a quick message to let you know I'm helping

with the Victor situation after all. Might not be in touch for a
while seeing where we are going. Love you.

I left the phone vibrating with a whole load of OMG replies from Angel and Misty and rather more restrained but encouraging ones from Marcus and Alex. I'd come to love my friends' soulfinders almost as much as I loved the girls; it was going to be a really painful kind of surgery to detach myself from the four of them. I was the Tin Man in reverse, wishing if I only *hadn't* a heart.

I couldn't think about that now. Still recovering from my mother's attack, I had to make myself relax. I stretched out on the bed and picked up my tablet. No sooner had I got into my Barchester novel, managing to forget some of the stresses of the last few days in Victorian cathedral closes, someone banged on the door. I checked my watch. It was only five-thirty. Feeling out to who was there, I couldn't sense anyone, which was a little odd. Most people leaked thoughts like that guy in the deodorant advert leaving a trail of scent for swooning girls to follow. The caller knocked again. Getting up, I opened the door. A cleaner version of Hal Robinson stood there, dressed now in denim and white shirt, water glistening in his close-cut brown hair, chocolate brown eyes burning with fury. OK, he did not want to be here. I got the message. But I was a lady if nothing else.

'Can I help you?'

'I came to apologize.' His tone made clear every word was paid out from a miser wallet of resentment.

I wasn't letting him off so easily. I wriggled my bare feet against the cold lino, shell pink nails gleaming. Check out my pedicure, Robinson. 'Sorry for what?' We both knew full well.

'For not being polite. OK, are we done here?' He managed to be rude making an apology for being rude: an impressive skill.

'I guess *you* are.' I made to close the door but a boot appeared in the gap, hand on the door frame.

'What does that mean?'

I tried to read his thoughts but couldn't get past the deep brown eyes. They kept distracting me from my purpose. Besides, with so much antagonism rolling off him, I hardly needed more information as to his state of mind.

'It means that you think you've made an adequate apology and I don't. But it doesn't matter enough to me to pursue, so off you go.' I made a little flicking gesture with my fingers that I knew would infuriate him. 'See you at supper.'

He gave a frustrated huff and moved his foot. 'It's dinner. Supper is what posh people eat.'

'I'll see you at supper.' I closed the door, giving him barely enough time to move his fingers. I leaned back against it, hugging my waist. Points to me, I thought, smiling at the ceiling.

I came purposely a little late to supper as I didn't want to risk being on my own with Hal Robinson without the Benedicts around me. As Will had said, the mess hall was well signposted: a long, low construction not far from my own quarters, designed as if the architect was entering Most Ugly Building of the Year competition. The smell of chips and burgers announced that my smart casual dress was a little too smart but I wasn't going to retreat. I was tired after a day of making the wrong choices so just gave up. I took a tray and joined the end of the queue. The majority were soldiers but there were a few civilians in line so I didn't feel completely conspicuous.

I reached the serving counter. 'I'll have the salad, thank you.'

The man looked at me nonplussed, lettuce pinched between his serving tongs. 'Yeah, but what do you want with the salad?' He gestured to the trays of chicken, chilli or burgers.

'Just the salad.' I felt I couldn't force any more down, still coming back from the shaky after-effects of my mother's attack.

I took the plate and headed over to the dessert counter to choose some fruit and a plain yoghurt.

'You're not one of those chicks on a diet are you? Because I can tell you from where I'm standing you really don't need to worry.'

Of course, Hal Robinson would be the one behind me in the queue at the counter, come to resume our match. He picked up some sponge and custard combination to add to his tray loaded with chips, beans and burger.

'It's too hot to eat much today.' I wasn't going to confess my weakness after an attack to him.

'You can't live on a lettuce leaf where we are going. The terrain is rough. You'll be fainting for lack of blood sugar.'

'Kind of you to worry, but I'll be fine.'

'I'm not kind. If you're really coming with us, then you'd better not add any more ticks in the liability column. You can't dick around with personal safety on a mission.'

I picked up my tray to look for a table. Saul waved to me from the far end of the room. 'Who died and made you my commander?'

Hal smirked and leaned in, trying to intimidate me. 'It's just my personality, babe.'

I put my tray down. 'No.'

He frowned and stepped back. 'No what?'

'No, that's a foul move in this little game of insults you've started. You don't get to call me "babe" just because I have two X chromosomes and you only have one.'

He added a chocolate bar to the tray which already contained enough calories to feed a family for a week. 'Between us, it's the Y that counts.'

'You respect me or I'll ask for you to be left off the team. Who do you think has the more valuable skill, Robinson?' I arched a brow, a not-so-subtle reminder of who was the savant here.

He gave me a go-to-hell smile and brandished the chocolate wafer at me. 'Well, *Whelan*, you might not be a guy, but you sure like picking a fight, don't you? Wanna arm wrestle to settle this?'

'How evolved of you.' I picked up the tray and stalked off, slamming it down on the table next to Saul with more force than I intended.

Saul stopped my apple from rolling off the edge. 'Making friends with Hal?'

If Mr Benedict had been of my generation I would have told him exactly what I thought of the idiot boy. Instead I settled for my usual politeness. 'I'm finding his manners somewhat lacking.'

Scott, the middle brother, leant across the table. 'She means she hates him. He has that effect on me too. You kind of either learn to love the verbal sparring or give in to your desire to kick him.'

'What do you do?' I asked.

'A bit of both.' He winked at me. 'But cut him some slack, Summer: he has to hang out with us Formula 1 savants knowing he's only ever going to be the rally driver in the low-power car. It hurts his ego and he has always liked to feel as if he is in charge of something. Sucks to be a non-savant younger brother sometimes.'

I felt a twinge of shame that I had gone for a vulnerable spot with my challenge. 'His ego seems to be doing just fine to me.' It was, wasn't it?

Hal arrived and circled the table to take the free chair beside me. He bumped his tray down next to mine, spilling my drink. 'Oops, my bad. Want me to get you another fruit juice or are you going to live it up with a diet coke?'

'Henry Robinson, play nicely or I'll put chilli powder on your toothbrush,' warned Scott.

'Yeah, yeah.' Hal sat down. 'Have you noticed what's she's eating? Or not eating? We can't take someone into the field on some stupid diet from a starve-yourself-stuff-yourself guru.'

I mopped up the spillage with a napkin, annoyed that there was nowhere to dispose of it. I crumpled it up and put it in my now empty cup. 'I'm not on a diet. I'm just not hungry. But thank you for your concern. It is duly noted.'

Will stood up. 'I'll get you another drink, Summer. Another apple juice OK?'

'Thank you.'

Hal squeezed ketchup liberally over his meal making it look like the bloody aftermath of some battle between chip and burger. 'Am I the only sane person here? We're going to one of the most dangerous countries in the world and you are thinking of packing her along for the ride?' He angled towards me, forkful of chips just ready to be shovelled in. 'It's not you personally, Made-in-Chelsea, but any untrained girl.'

'And if I were a boy?'

'Same goes—though I'd say that a sex change would be a great waste of your obvious . . . talents.'

It was like sitting next to some Neanderthal throwback. I wondered why the others weren't coming to my defence as they had earlier. Brushing lightly over their thoughts I could tell the Benedicts senior and junior were waiting to see if I had the courage to defend myself. I sensed that was based on a deep confidence in my abilities, which was heartwarming. As for the Robinsons, I couldn't read them.

Strange. I sliced a tomato in two, buying myself time. Why couldn't I sense them? Some people did have naturally high shields and I guessed it would fit with their job. What would happen if I pushed a little harder, tried to land behind the enemy lines, so to speak? I contemplated doing just that but Hal wouldn't give me the space for the attempt.

He unscrewed his bottle of coke, letting the hiss erupt like an audience disapproving a first-night performance. 'See what I mean? She gives up at the sign of a real attack. I've been testing her and she falls back on politeness then blanks you and runs. That isn't going to work if we're going in as a team.'

'What are you saying, Hal?' asked Lucas. Fresh from the shower, his hair was revealed as a gingery brown, eyes a shade lighter than his brother's.

'I'm saying that, however good her powers are, she's too much of a risk. It's not safe for her, or us.'

I wondered if my dad would agree that our contract was void if I got chucked off the team without even leaving the country. Knowing him, he would probably insist on holding me to it as he hadn't reneged on his part.

'Summer?' Saul was gently prodding me into defending myself. I couldn't think how to do that as my defences were pretty low at the moment.

I played it cool. Never let anyone know how much you want something or how hurt you are. 'It's fine if you decide to leave me off the mission. I came because I wanted to help Victor and I was told that I was the only one who could track him.'

'You are,' said Trace, the oldest Benedict brother and a police officer in Denver when he wasn't chasing Victor across half the world.

'I'm feeling a little shaky today. I should be recovered by the time we get on a plane.'

Hal put down his fork, ketchup-boarding a tortured chip in the process. 'You've been ill? Why didn't you say? I thought you were on some diet thing. Extra reason why we shouldn't cart you off into a war zone.'

Saul covered my hand with his. 'No, it's not that, Hal. Summer had a run-in with a savant vampire the day before yesterday. It makes us all a little shaken just to think about it.'

Lucas paused in buttering his bread roll. 'Where is he now? Did you put him down?'

'Put who down?' asked Hal, eyes shuttling between his brothers' faces.

'Savant vampires are bad, Hal,' explained Scott. 'They drain the brain, really dangerous stuff.'

Hal shook his head. 'Geez, you are all so weird. What did I do to get a couple of you for brothers?'

'No, she wasn't put down but she's under control,' replied Saul, pretending that the insults to savants hadn't just been flying.

'She?' probed Lucas. 'Your mother?'

He said it just as I said 'My mother', proving his anticipation worked just fine around me.

He winced but then dredged up a smile for me. 'Tough break, darling.'

I kept my eyes on my salad. The army didn't do good ones: lettuce, cucumber and tomato with a few curls of onion. 'If everyone has stopped eviscerating my personal situation, maybe we can get on to the purpose of us all being here.'

'Waiter, waiter, bring us the dictionary!' Hal pretended to summon one with a click of his fingers.

Will returned with my apple juice and set it down on my tray.

'You can be a real jackass, you know, Hal?' muttered Scott.

'Eviscerating means knifing her in the gut,' said Lucas. 'Leave Summer alone, Hal. If she's survived being raised in a family of vampires, then she'll find Afghanistan a walk in the park.'

Just one vampire, I wanted to say, but the moment passed before I could defend my family.

Hal didn't say anything to that but waited for the attention of the group at the table to move on to talk about choosing the right hotel base. 'Sorry.' This time Hal did at least sound genuine. 'Scott's right: I can be a jerk.'

I gave a nod, not trusting the tight feeling at the back of my throat.

'That salad looks like something my pet rabbit would've rejected. I got this for you.' He held out the chocolate bar on the tray.

He was right. If there was one thing I could force down that was a little of the sweet stuff. I cracked open the wrapper, red band giving way to my fingernail. 'You had a pet rabbit?'

'Yup. Named it Napoleon until it had babies. Then it became Josephine. My dad wasn't great at telling rabbit genders and the shop must have had a laugh when they sold him a pregnant doe. I liked it though. I got to be a daddy.'

I caught a flash from him of a grinning boy with spiked-up hair and big brown eyes, gap in the front of his teeth, holding up a clutch of baby rabbits for the camera. 'I hope they all found good homes?' Perhaps we could have a half-decent conversation.

'You could say that. I went all *Madagascar* on them and decided it was cruel to keep them in the cage. Released them onto the nature reserve near our house. I imagine I made some foxes very happy.'

'Oh.'

He nudged me. 'Alternatively, they went on to create a whole race of super rabbits who are running free to this day, kicking fox butt. Got to think on the bright side. Cheer up, princess, you don't always have to be so pessimistic.'

I couldn't tell if he were joking or not. It was strange not hearing anything but the tiniest stray thought and I wondered if whoever was shielding him had let that one about the rabbit leak on purpose to make me warm to him. I glanced at Lucas and Scott but they seemed not to be paying us any attention. 'Are you sure you're not a savant?'

He had already polished off the main course and was now onto dessert. 'Last time I checked my head for freakiness, yes. Why do you ask?'

'I can't hear you.'

He choked. 'Sitting right next to you, princess.'

I let the stupid nickname go. 'I meant I can't hear your thoughts. Normally I get swamped.'

'Maybe I don't have any? Have you thought of that?' He gave me a devilish grin. Oh, he had thoughts but I wondered if I should be thankful I wasn't party to them right then.

'Do your brothers shield you?'

'They might. I'm not sure how their gifts function. You'd know more than me. I know they like to work under what they call radio silence.'

I broke off a wafer of chocolate and tapped it on the silver paper. 'It would follow or you would be a risk in a savant operation. A powerful mind reader could pick up their plans from the weakest link.'

'Are you calling me the weakest link?'

'I didn't mean it like that.'

'Keep telling yourself that, babe. It's what you're thinking and, no, I don't need to be a mind reader to know that.' He pushed back from the table, spoon in empty bowl rattling. 'I've got to set up the conference room. Be there in five.' He stalked out.

My comment had needled him when I really hadn't intended anything of the sort. I hadn't meant to score a point off him. Or maybe I had? I could do without a Hal Robinson on this mission. He was making me doubt myself and bringing out a bratty side that I didn't recognize.

'You OK, Summer?' asked Saul in his rumbling voice.

Was I? 'Nothing I can't handle.'

He chuckled and covered my hand with his, his calloused palm strangely comforting. 'I'm sure you can. That boy is only going off the deep end because he doesn't know how to handle a real lady. I doubt he's ever met anyone like you before.'

'How do you know?'

He winked. 'Father of seven boys. I've seen it all, sweetheart.'

Chapter 6

The military flight was much noisier than a civilian airline; I could feel my teeth humming with the vibrations, bones in some sonic scan like a giant MRI machine. My allocated seat was surrounded by cargo strapped to the walls in camouflage netting and nothing by way of a window. I had given up trying to listen to my music as the background roar of the engines drowned out even Florence and the Machine at full volume. I studied a map of our destination instead. We were headed for the northern Afghan city of Mazar-e-Sharif as Crystal's clues about the location of Victor's soulfinder included some glimpses of sites that sounded like local landmarks.

I ran over the plan in my head. Set up a base in a small hotel. A contact of the Robinsons in the Secret Services had provided me with a new identity so we were able to travel as part of the same extended family group. My wish had come true: temporarily I was Summer Benedict and Saul was now officially my adopted father, Will and Trace my brothers. The Robinsons were to claim to be our cousins. The fact that I spoke with an English rather than American accent shouldn't matter as I wasn't expected to do any of the talking to the local authorities, or indeed any man outside our family group. Saul and Will were going to provide a ring of security while Trace made enquiries as to whether anyone had seen his brother. Once we got a lead, my job was to close in on him so Trace could pick up the physical trail and catch up with his brother with the Robinsons' assistance.

Easy, huh? I doubted it would go so smoothly.

And what were we to say about our presence in the area, which was hardly on most people's holiday itinerary? We knew from his colleagues that Victor often travelled as a journalist when undercover. Our story was that Victor was writing a good news story on the security improvements in the area—no need for anyone to think that he was there to sniff out trouble. Saul was pretending to be an expert on the art of Islamic cultures and we had come to join Victor as he had spoken so highly of the Blue Mosque and the nearby historic town of Balkh. So far it was clear, but what were we going to do when we actually found Victor? He might not be ready to leave. I hadn't told the team that I had the ability to take people over, as I did my mother during one of her episodes. I hoped it wouldn't come to having to employ mind-force as I didn't think I had it in me.

Unless I was saving a life. That was my one exception.

If Victor had found out some bad news about his soulfinder and was in a desperate place, I might have to do something drastic to tear him away. But if he resisted, would I even be strong enough? I'd never tested myself against him. With the two-way channel my gift opened up, he could just as easily take me over.

Hal dropped a chocolate bar in my lap. 'Hey, Pink Lady: you're looking on the dark side again.' He wasn't letting my suitcase go without a few jabs.

'Everyone has a dark side.' I gave him a fake smile.

'So says the song. But what about everyone has a bright side? When is someone gonna sing about that?' He dropped down into the spare seat beside me. 'Comfortable?'

There was no way I was going to show him that I was the least bit disturbed by the decibels. 'Just like flying first class on Emirates.'

'Yeah, you look the type to be a frequent flyer, racking up the air miles.' How little he knew about me. 'This is the pits but it was all I could arrange at the last moment.' He opened a packet of crisps and offered me one. I shook my head. 'We were lucky the mine clearance team were headed the right way.'

The experts in clearing up the unexploded ordinance left by the many wars in the region were sitting down the front of the plane, keeping themselves to themselves. They'd been told not to take too much interest in us, though I could sense that their minds were whirling with questions. 'So you're responsible for the hitchhike with them?'

'Yeah, this is my job. I may not have your fancy ESP but I can run a mission. Lucas has been training me since I turned sixteen.'

'You've left school?'

He nodded. 'Last year. Couldn't wait, felt like I'd been sprung from prison. I'm officially signed up to the army but Lucas has a deal with them and I'm his recruit. We have a special semi-detached status with the British military. He did the same for Scott a few years earlier when he hit sixteen.'

I was curious how this family worked. 'And your parents really don't suspect there's anything different about their older sons?'

He laughed. 'Nope. And why would they? Lucas and Scott don't go using their gifts around them like that telekinetic stuff where you move things with your mind. Can you do that?'

'A little. It's not my strong suit.'

'But I bet telepathy is.'

'Yes.' I rubbed my palms on the thighs of my trousers, awkward that I was having a proper conversation with him. It was easier when he kept his distance. I found his mixture of good looks and obnoxious behaviour confusing, like dipping a toe in a bath and not knowing if the wince was because it was too hot or icy cold. 'What are your parents like?'

He scrunched up the packet and tossed it into the air to catch. 'Dad is a football coach in the Championship League now he's retired from his playing career. He's used to barking orders.'

'So that's where you get it from.'

He smiled. 'Mum's originally from Munich, sister to a football player friend of Dad's, and now a music teacher.'

'Which instrument?'

'Drums and percussion. She teaches music in a secondary school. Before that, before having us, she was in the German army and played in a marching band, ceremonial stuff, when she wasn't looking after her regiment's logistics. See, rapping out orders really does run in the family.'

'And when your dad barks, what does she do?'

'Laughs, or barks right back. You should picture them as Mom being a Jack Russell to his Rottweiler. But he doesn't do much barking round her. It's his boys he likes to keep on their toes.'

I could imagine that theirs must have been a tempestuous house, no place for a shrinking violet. Little wonder Hal and his brothers were all so forthright. 'They sound like good parents.'

'The best. You see, it doesn't matter to us if they are savants or not. They are just Mum and Dad.'

He didn't know how lucky he was. 'That's nice.'

'And you? What's the family like?'

I recalled my last telephone call home before we took off, Dad failing to hide his delight that I had agreed to settle at home for another few years after this trip. 'My dad likes to bark orders too.'

'And your mum? The vampire lady?'

From the tone of the question, I could tell he didn't get it. 'I'd prefer not to talk about her.'

He shrugged. 'OK. Brothers or sisters?'

'One. A brother.'

He tossed the packet at the back of Scott's head, catching him dead on. 'You're not good on the old sharing assembly stuff, are you? Older? Younger?' The packet came back, hitting my knee.

'Sorry, Summer!' called Scott.

'It's OK. My brother is older but he's not well. Look, I know your intentions are good with the getting-to-know-you questions but I think I'd like to sleep now.' I tried to hand him back the chocolate. My stomach was churning again with the memories of what I'd left behind.

'Keep it, princess.' He got up and went in search of someone else to bug.

'Sorry.' He was too far away already to hear my apology. I didn't open the bar but left it lying on the map. Hal had protested vociferously about my inclusion in the team right up until the moment we took off and now he decided to play nice. What was that about? Maybe he was the kind of guy who didn't hold grudges, flare up and forget, like Angel? She and Marcus both had tempers but fortunately didn't hold on to them. She had tried to persuade me it was healthy but I had never been allowed to show emotion around my mother so I couldn't get over the impression that something indecent was going on in the casual way Hal treated his moods; it felt embarrassing, like he was walking down the high street in just his boxers.

Stop. I so did not need that image in my mind. I got out my tablet punishing myself with a bit of Dr Johnson, the least sexy writer in the English canon.

The plane descended into the airport at Mazar-e-sharif. I clutched the armrest as the wheels touched down. I didn't normally mind flying but somehow this stripped-back aircraft made me think too much about the thin layer of fuselage between me and disaster. We taxied to a standstill and Saul was immediately out of his seat, freeing our bags from the netting. We had strict instructions to separate from the mine clearance team as soon as we got there so they didn't get caught up in our problems. I was already wearing the shalwar kameez, tunic and loose trousers, Hal had given me to wear. He might be rude on occasion but he was ruthlessly efficient and I was grateful he'd silently solved my inappropriate clothing problem. He had bought it from a market stall in Bristol when he'd done a supply run for the team and, as he'd picked a pretty shade of blue, it could have been much worse. I covered my hair with a matching scarf. I wasn't going for a full burka because I had been told it was OK in a city to leave my face visible, another Hal-ism, so I hoped he had got that right.

'You ready?' Saul handed me my pink case. What had I been thinking? It had been visible all flight stowed among the khaki boxes and kitbags.

'Yes.' I slipped the chocolate bar into a front pocket, despite myself touched by Hal's attempts to keep me well fed.

Our team walked down the ramp at the rear and crossed the tarmac to the immigration hall, Saul holding my hand to steady me on the slope. Heat rose in shimmers from the runway. I caught sight of a dusty plain beyond the airport and a line of blue mountains on the horizon.

I'm not liking this, said Will, using telepathy. *Threat levels are rising the nearer we get to that building.*

I glanced over to Hal to check he had got the message. His brothers were flanking him and from the looks passing between them they had warned him. I kept quiet. This wasn't my role, but I wished I could order us all to scuttle back to the plane.

The danger is not life-threatening, Saul said calmly. *I think we are in for a major bureaucratic hassling.*

I'm reading a darker edge, Dad. Will really wasn't happy. *Something to do with Victor.*

Saul dropped my hand and moved a little way away from me to get a clearer reading. *I get it now. Lucas, what do you anticipate?*

Behind us, forklift trucks were already unloading the plane. There was no chance of a fast getaway. Besides, the mines clearance team had a clear mandate to be here that we couldn't mess up with our shadier purpose.

Trouble. But I guess we have to play this out. Lucas' voice went deep in my head, like the low notes of an organ. I realized I'd not connected with either of the Robinsons before. *Summer, fall back with Hal. He knows what to do. Don't bring any attention to yourself, OK?* Lucas nudged his brother over to my side.

Saul and Lucas went first into the immigration building. Though they tried to look unthreatening, no one would mistake them for ordinary civilians. The men all walked like they had training—which they had—only me with my pink suitcase looked anywhere near normal. And I had thought until now that I was the one that stuck out.

Saul went to the kiosk where a guard sat watching us. He pushed over the bundle of passports and the letter in Dari explaining our purpose for coming, countersigned by the embassy in London. The guard leafed through each document languidly. I dipped into his head and found gleeful anticipation. He was playing indolence with us. I sent the group a warning.

There are six policemen coming our way, said Will. *Vick, what have you been doing to enrage so many people?*

'Mr Benedict, I wish I could welcome you to Mazar-e-Sharif but I'm afraid there are some difficulties with allowing your party into the city,' the guard announced in good English, keeping hold of our passports. He had had warning of our arrival from the embassy in London but something had happened to make the expected welcome turn sour.

Saul didn't blink. 'Oh? How can that be? This is my first time in Afghanistan. I wasn't made aware of any problem when we got our visas.'

The man gave a sly smile. 'This is not a matter which concerns the Kabul authorities. You will find that in our province we run things ourselves. Before we can let you free to visit . . .' he picked up the letter and waved it tauntingly, '. . . the Blue Mosque, you and your family will have to go with our chief of police and answer some questions about this journalist you claim you are meeting, this Victor Benedict. First matter that needs clearing up is your relationship to him.' I caught a confusing flash in his thoughts of a crown made of tiny little golden discs but I couldn't place its relationship to Victor.

'He's my son.' Saul's hands flexed at his side. 'I've an academic interest in Islamic culture. He invited me to join him, as it says in the letter.'

'We shall see. And these others.' He gestured to the rest of us as the policemen entered at a fast walk from the other end of the building.

'Two more of my sons, my daughter, and my nephews.'

'You have a big family.'

'That's right.'

The guard got up and exited the kiosk by the door at the back. Leaving us standing there, he walked over to the policemen and handed over our passports.

Hal swore softly beside me. He reached for my hand. 'Don't get separated from us, OK, princess?'

I nodded and clutched his fingers tightly, his warm grip reassuring despite the deteriorating situation.

What are they saying, Summer? Saul asked.

I can't understand the words but the intentions are reading strongly. I got more flashes of images as they passed through the policemen's heads. *They want to take you to the police station and interrogate you. They don't want you to contact the consular authorities of either of our countries. I keep getting images of golden artefacts, particularly a crown. It doesn't make much sense to me.*

We can fight our way out, said Lucas, giving us the option in a series of brief mental pictures.

Too risky and would mean we would have to evacuate immediately without Victor. I still don't get physical violence from them, just ill will, replied Saul.

I agree. They really are just thinking about questioning you. I had not featured in any of those thoughts. As Saul had said earlier, my gender and age made me of less interest to them. *I think they are OK about leaving me free. What do you want me to do?*

I'll see if they'll let Hal stay with you. Go to the hotel and wait there. If we don't get out by tonight, contact the authorities, British and American. It will mean double trouble for Victor and his friends in the Secret Services who have helped us get this far unofficially, but I don't see a choice.

OK, Saul. I squeezed Hal's knuckles. 'Saul is going to try to persuade them to let us go.'

'Stay close.' Hal was on full alert, preparedness thrumming through his body.

I nodded. For all his annoying side, Hal projected an air of someone you could rely on in a crisis.

The guard came back with the policemen. 'Mr Benedict, go with the officer here. He has some questions for you.'

'Of course, I'll cooperate.' Saul stepped forward. I could tell he was hoping that he could get away with being the sole sacrifice.

'And the rest of your party too.' The guard beckoned us forward.

'Not my daughter or my nephew surely?' Saul waved dismissively to us. 'They're both minors, under eighteen. They can't be of interest to you.'

I pulled my pink suitcase forward so it stood in front of Hal's army boots. He slouched, trying to take a few inches off his height.

The policeman shuffled through the passports until he came to ours. I caught a stream of language I didn't recognize, accompanied by a general impression of fuss and concern about bad publicity for detaining underage westerners. Reaching a decision, he said something to the guard.

'My colleague says they can go as long as they give him the address where they will be staying. The rest of you will have to go with him and wait for an interpreter.'

'They'll be at the hotel we booked for our vacation.' Saul handed over a copy of the reservation.

The policeman gave our passports to the guard, who stamped them for entry into the country. I felt a huge wave of relief when he passed them to Hal. At least we had travel documents. With us free, the others were a lot safer too.

Find out what you can about Victor and this crown, Summer, and let us know how they knew to expect us, said Saul.

Will do.

Hal made to pick up his holdall but a policeman stepped up and shook his head, order reinforced by the gun held across his chest.

'They want to search your luggage,' said the guard. 'You can collect it later from the police station.'

'They can do that?' asked Hal, failing to hide his resentment as the policemen piled all the men's bags onto a trolley.

'This is Afghanistan, not America.'

The policeman came back for my suitcase but Hal put a hand on the wheelie handle. 'Hey, tell him it's girl's things. He wouldn't want to part my cousin from her hairdryer, would he?'

The guard smiled, showing he had a sense of humour too, or possibly a teenage daughter. He exchanged a quiet word with the policeman, who replied gruffly. 'He says if she unzips it here then he'll check it now.'

I knelt down and opened up the bag. The policeman gave my neat clothes a cursory look then nodded and waved it away.

'You can take it,' said the guard.

I quickly zipped it up and Hal started walking away with it as soon as I stood up. 'We'll get a taxi. See you later, Uncle Saul,' Hal said.

I jogged after him, understanding that he wanted to get clear before they changed their mind about us leaving. Once outside in the blistering sunshine, Hal flagged a taxi from the short rank of six vehicles and threw my suitcase in the back. I slid in beside him.

'That went well.' Hal hit his forehead with his fist. 'Now what do we do?'

'Our job.' I crossed my arms, feeling chilled inside even though it was over thirty-six degrees outside. 'Give him the hotel address.'

Hal handed over the piece of paper to the driver who gave us a broad smile. 'Yes, yes, I know. Welcome to Afghanistan,' he said in thickly accented English.

'So happy to be here,' said Hal sourly.

We checked into the hotel, relieved to find that the staff spoke some English. It hadn't been our plan that we would be the ones to do the talking, as Will and Lucas had done the crash course in basic Dari to make the local contacts. The clerk

76

picked up my suitcase to lead the way to our room. The hotel was in fact more like a guest house, a large private residence set in a walled garden not far from the tourist destination of the Blue Mosque. Our party had been allocated one wing, which had a sitting room and three bedrooms. I was given a little one on my own, the Benedicts and the Robinsons were to share out the other two. The family who owned the hotel lived in the other part. I could hear the chatter of girls and the laughter of a young child in the distance, friendly, normal sounds after the hostile reception at the airport. Opening the door to our quarters, the clerk wheeled my case to the centre of the living room and waited, holding on to the key. Hal was already exploring the rooms, opening doors and cupboards.

'He expects a tip,' I explained quietly, knowing I couldn't be the one to give it.

'Oh.' Hal dug into his pocket and pulled out a five dollar note. 'Will this do?'

'He'll be delighted.'

With a grin as the banknote disappeared into his fist, the clerk bowed slightly and left us alone.

'I overpaid him, didn't I?' Hal flopped down on the sofa and eyed the bowl of fruit in the centre of the coffee table. He helped himself to a grape. 'Well, hell.' He meant more than just the generous tip.

After opening the French windows to let in some air, I took a seat in the armchair. 'Exactly.' A burst of birdsong from the garden entered, followed by the scent of the rose bush just outside.

'How long do you think they'll be? Don't answer that: how could you know?' Hal peeled an orange. 'I can't think they can be charged with any offence as we hadn't even entered Afghanistan when they were marched off. But do you have any idea what it's about?'

I remembered that he hadn't been part of the telepathic conversation. 'It's weird but I think it's something to do with a gold crown.'

'A crown? You mean like in a badge or symbol?'

'No, the real thing. An archeological artefact, the kind of thing you'd see in a museum.'

'What has Victor Benedict got to do with that stuff?'

'I would guess it might make more sense if we knew who his soulfinder is.' I was beginning to wonder. I'd leapt to the assumption that she would be a political prisoner, or kept behind closed doors at home because she lived in a strict household, but what if the explanation was something much more straightforward? Maybe she was implicated in a crime involving the crown I'd seen? 'What's the Wi-Fi like?'

'I booked this place because it claimed to offer it to guests.' Wiping his hands off on a serviette, Hal grabbed his phone. 'It's OK but not great.'

'Can you run a search on key terms to do with gold crowns and this part of the world?'

'Are we starring in *National Treasure* now? Can I expect Nicholas Cage to burst in with a map and a flashlight?'

I smiled, slightly mystified.

'Don't tell me you haven't seen those films either? Where've you been, princess?'

'Living under a rock, I expect you'd say.'

'Yeah, a sparkly princess one, I bet. With a concierge.'

'Don't all the best rocks come with one?' I stole a segment of orange from him. 'You wait out here for Nicholas Cage while I take my case into my room and get us some drinks. I've got a feeling we might have to go out as soon as the others get here, to see what artefacts like that they have on display.'

'Yeah, museums, just my thing.' Hal groaned and settled down to wait for the painfully slow page loading.

I returned five minutes later with two bottles of cool water from the in-room fridge. I'd also sent Misty an update couched in a kind of teenage speak laced with emoticons. It had to be by phone as telepathy over such huge distances is extremely difficult, top end of my range about five hundred miles. If the local police looked at my text messages they would think I was just bleating to a best friend about the delay to our holiday plans but she would know to pass the message on to the rest of the Benedicts. I put the drinks down. 'Found anything?'

Hal was frowning at his screen, little lines appearing at the top of his nose. His hair looked velvety soft in the light filtering through the net curtains; I had a strange urge to stroke it to see what it felt like. There was no doubt that I was inconveniently attracted to him physically. I felt like a phone on recharge while with him, battery bar climbing to full desire.

'Maybe. Have you heard of Bactrian gold?'

I shook off the distracting thoughts. He wasn't a savant, wasn't for me. No one could be for me with my family, as I couldn't risk bringing anyone home. 'No. I've heard of a Bactrian camel so I guess it must refer to a place?'

'Yeah, it's the old name for a civilization that used to rule parts of Afghanistan. Archaeologists have found hoards of gold in burial mounds, left as part of the funeral practices. It says here that the stuff that hasn't been looted makes its way to the museums: belts, jewellery, but also crowns. Hang on, the next page is finally loading. Just running it through Google translate.' He angled the screen so I could see, meaning I had to sit next to him on the sofa.

'Oh my word!' I whispered. Hal had hit the mother-load. A regional newspaper carried a story about a female museum worker who had been arrested on suspicion of smuggling a priceless cultural relic out of the country nearly two years ago. Atoosa Nawabi, who graduated with a PhD from the

National Museum Institute, New Delhi, in the Art of Central Asia, received a ten-year prison sentence for the theft of the Bactrian crown but the object was still missing. 'Run a search on her name.'

Hal was already a step ahead and a new page was loading. 'Wow. I guess this is why they were so angry at the airport.' Nawabi had escaped from her captivity in the Mazar-e-Sharif women's prison just yesterday while we were in the air and was reportedly on the run. She was suspected to have had help from her last visitor, an American travel writer, name not reported but the picture taken on his entry to the country identified him clearly to us as Victor. 'My brothers need to know this. The police must think that we've come to help smuggle her out of the country and I have to admit with that timing we do look very suspicious. I'd arrest me too if I were them.'

My brain was still reeling with the news that Victor's soulfinder was an international jewel thief. 'Victor must have found himself in a very difficult spot: save her or abide by the laws of the country.'

'He doesn't strike me, from what I've heard, as a guy who is content to play by the rules.'

'But he wouldn't like the stealing angle. He has his own morality.'

'Doesn't matter: our team needs to know. I'll have to go and see if I can get in to visit them at the police station.'

I put out my hand to stop him rising. 'Hal, you're with a savant. I can do that from here.'

He shook his head, shrugging off my touch. 'They might be miles away.'

'Powerful telepath, remember?' I tapped my temple. 'Maybe your brothers can't do this but for me it's simple. Just let me do my thing while you have a drink.'

I quickly sent out a call to Saul, hoping I wouldn't be intruding at a bad time. I found him in the middle of an interrogation so had to wait a second until he was free to concentrate on my message.

You and the boy OK? he asked, his calmness very reassuring.

Yes. And you?

Just questioning, nothing to alarm Amnesty International.

There's something you need to know. I quickly recapped on the news we had gleaned from the internet.

I felt Saul's mood brighten a little. I think he had been suspecting something far darker about his son's soulfinder, some radical religious angle that would make a connection between an FBI agent and an Afghan impossible. That was the only kind of bad news story about Afghanistan that reached America; it was almost a relief to hear they had ordinary crime too. Theft, the Benedicts could handle. *Thank you, Summer. You and the Robinson boy stay where you are. This gives me enough information to know what they want from us. I hope we'll be with you in a few hours. I'll break off now so I can concentrate on the interrogator; he's already giving me a strange look. I'll have to tell him I was having a senior moment.*

No one would believe Saul was reaching that stage in life. He was far too switched on. *See you later then. Take care.*

I broke off the conversation to find Hal studying me with a bemused expression. 'What?'

He shook his head. 'It cracks me up every time how you lot take such extraordinary abilities in your stride.'

'It's just like using a mobile.'

'Summer, it is not the same at all. Don't kid yourself.'

'I can't help being this way.'

'I'm not blaming you, just reminding you that it's not normal for the rest of us. So, ready to hit the museums to see what else we can find out?'

I rubbed the side of my bottled water. 'I told Saul we'd stay put.'

Hal stood up and stretched out his cramped limbs, arms locked above his head. I really wished he would stop doing that in front of me. I was finding the display of toned midriff distracting. 'I don't know about you but I've been sitting too long and I didn't promise him anything. You can stay here if you like but I'm going out to be an innocent tourist.'

'But what if something happens to you? You wouldn't be able to let us know you were in trouble?'

He dropped his arms. 'Princess, I can't wait around for my savant escort, not when we've got a prison break to investigate.'

His mind was made up and I couldn't let him go alone, could I? 'We have to tell the others.'

'Look, we're on the clock here. I know my brothers would expect me to start intelligence gathering. I don't know about your Benedicts but they strike me as the kind of guys who would want to get right down to work. We'll leave them a note. They can come and join us if they get out early, otherwise we'll be back before they know it. We can't afford to lose even a day if Victor has a head-start on us.'

I bit my lip. Was I being too cautious or merely sensible?

'We're not doing anything illegal; stop tying yourself up in knots.' Hal stuffed our water into his backpack, along with our passports and money. 'Are you coming or not?'

I held up my hands in surrender. 'OK, OK, I'll come.'

He flashed me a grin. 'I knew there was a rebel in there somewhere. Had to be, seeing how you're part of this crazy mission.'

I arranged my scarf over my head and slid on my sunglasses. 'You're leading me astray.'

'Hell, yeah, princess.'

Chapter 7

We started where the tourists who made it to Mazar-e-Sharif always began their tour: heading for the Blue Mosque. It wasn't hard to find as all the roads led to it in a carefully laid out grid, the spiritual heart of the city still beating after centuries of turmoil. As we drew closer on the traffic-choked streets, we could see that the mosque was a series of turquoise domed buildings and one taller tower for the muezzin to broadcast the call to prayer. Pale gold and sky-blue tiles in intricate patterns covered the walls, moulded into arches that spanned the walls. The courtyard was paved with pale stone that reflected like shallow water in the baking sun, flocks of doves strutting between the legs of the visitors, waiting for handfuls of corn to be scattered. I watched a boy throw the contents of his paper bag high in the air; the flock billowed in pursuit, before settling back once more on the ground. It reminded me of a scene from one of the drawings of the Oriental miniaturists, conjuring Arabian Night phrases like the Silk Road, Samarkand, enchanted palaces and treasures of the East. I could easily imagine Aladdin coming to worship here in curled slippers and purple and gold waistcoat.

Hal consulted the guide he had downloaded on to his phone. 'It says here the mosque has a small museum.'

'Lead on, MacDuff.' I kept an arm's length from him, having been told in our mission briefing that men and women touching in public might offend some locals.

Hal turned to look down at me. 'What's that?'

'You don't know Shakespeare?' I pulled the tail-end of the scarf across my face to hide my smile.

'Not personally, no.'

'It's a famous line from *Macbeth*.'

'Was that the best he could do?' Hal picked up the pace.

'I'm sure even a Yahoo such as yourself knows that Shakespeare wrote amazing verse. That's just a fragment people got into the habit of repeating.'

'So what's a search engine got to do with anything?'

Where to begin? 'Yahoo didn't start life as a search engine, Hal. There are things worth knowing in books too.'

'Really?' From his cutting tone, it was plain he wasn't appreciating my correction. 'And tell me why I should care?'

'Because they're interesting, enriching, they tell us who we are, what people have thought and felt.' We'd been doing so well since the flight but now our relationship was sliding off course again. 'If you go through life with only a slender diet of references taken from TV shows and pop singers, then you'll live an impoverished existence.' Something about him made me more of a know-it-all; even I didn't like myself when I talked like that, but I couldn't seem to help it. Normal instincts went haywire round him, tact left back at home.

'Just listen to all those fancy words from the princess to her minion. Spending any time with you is as much culture as I can take.' He checked his map and took a turn around the eastern side of the building. 'So what's a Yahoo then? Do you even know?'

'A race of crude and boorish humanlike creatures met by Gulliver on his travels.' I felt a little ashamed as I explained.

'OK, so you get to insult me and I don't know it because your clever references sail over my head. Very stylish.'

Put it like that, he showed me an unedifying side to my

character. 'Sorry. You're right. But the word came to mean something less strong, a reference to someone who didn't appreciate refinement or culture.'

'Save it, princess. At least if I google your comments I'll know what you really think of me—or maybe I should ask Yahoo, seeing how it's my natural home.'

Point to him. I felt disappointed in myself for mocking him for something that was none of his fault. I had been brought up by my father to read widely, attend classical concerts and operas. I was probably far more of a cultural oddity than Hal in my generation. Most of my contemporary music education was thanks to Angel rather than my own listening. Ask me about football or that rapper guy named after a sweet and I'd be the one at a loss.

'OK, we're here,' said Hal. The door to the museum was wedged open, a cool black vault, an escape from the heat outside. He paid the entry fee to the attendant sitting at a table on the threshold. The man eyed us with interest, not, I was pleased to find from his brain patterns, because he suspected us of anything but for the reason that western tourists were rare. We wandered into the rooms and peered at the displays. It was a bit dull to be honest. I could see why Hal wasn't a fan of museums.

'What kind of clues are we looking for?' asked Hal.

'I'm not sure—references to the crown or Victor's lady.' I didn't dare speak her name aloud. This conversation would have been much safer if we could use telepathy. I spotted a knot of museum workers in discussion at the far end of the room; they were gathered around a newspaper which gave me hope they were talking about recent events. 'I'll take a seat and listen in.' I flicked my gaze towards the people. 'Why don't you see if you can find anything in the exhibition.'

Hal nodded and moved off to a row of cabinets we hadn't yet examined. I sat down on a bench and closed my eyes to help my concentration. When there is more than one unfamiliar mind to shadow I have to untangle the threads, learn each specific brain signature. I caught hold of the first quite quickly as it belonged to the one holding the newspaper. His thoughts were filled with cold fury, outrage at the escape, a sense of his own importance. *Museum director?* I wondered. I nicknamed him Sultan. Another mind was more slippery. I couldn't understand his thoughts but it seemed like he was looking to take advantage of Atoosa Nawabi's disgrace, perhaps step into her position. I decided to call him Jafar. The third person, the youngest of the three, I nicknamed Aladdin for his handsome dark looks; he was sincerely distressed and personally involved as his thoughts of Atoosa were a blend of many life-stages, flashes of domestic scenes and celebrations. A family member perhaps? I couldn't understand his words but I sensed an intention to protest her innocence. Interesting. That was the first person we'd encountered who had any question that she was involved in the theft. The police certainly hadn't had any shadow of a doubt that they were chasing a guilty person.

Hal returned and placed a leaflet on my knee. 'I found something. This was at the back of the stack of information material.'

I opened out the folded paper to reveal a picture of the very crown I'd seen in the minds of the Afghans. The curling script was in Dari but there was a brief English summary at the foot of the page. It advertised a special exhibition of Bactrian gold artefacts two years ago, organized jointly with the National Museum in Kabul. The curator was named as one Dr A Nawabi, originally from Mazar-e-Sharif but now returning on secondment from the capital for her first big exhibition. 'That answers quite a few questions but doesn't explain how it went missing. Would you really set up a special show in your home town and then steal the crown jewels? It's career suicide.'

'But you're also the one who knows most about the weaknesses in security and have local links. If it were her, then she might have hoped someone else would take the blame.'

'And yet it also makes her the perfect scapegoat.' I preferred to think that she might be innocent for Victor's sake.

'I guess we won't know until we catch up with her. What have you learned?'

The conversation at the end of the room was breaking up. Sultan stalked back in the direction of his office, Jafar put an arm around Aladdin, guiding him out. From the flickering images in Jafar's brain, he appeared anxious to get rid of the young man, embarrassed to see him in the museum.

'Aladdin there—I think he's connected to Atoosa somehow.'

'Aladdin?'

'My nickname for him. Can you find a reason to talk to him? I'd do it but it wouldn't be right round here for a girl to approach a stranger.'

Hal nudged me. 'So I'm the Genie now to your Princess Jasmine?'

'I'm not asking you to arrange a date but to question him, if he speaks English. I think he'll be sympathetic. But wait until that creepy guy is out of the way.'

Hal cast a look at Jafar, who was now brushing away tears and shaking his head. 'Yeah, I see what you mean. I look at him and I think, "There's a snake in my boot."' He arched a brow at me. 'That's a test for you: where's that from?'

I shrugged, not sure what he meant.

'*Toy Story*, film classic even you shouldn't turn your nose up at. Seems like there are holes in your education, princess.'

He was enjoying getting one over on me and we were in danger of losing our lead. I waved my hand at him. 'Quick—go!'

'Cool your jets, flower; I'm on it. Follow in about thirty seconds.'

Flower? But he'd gone before I could challenge him on his latest nickname for me. Hal sauntered off looking as if he had all the time in the world. Was he taking this seriously or did he just have a problem following orders from a girl? I didn't wait thirty seconds but made my way to the exit to watch him in action. He had overtaken Aladdin without appearance of hurry by the simple fact that his stride was much longer than the other boy's and his target was ambling, shoulders hunched, hands in pockets. Hal was holding out his phone, asking if Aladdin would take a photo of him against the backdrop of the impressive entrance of the mosque. It was a smart way of ascertaining if the boy spoke English and, as the encounter was prolonged, my hopes began to rise. I crossed the paved stretch of courtyard just as Hal posed for his photo.

'Where were you when I needed you, Summer?' Hal said, as if my absence had been all my fault. 'I had to ask this guy to take the picture for me.'

I scrambled for an explanation. 'Sorry. I needed to sit down for a moment. The heat.'

Aladdin's attention had transferred to me, brown eyes sweeping me from head to toe. His close focus made me feel uncomfortable as I knew it was not common practice to stare at women who were not family members. I touched the edges of the headscarf to check it was still in place. Hal took a step between us but Aladdin only shifted so he could see me.

'Hey, man, that's my cousin you're staring at,' said Hal softly.

Aladdin held up his hands and took a quick look around to check we weren't in hearing of any of the other visitors. 'I apologize. But you, you are a savant? I've never felt such a strong energy before.'

'Oh, er . . .' I looked to Hal, unsure how to answer. For all I knew they could imprison people here for having ESP and I hadn't been shielding.

Aladdin's face broke into a pleased smile, white teeth gleaming against bronzed skin, increasing his handsome score yet further. 'I am one too. All my family are savants. My gift is to detect it in others.' He closed his eyes briefly. 'You are . . . you are very powerful mind savant and very beautiful.' He turned to Hal. 'But you are not gifted. I don't sense you.'

Hal scowled at the kick to his ego, but at least we had confirmation that the boy was a savant. We were standing in the middle of the most public place in Mazar-e-sharif; it probably wasn't a good idea to have this conversation out in the open.

'Look, man, can we go somewhere else to talk about this?' asked Hal. 'It wasn't by chance I approached you. I want to ask you what you know about Atoosa Nawabi.'

Aladdin grabbed Hal's wrist, a flare of hope in his eyes. 'You know where Atoosa is? Tell me!'

'No he doesn't. We're here to find her and the man she is with,' I explained.

'My sister would not run off with a man. She has more honour than that!' Aladdin had clearly heard this accusation before and it was at the root of his distress.

'Maybe she would if he were her soulfinder. Please, who are you?' I couldn't keep calling him Aladdin in my mind; next thing would be calling him that out loud by mistake.

'My name is Javid. I am Atoosa's youngest brother, the seventh child of my parents.' That would make him an extra-powerful savant, like Zed was in the Benedict family, I noted. 'Welcome to my city.' He made a formal bow to me and held out his hand to Hal to shake.

'I'm Hal and this is Summer.' Hal held himself a little stiffly, taking half a step so he had his shoulder between me and our new acquaintance.

'Javid, can we go somewhere to talk?' I asked, side-stepping

Hal. 'There's a lot you need to know and questions we have to ask.'

Javid cast a dubious look at Hal. 'I don't trust people who aren't savants. Your gift makes you one of the family; he is not.' Perhaps his limited English was making him less than tactful, but I felt for Hal under this dismissal.

'But you wouldn't expect me to allow you to go off with my cousin, would you?' said Hal, swallowing any insult he might feel for the sake of the mission.

Javid frowned. 'No.'

'So I'm part of the package. The police will be watching our hotel so I suggest you pick the venue for our conversation.'

I hadn't thought of that. 'Do you think they'll have followed us here, Hal?'

'No, princess. I've been keeping a watch.'

'I take you home,' said Javid, coming to a decision. 'You are right. This is bad place to talk.' I followed his gaze back to the museum where Jafar was standing at the door talking to the attendant at the cash desk.

'Who is that man you were with just now?' I asked.

Waving us on, Javid started walking away. 'Dr Abdullah. He was Atoosa's, how do you say, colleague? He is the only one who agrees with me that she is innocent.'

That didn't tie with my impression that Abdullah was quite pleased with the outcome of the trial but again, the street was not the right place to discuss this.

Will's voice nudged into my mind. *Summer, good news: we're free to go and are heading for the hotel.* He must have detected my flustered reaction. *You're not there? But I can't sense that you are in any danger.*

No, we're not. We found Atoosa Nawabi's brother. He's a savant. We're going to his home.

That wasn't the plan.

I sent him an image of shutting the door after the horse had bolted.

He sent a telepathic resigned sigh in response. OK. *Let us know where you are when you get there.* There was a pause. *Don't worry: Scott says he can find his brother with his gift, some kind of local positioning link-up he can do with people he's met. We'll join you.*

Thanks, but I think it's best if it's just us for now. Her brother is around our age I'd guess; we're less threatening than you all would be turning up on their doorstep. I'll let you know if we need backup.

Javid took a left down an alley and opened a grey-painted gate into a courtyard of a private house, a smaller version of our hotel but set apart by the amazing lushness of plants inside. It was like stepping into a jungle with musical birds calling from hidden perches. Javid laughed at our surprise.

'My mother is good with growing things,' he explained. 'Father finds water. Brother has a gift for calling birds to him. Our family is why white doves come to the Blue Mosque. We always have that gift among us. But still our neighbours are thankless people. They complain that it is bad for their laundry.'

His vocabulary was impressing me more and more as his fluency picked up with use. 'Where did you learn English, Javid?'

'When Atoosa studied in New Delhi, I lived with her and went to school. I am good, yes?'

'Very good.'

'I am thinking of being UN interpreter when I finish school.'

I could feel the brush of telepathy from him like wings passing overhead as Javid sent out a message to his family that he had brought guests. A middle-aged woman emerged from the nearest doorway, throwing a scarf over her head as she saw foreigners standing with her son. Her rapid speech poured from her like water from a high-pressure hose. Javid made his explanations, using his hands elegantly to illustrate his words. The lady responded by beckoning us inside.

'My mother wants you to meet the family,' Javid explained.

We entered the cool interior of the house, walls painted a soft orange, furniture a dark blue. Two men and three young women sat on cushions around a low table. Two of the girls were working on a long piece of embroidery, each approaching it from the opposite end, while the other studied from a pile of weighty anatomy textbooks. They rose on our entrance, faces disappearing behind scarfs. The mood in the room was sombre compared to the carnival atmosphere of the birds outside. One of the men had a white dove perched on his shoulder.

'Welcome to our house,' said Javid, gesturing to two cushions. 'Please sit.'

'Do any of your brothers and sisters speak English?' asked Hal, shaking hands with the men, nodding to the girls and then taking a seat on the rug.

'Poonah speaks a little as she is studying medicine but she understands more. Ramesh and Jahan also.' Javid indicated his brothers. Ramesh was the one serving as a perch. 'I speak best though. I will translate.'

I exchanged shy smiles with the sisters and mother and then sank down slightly behind Hal and nearer to the women.

'You have news of our sister?' asked Ramesh, feeding a corn kernel to his pet.

Hal was about to explain but Javid motioned imperiously for him to be quiet. 'I will tell them what you told me about Atoosa's soulfinder. It will lessen our family's disgrace. The disapproval of our neighbours has been very shaming.'

He began speaking rapidly in his own tongue. Mrs Nawabi greeted the news with a little cry of joy. She clapped her hands to her chest, then tugged at her son's sleeve, her questions pouring from her.

'My mother wants to know if Atoosa's soulfinder is a good man.' I'm sure Javid wasn't doing justice to the flow of words spilling from the lady but maybe he had gone straight to the heart of her concerns instead.

Hal looked to me. 'I don't know him. You'll have to answer that.'

'Victor is a very strong savant, a decent man. He will sacrifice everything for your daughter.' He had shown that much by putting his career at risk. 'His family are with us—his father and two of his brothers. We want to find Victor and Atoosa to help them,' I assured her. 'Can I ask something? How did your daughter come to be accused of theft? Forgive me, I've not met her, but is there any chance that she was involved at all in the crown going missing, maybe because she was tricked?'

Javid translated my question for his family and it was answered by vehement shaking of heads.

'We have told the courts and the lawyers again and again that she is innocent,' said Ramesh, 'but most people do not want to hear. There are some who said that allowing a daughter to go to Delhi to take doctorate rather than marry would bring shame on us. They see this as their words coming true. They do not understand that a savant must wait for her soulfinder.'

'And who will now marry any of us if this shame is not lifted from our family? We will not disown our sister. We know she is not guilty,' added Poonah softly. Her sisters murmured their agreements, showing they too understood a little English.

'What have you done to find her?' asked Hal, shrewdly guessing that this close-knit family would not be sitting on their hands now Atoosa had escaped prison.

'Our father and Uncle Maiwand have gone to find them,'

said Javid. 'Uncle is strong. He senses noise from very big distances and can send sound waves to make silence.'

'Like active noise reduction used in some military tech?' asked Hal.

'Yes, like stealth machine,' agreed Javid. 'He can follow anyone anywhere as long as they make sound.'

I dipped into his thoughts to see what he was picturing. 'You mean he can catch them by listening out for Atoosa's voice as well as hide the sound of his approach?'

Javid nodded.

'Cool. And has he found them yet?' asked Hal.

'Not yet. They have travelled into the Panjshir Valley. We expect more from them in a few hours.'

The valley was the route to Kabul but also meant heading into the Hindu Kush, and could be the start of a journey towards the border with Pakistan. 'So they think Atoosa went that way?'

'The journalist—this Victor—had a car. An SUV with the same number plate was seen leaving town in that direction late yesterday.'

Hal rubbed the bristling short hair at the back of his neck. 'Sounds a solid lead. Your father has a vehicle also?'

'Yes. He has gone in Uncle's pickup. Uncle is a big merchant, very rich. But the police are also looking in the valley. And the army.'

A suspicion came to me. It didn't sound like Victor, to run off with the entire law enforcement contingent on his tail. He was subtler than that. In his place I would send out a decoy and take quite another direction, or even stay put.

Victor, are you here? Amazed that I hadn't thought to try it before, I sent out a narrowly focused call on the telepathic wavelength I associated with him from the wedding. It should be good for ten miles or so at that strength. I waited, then there was a slight tug on the end of the thread, like a spider sensing disturbance in its web, but it vanished. Either someone else with the telepathic skill of eavesdropping had listened in— such people existed in most savant communities I'd visited— or I had brushed against Victor's mind. I had to hope if there was an eavesdropper he didn't understand colloquial English because I couldn't pass up this opportunity to send a further message. *It's Summer. We've rocked up with some BFFs.* I added the address of the guest house. *Boys in blue are watching.*

I wasn't sure this time if my words had reached anyone; they were such a weird mix I hoped a non-English speaker would be spending the next while puzzling over a dictionary.

Hal tapped lightly on my knee. 'You OK, princess? You checked out for a moment there.'

While I had been putting my concentration into communication, one of Javid's sisters had fetched a tray of dates, apricots and mint tea. She was holding out a delicate little cup to me, puzzled by my lack of response.

'Oh, sorry. Thank you.' I took the cup and sniffed in the delicious scent. It cleared my head wonderfully.

'What's up?' persisted Hal.

'Tell you later.'

Javid was staring at me again. 'You used telepathy. I felt it go out from you.'

Had it been him I had sensed listening in? 'How do you know?'

'I can see the gifts more clearly when they are used. No, not see,' he frowned, trying to describe his experience, 'I just know.'

'So you can't listen in?'

'No. It is like watching someone making a call from a street phone box. I am outside the kiosk.'

'I understand.' So it probably hadn't been him I had felt. 'Thank your family for the tea but we really need to return to

95

our hotel.' I allowed everyone to draw the conclusion that I had been talking to our party.

Mrs Nawabi said something rapidly to her youngest son.

'Mother says I am to go with you, meet the rest of Atoosa's new family and do all I can to help you. Is that acceptable? My older brothers have to stay here to look after the girls. The neighbours are not being nice to us.'

I imagined that was an understatement. The Nawabis probably didn't dare venture out in case of insult.

Mrs Nawabi surprised me by leaning over and pinching my cheek, yet more words tumbling from her.

'My mother say you are very pretty. She wants to know how old you are. Her boys all need their soulfinders.'

I now found myself the focus of all eyes of the room. I knew I was often mistaken for being older than I actually am so Ramesh was particularly interested in my answer, his dove equally so, head cocked to one side. Hal was looking amused at my embarrassment.

'I'm seventeen.'

The dove cooed in disappointment.

The issue of my impossible vampire inheritance rushed back. Finding I had a soulfinder in Afghanistan would be horribly complicated and all outcomes likely to be tragic. No one in their right mind would want to take on my burdens.

Javid struck his chest triumphantly. 'I am seventeen. I was born 30th November.'

Just a day before me. I swallowed: it was entirely possible he could be my soulfinder. 'Oh, I doubt we're a match then.'

'Funny: mine's the 28th, Javid. So when exactly is *your* birthday, princess?' asked Hal.

'Later than that.' Which was absolutely true.

Mrs Nawabi clucked her tongue, maternal disappointment plain.

'We could talk telepathically to check,' said Javid, not yet giving up on the idea.

I stood up. 'Yes, maybe, if there's time. But we've got to find your sister first, remember, and to do that we have to get back to the rest of our group. Hal, are you coming?'

He unfurled his long length from the cushion. 'Princess Jasmine giving Aladdin the brush off?' he asked so only I could hear, seeming quite pleased at the idea.

'There's no time for that.'

'I thought you savants always had time for your soulfinders?'

'He isn't my soulfinder.'

'How do you know when you're too chicken to try him out?'

I felt like thumping Hal. He just didn't get the savant life. It was no small thing to discover your partner; it would unleash a whole torrent of its own problems, drowning you if you weren't careful. Just look at my dad. He made no secret of the fact that he wished now he had been more cautious. Besides, there was no tingle factor between Javid and me. 'Can we get a move on please?'

'Yes, ma'am.' Hal gave me a mock salute, two fingers to his forehead.

We made our farewells quickly, promising to bring Victor's father and brothers to meet Atoosa's family as soon as we were able. Mrs Nawabi patted my cheek on the same spot she had pinched it and then pressed a little parcel in my hand. I made to open it but she shook her head.

'You must open it in your hotel,' Javid explained.

'What is it?' The present was beautifully wrapped in pink silk.

'A blessing from mother. She gives them to those she likes.'

'And I don't get one?' murmured Hal, eyebrow arched as his eyes twinkled at me.

97

'It's for you both,' explained Javid, not catching the irony.

'I'm relieved. I thought I'd done something wrong. Lead the way, Aladdin.'

I elbowed Hal in the ribs. How could he?

Javid paused at the gateway out of the lush courtyard. 'Aladdin? No, I am Javid.'

'Yeah, I know.' Hal winked at me. 'Just a joke with Princess Jasmine here. It's her name for you.'

'Hal!' Kill me now if Javid knew about Disney.

'Ah, I understand.' Javid smiled and then started singing in an oddly accented voice, *'I can show you the world . . .'* Disney had made it this far, or at least to Delhi where he had gone to school. Hal responded with a terrible falsetto, adding in the Jasmine lines. Bonding over teasing me, they continued their torment as they led us back to our hotel, Javid pretending to conduct us on a magic carpet. It was nice to see he had a sense of humour but I wanted the ground to swallow me up. No, strike that out, I wanted the ground to swallow *Hal* up.

Dropping the song, Javid stopped at the entrance to the guest house. Expression sombre, he took my hand for the first time and pressed my fingers in his. 'We will talk telepathically soon, yes? I understand that you want to keep our minds on Atoosa and this Victor but we must try.'

Just a mention of a possible soulfinder link and he was acting possessive. It made me deeply uneasy. I glanced over at Hal, who was watching us with arms folded, probably relishing my dilemma. He had no idea or he wouldn't be so cruel as to be smiling.

'There's a lot you don't know about me, Javid.' I slid my hand from his.

'Then I look forward to finding out more.' Javid opened the gate and entered the guest house grounds. 'First, we save my sister.'

Chapter 8

'Hi, honey, we're home!' called Hal as we entered our rooms. He didn't give the others a chance to criticize our decision to go out but entered straight into a round of introductions. I would have to learn how he did that: it might be useful with my dad. With that distraction taken care of, I took the chance to slip off to my bedroom, wanting a moment to catch my breath. Kicking off my shoes, I sat on the foot of the bed next to my open case, unwrapping the present. A packet of sweet-smelling dried rose petals fell out. Mrs Nawabi must have sensed I was in dire need of a long perfumed bath. I only felt comfortable when I believed I had some semblance of control over my situation; I wasn't a fly-by-the-seat-of-the-pants kind of person like Hal was. I couldn't be. The last few hours of impulsive decisions had tested me and I felt giddy, like someone just coming off a spinning teacup ride at the fun fair.

With no time for the bath, I found solace in routine. I started laying out my toiletries on the little dressing table, brush, small bottle of moisturizer, and make-up bag. I glanced up at the mirror and saw that my mascara applied back in the UK so many hours ago was working its way down my face. I took a cotton bud out of my wash bag and dipped it in the miniature face cream I'd packed, each little step in the ritual another brick reinforcing the wall I built mentally between me and life's chaos. I couldn't win in the long run but it helped for the moment.

A fist thumped on the closed door. 'You OK in there, princess? The team wants an update.'

'Just a moment.' I got out the mascara wand.

Hal opened the door, not waiting for an invitation. 'Geez, flower, you don't need to pretty yourself up for Aladdin; he's already sold on you in case you haven't noticed.'

I wasn't doing it for Javid, or for anyone, only myself, but that wasn't a conversation I wanted to have right now. 'Closed door, Hal. That should've been hint enough. I could've been changing.'

He grinned. 'I live in hope.' He shut the door behind him with exaggerated care. That boy was chaos theory in human form, each little flutter of his butterfly wings driving me into a tornado of feelings, most of them angry ones.

'OK, Summer, take a breath and then go back out there.' I wasn't happy with the daunted expression on my face. 'Keep your focus: Victor, the mission, then go home and disengage from savant friends.' I slid into some black canvas soft-soled shoes I'd packed to wear indoors and went back into the living room. Supper had been delivered while I had been in my bedroom and the others were already crowded around the low table, scooping up curry in flatbreads while they chatted with Javid. There didn't look as though there would be much left for me, which was bad news as my appetite had finally returned.

Saul got up and came over. He put a gentle hand under my chin, tilting my face, and waited for me to meet his eyes. 'You OK, Summer?'

'Yes. And you?'

He dropped his palm to my shoulder and gave it a squeeze. 'We're good. The police have ordered us to report again tomorrow but they let us go for the moment.'

'They think we might lead them to Victor,' said Trace, patting a space next to him on the sofa. Javid was staring at my hair loose on my shoulders with an appreciative glint in his eye.

'Stands to reason.' I tucked my hair behind my ears and sank down on the cushion, noticing that the bowl of rice in the middle of the coffee table was down to a few grains.

Hal appeared behind me and put a covered plate on my placemat. 'I made them save you some. Swarm of locusts the lot of them.'

'Oh, thanks.'

He shrugged as if it was no matter requiring gratitude. I hadn't seen him take such care of the others but maybe he'd decided his logistics role in our team included keeping me on my feet. Whatever the reason, it was lovely to have a plateful of warm lamb curry and fragrant rice that hadn't been chased round the bowl by eight other spoons.

Will tweaked the curtain over the window back into place. 'I sense three policemen keeping us under surveillance. Javid, you'll have to watch your back when you go home.'

Javid smiled slightly as if he wasn't worried. He already fitted right in among his fellow savants, picking up the ready-for-anything vibe the Robinsons and Benedicts radiated. Maybe I was the only cautious one in the room?

'So, Summer, we've heard about your discoveries this afternoon from Hal, and Javid has filled us in on what his family is doing, but do you have anything to add?' asked Saul.

I put down my fork and pushed the plate away. 'Oh, yes, sorry. I think Victor is still in the area, not in the Panjshir Valley at all.'

'What?' Hal shot to his feet. 'When exactly were you going to tell me this?'

I laced my hands together on my knee. 'I am telling you, Hal, along with everyone else.'

'And this brainwave came when? While putting on your

war paint in there?' He exchanged exasperated looks with his brothers.

'Hal, calm down. Let her tell us,' said Scott, though he was frowning at me too. Perhaps I had made a mistake not blurting it out immediately when I entered, but I didn't see what a few minutes' difference would make to something that was essentially a hunch.

'When Javid told us his father and uncle had gone off after the car, it struck me that Victor is too wily to be so obvious about his exit. I decided to try and contact him.'

Hal slumped on a stool by the French windows, head in hands. 'Without clearing it first with me? This was all back at his house, wasn't it? I knew you'd tuned out for a moment. I should've pushed you for a proper answer.'

Javid grimaced, a step behind everyone else in the conversation. 'What is "wily"?'

'Ask flower here: she's the one who talks like an encyclopaedia.'

I rubbed my knees. 'It means clever or cunning, Javid. Like a fox.'

Saul nodded. 'You're right, Summer. It is obvious now you say it. He wouldn't leave flying so many obvious flags like using the same car. So what happened next?'

'You know I'm a powerful telepath?'

'Yes, Sky and Phoenix told me.'

'I do this by learning the brain signatures of the people I contact. Once I know what they are like, I can narrow my telepathic wavelength and make it travel over longer distances, a bit like having someone's private line rather than having to go through a switchboard. I think we all manage this to a certain extent but I've just trained myself to do it accurately.' And so that Mother couldn't listen in to my conversations with my friends.

'I guess you're right. We all have some instinct for channelling. Sky and Zed almost managed to communicate between our home and Las Vegas once, getting a few fragments through. I thought that was the maximum range anyone could manage unless they had a soulseeker gift like Crystal.'

'You know a soulseeker? That's wonderful!' Javid gave me a very direct look.

'Yes, it's how we knew to come here, for Victor I mean.' Javid was flustering me. I couldn't deal with his expectations right then. Keep to the mission. 'Her telepathy works differently from the rest of us. Hers is through our connection, our love for the person; I don't have to love or even know my target very well as long as I recognize the brain pattern.'

'How far did you reach?' asked Trace.

'It's ultra reliable for about ten miles so I tried that first. I felt a presence but it was cut off too quickly to confirm if it was Victor or an eavesdropper.'

'But an eavesdropper would have to be very skilled to listen in if it is as focused as you say?'

'Correct. Which is why I'm leaning towards thinking it was Victor. I sent him a message in a kind of code, hoping he'd open up a channel when he thought it safe to do so. He's not done that yet.'

'If he's not answering telepathy, can you mind-shadow him now you've had a bite on the line?' Saul looked hopeful. It was why I was here after all.

'I think so, but I'll need to rest first. It's exhausting searching for the right brain pattern. I'll make mistakes if I'm not at the top of my game. I also need to get closer to make a full insertion into someone's mind.'

'How far can your gift stretch? At its upper limit, I mean?' asked Lucas. He had been standing with his back to the kitchen counter, arms folded, but his soft question reminded me that he was in charge of the military parts of this mission and would want to know the strengths of his team.

'I'm not sure. I can speak telepathically to a really good friend over several hundred miles if we are both sustaining the link. I once managed nearly five hundred but that was with Alex—he's soulfinder to one of my best friends—and he's a very powerful telepath too. The message gets a little frayed at that distance.'

'Listen to her. She thinks this is normal and that we didn't need to know,' said Hal, bashing his head on his palms.

'But you said you needed to be really close to mind-shadow?' continued Lucas, ignoring his brother's commentary.

'That's true too. It's not quite the same skill, but I suppose the telepathy is one of the doorways in.'

'But not the only one. You can mind-shadow without having made telepathic contact?'

'Of course. They don't even have to be a savant. I thought you all knew that?'

'I didn't. You?' Lucas turned to Scott.

'No, but I think you should recruit her for our team after all this is over. She's got capabilities we need.' Scott winked at me.

'We knew,' admitted Saul, 'I'm sorry if I neglected to mention it. What I didn't realize was how far she could send her telepathy. That's amazing, Summer. Zed and Sky managed because they are soulfinders; you do it even without that special link. You remind me once again that we should never judge a savant by her cover.'

'Would Victor know it was you?' asked Will.

'Yes. I didn't try to hide. I even told him where to find us.'

'And the person on the line didn't seem the least bit surprised you were here?'

Will was right: I hadn't thought of that but it was a clue.

'No. He just heard and then ducked out as soon as possible before I could gain a fix on his location.'

'So the telepathic door was shut in your face?'

'Yes.'

'How would you mind-shadow him now?'

I wished the focus of the conversation would move on to someone else. I desperately needed to rest. 'He has to be close. I have to sift through all the mind-signatures I can sense looking for the familiar one. It's like scanning a room for a known face: your eye can disregard the majority quickly if it knows what it's looking for.'

Scott walked past his oldest brother to pour himself another glass of water. 'As I said, Luc, recruit her.'

Trace sat forward. 'Wait a moment: there's another part of the picture we don't know. We're already guilty of underestimating the ladies once; let's not make it twice. Javid, what's your sister's gift?'

Javid smiled proudly. 'She is super-smart. She sees patterns, decodes computer programmes, reads languages very quickly once she picks up a few signs. They called her Rosetta at college.'

'Why?' asked Hal.

'After the Rosetta Stone, the archaeological find responsible for unlocking Egyptian hieroglyphs,' I explained.

He rolled his eyes at me and mouthed the word 'encyclopaedia'. At least his initial flash of anger had passed. I hoped that meant I was forgiven.

'Does she have any military-grade skills?' asked Lucas.

'What does that mean?' said Javid.

'What's she like in a fight?'

Javid sniffed. 'My sister does not fight.'

'But if she had to, what could she do?'

'A little moving with the mind, nothing more. She has my brothers and me to defend her.'

'And yet she ended up in prison,' murmured Hal, unable to resist the dig.

Javid glared at him. 'We were working on her release. We were making progress until recently when new evidence was produced that had not been at the trial.'

'New evidence?'

'Dr Abdullah found a photo of what he thinks is the crown on an auction house website in Delhi. The museum director took it as proof Atoosa had smuggled it out of the country into the hands of black-market dealers, people she knew from her time at university there.'

'When is the auction?' asked Saul.

'It didn't take place. It was sold to a private collector before it reached the market. We were not able to use it to prove her innocence, or even return the missing item in hopes it would earn her a reduced sentence.'

'So she gave up waiting and broke out.'

'My sister would have followed our laws. Your son is responsible for her escape.' Javid's eyes glittered.

'Indeed he is. But I would bet the farm on them having a plan to clear her name. If she is an honourable woman as you say she is, and knowing my son, they will not be content to let this rest there with her having to live the life of a fugitive. If we can't find them here, then we should follow that same trail to the crown.'

Trace got out his phone. 'I'll text Yves and see if he can hack the auction house website, find out who bought it.'

Saul offered me a hand to pull me up from the low sofa. 'You go rest, sweetheart. As soon as you are ready, I want you to do your thing.'

'And the police surveillance?' asked Will.

Lucas exchanged a grin with Scott and Hal. 'We'll take care of that.'

'What if they sense you?'

'They won't. We reconvene in six hours, OK? Everyone to get some sleep. If we're going out, it will be under cover of darkness, so we meet at midnight.'

Trace got up. 'Will and I will walk Javid home.' Javid began to protest. 'No, really, we want to meet our brother's new family. It's no trouble.'

After allowing myself a desperately needed four hours of sleep, I started work in my room on sifting through the minds I could sense. Assuming a comfortable position, I sat cross-legged on the bed, hands folded palms up in my lap. Victor's mind-signature was still fresh in my memory from the wedding so that made what otherwise would have been a nearly impossible task a little easier. Rather than looking for a needle in a haystack, I had more like a bale of straw to search. It was exhausting though. A headache edged in like a tall spectator sitting in the row in front of me at the cinema, partially blocking my view. I screwed up my eyes and tried to bend round it. I could sense something faint, hard to describe, like an emerging bruise just below the skin. *Victor?*

Hal came in quietly and put a cup of tea on the bedside table. He didn't say anything, having gathered that his wake-up call was unnecessary and I was already at work. I broke off for a breather, the faint trace of Victor fading.

'Thanks.' I cradled the tea. He'd made it just as I liked it, not too strong.

'Problem?'

'This makes my head ache.' I rubbed my temples.

'Let me.' He knelt on the bed behind me and started massaging my shoulders, releasing tension in muscles I hadn't realized had stiffened. 'Got to keep our top prize-fighter in condition for the next round.'

While he was thinking of me as a female boxer, I was thinking how lovely it was to be massaged by him. Few people touched me—Misty and Angel, my dad occasionally, my mother . . .

'Hey, you just went all tense again. I'm supposed to be making this better.'

'Sorry, you are. I was just thinking of something I don't like remembering.'

'Ah.' He went back to work again on my shoulders, taking the massage a little higher up my neck. 'Yeah, I guess we all have those things inside us. Best to shine a light on the dark spots. Takes away their power.'

'Is this philosophy according to Hal?'

'Yep. Shine a light and you'll see that the Bogie Man is really your dressing gown hung in a funny way on the back of the door.'

'Speaking from experience?'

'Absolutely. I was terrified of going to bed when I was little until my mum realized what the problem was.'

'She solved it?'

'Took the damn thing off the back of the door, shook it out and took it into her bedroom until I got over it. She knew if she just hung it in my cupboard I'd imagine he was hiding in there, but he wouldn't dare go anywhere near my parents.'

My headache was beginning to turn from tall man to dwarf. Surrounded by the scent that was uniquely Hal, the rub of his fingers, I felt like a cat with her fur being stroked. I was dangerously close to purring.

'So, do you think you and Javid are . . . you know?' His fingers stilled as he waited for my answer.

His question pulled me from my lovely dream with the abruptness of the cat getting dumped in a bath. 'I don't know. I doubt it.'

'And you don't want to find out? I thought this soulfinder thing was the Holy Grail for you savants. My brothers haven't said much but I know they'd love it if your friend Crystal could help them find theirs.'

'She will if she can. Just there's only one of her and a whole world network of us.'

'But you and Javid?' His fingers were pressing lightly again, giving me little brushes that felt more like caresses than a massage. What was going on here?

'I don't think that there's a me-and-Javid. I don't feel anything for him.' It struck me that if I couldn't have a soulfinder, maybe I could have someone like Hal. A guy who knew about us but wasn't one would in so many ways be perfect, at least for a little while until he tired of me. Maybe he'd even cope with my home situation as he seemed pretty resilient. That's if we could get past our desire to fight each other at every turn. I suspected in my case that my belligerence was frustrated attraction speaking. Was it the same for him? Our interactions felt like a twisted flirting, very stimulating.

'Good.' He cleared his throat. 'I mean he's a nice guy, but I can't see you happy out here. Too rough and ready.'

'I'm not high maintenance, Hal, despite what you think.' I wanted Hal to like me, feel the same sparks that I did.

He chuckled, his breath warm at the back of my neck, sending goosebumps down my spine. 'If you say so.'

'I'm not holding you back here, am I?' I felt a little wounded that he might still object to me being on the team.

'I didn't say that. No, you're doing great, apart from the withholding information from your team leader this afternoon.' He gave a little tighter squeeze, part tease, part rebuke.

'Team leader?'

'Team mate then.'

'You are so bossy.'

'And you, flower, are stubborn. I was angry because when a team doesn't share we are all put in danger.'

Once again, he had a point. 'I'm used to keeping things to myself. And why are you calling me "flower"? I'm not sure I like it.'

'You like it. Anyway, it's pretty and delicate like jasmine—I think it suits you.'

That sounded a little insulting. 'Really, I'm not delicate.' That wasn't an argument I was going to win today. 'But I'm sorry if I let you down, not telling you what I'd done.'

He bent forward and I felt his chin rest briefly on the crown of my head. 'You didn't let me down, but on another occasion it might matter. Try to learn to be a bit more of a team player, OK?'

So that's what he had come in to say. I was getting the pattern now: he would flare up in a temper, shake it off, then put his point more seriously when he calmed down, like he did over the not-eating thing and now again over my decision to try to contact Victor without checking with the others. This time, he'd been relaxing me so he could read me his lecture in a more receptive mood and I had fallen for it. I'd found the neck massage sensual and started thinking about romance; for him it had been business. I was very close to making a complete cake of myself. I had to put some distance between us.

'The headache's gone now.' Well, almost. 'Thanks for the massage.'

'You've pulled away from me again. What are you thinking?' Hal's hands cupped my shoulders, warmth seeping through the skin.

I didn't want to say. I bit my lip, emotions see-sawing wildly. Why was I reacting like this?

He shifted to sit beside me. 'Drink your tea and tell me what's wrong.'

'You confuse me.' I reached for the cup.

He laughed at that. 'Princess, I am the most straightforward guy you'll ever meet. I'll give you an answer to every question. Don't guess; go ahead and speak out.'

He asked for it. 'Were you massaging me to soften me up for your lecture?'

'Yes.'

'Oh.'

He grinned and then leant forward quickly and kissed the tip of my nose. 'But if you think I didn't enjoy getting to touch all that gorgeous skin of yours, then you don't understand guys at all. I feel good; you feel good; you get to hear my thoughts without us both scratching at each other: I consider that a positive result.'

'Thoughts? Wasn't it more of a reprimand?'

He dropped his gaze to my lips. 'That vocabulary of yours is a serious turn-on, princess. You've got to be careful. It makes me want to kiss you so badly and I really think that would be the wrong way to treat a team mate.'

Oddly, the idea of him kissing me didn't sound so disastrous right now. His lips were rather nice too, generous, quick to curl into a smile which brought out two grooves in his cheeks, which would've been dimples when he was little. That was a killer thought.

Hal groaned, lids hiding his dark chocolate eyes for a moment, breaking the spell of their gaze. 'OK, enough. I'm gone. You can't look at me like that and expect me to behave.' He got up. 'I'll let you get back to work.'

Right, yes, work. I had to find Victor. 'Thanks for the tea.'

He paused in the doorway to give me a smouldering look. 'Any time, flower.'

Just before midnight, I caught hold of a definite lead. I was shocked to find Victor was close, much closer than I had felt him this afternoon, which was why I hadn't sensed him more quickly. I'd started looking too far out. It took me a second to realize that he was coming to us.

I dashed out of the bedroom, finding the team gathered on the sofas.

'Are the police still watching?' I asked.

'Hey, calm down, Summer,' said Lucas, getting up, but Hal reached me first.

'What's up, princess?'

'Are the police still watching? Tell me!'

'No, we dealt with them.' Hal rubbed his palms up and down my upper arms.

I was torn between leaning in on him and standing alone. I ended up in a halfway position that looked as if we were about to start a waltz. 'What did you do with them? Will they come back?'

'Not for a while. We led them on a wild goose chase. They think we've headed for the Panjshir Valley too.'

'Thank God.' I rested my head against his chest.

'What's going on, Summer?' asked Saul.

'I think she is about to tell you that I'm here, Dad.' Victor stepped through the French windows. 'And she's really going to have to explain to me one day how she can track me when no one else can. It's damn inconvenient.'

Chapter 9

Saul was across the room in the blink of an eye, grabbed hold of Victor and crushed him in a bear hug.

'Victor!' he exclaimed, rocking to and fro. 'Your mother's going to give you such grief over this.'

'I suppose I'll be eating meals out in the barn for a month?' Victor asked wryly, hugging his dad back.

'At least.' Saul held him at arm's length. 'Are you really all right?'

'I'm truly great, Dad,' he said in a soft tone I'd never heard from him before.

'So she's really the one?'

'Yes, she is.'

'Then this is all worth it.' Saul let go, allowing Trace and Will to greet their brother, which they did in the form of rubbing knuckles on the crown of his head and mock-punching him in the physical tussle that spoke the love the Benedicts had for each other. Finally, a little breathless, Victor stood up straight and only then directed his attention to the rest of us in the room. You had to forgive him as they were all a little drunk with happiness at being reunited.

'I guessed you might come after me but I didn't realize you'd bring others to the party.' His usual cool manner had regained the upper hand. 'You're the Robinsons, right?' He shook hands with each in turn. They gave him wary nods rather than smiles. 'I know your reputations. You always get your mission done, no matter the odds. Thanks, guys, for coming to help. Dad, I hope you didn't mortgage the house to get them. They're the best and I know that doesn't come cheap.'

Saul coughed. 'Yves is bankrolling the operation.' The second youngest Benedict had made himself a digital fortune. 'He and Phoenix insisted as I wouldn't allow them to come.'

'I should think not. This is no place for anyone without the proper training. But Summer? You thought it OK to risk her?' Victor reached me and took my hand. 'You shouldn't be here.' He kissed my cheek, beard prickly on my skin.

'I had to come.'

'Emotional blackmail? Want me to kick some Benedict butt for you?'

'I think that's what they intend for you, Mr Runaway.'

'Correction: Mr Rescue Party.' His grey eyes sparkled. The change in him since meeting his soulfinder was the difference between seeing the decorated Christmas tree dark and then with the lights on, all the potential warmth and gorgeousness revealed.

'So where is she?'

'I stashed her somewhere safe while I come tell you all to get the hell out of here. Will, Dad, are we clear for the moment?'

'Yes, the perimeter is secure. No police near enough to see you,' said Will, adding a quick visual scan of the garden to his savant one.

'I haven't got long because I can't leave Atoosa alone. She's brave but the last eighteen months have been devastating. She's feeling fragile.'

A picture of her like an ancient vase painstakingly glued together by a museum conservator, Victor the foam surround in the box to keep her from shattering again, came into my mind. He'd sent the image to all of us, apart from Hal. Sensing

114

the failure to communicate, Victor turned to look at the youngest Robinson more closely.

'You don't connect telepathically. Why's that?'

'That would be because I'm not a savant,' replied Hal.

'OK.' The consummate professional, Victor noted the information without a ripple and moved on. 'Then I'll say the rest aloud. No eavesdroppers?'

'We're clear,' confirmed Will.

'Here are the headlines then. Atoosa Nawabi is my soulfinder.' He shook his head with a disbelieving smile. I felt something crack inside me, a little sigh of happiness for him but sadness for myself. 'She was set-up, most likely by someone local. The crown was stolen the night before the opening of the exhibition and immediately taken out of the country. She didn't have time to investigate as the theft was reported before she knew about it and then she was arrested. A document explaining the origin of the crown was falsified, allegedly with her signature on it, and the crown was put up for sale, but from the photos online she can tell that it is definitely the same piece. It's now been sold on.'

'We've got Yves working on that,' said Saul.

'Oh?' Victor looked over at him in surprise. 'So you know all this already. How?'

'Summer and Hal. They also pointed us in the direction of your soulfinder and we've made contact with Atoosa's family.'

Victor did a quick rethink, editing down his explanations. 'I've underestimated you guys.'

Hal bumped my shoulder with his. 'It helps having a kick-ass mind reader on your team, even if she doesn't obey orders very well.'

I narrowed my eyes as he chuckled. His compliment pleased me though.

'The hunt for you is heading for the Panjshir Valley,' said Trace, getting us back on track.

'Good.' Victor rubbed his hands. 'The guy I paid did his job then?'

'Paid?'

'I said he could keep the SUV if he drove it far enough away that the police lost him.'

'Good incentive for him to be clever.'

'I expect he has a cousin who'll switch the number plates and give it a paint job. That lead should keep the local authorities busy for a while though, so we can get back to the main mission.'

'Sorry, but our orders are to pull you out,' said Lucas. 'You're standing right here so I say we're done.'

'That's fine. Feel free to go. In fact, it's what I want you to do. I've still got to clear Atoosa's name.' Victor folded his arms, unconsciously mimicking Lucas's commanding stance. I had a sudden inkling that there were too many commanding officers in the room and not enough soldiers for this to go well.

Lucas glanced at his brothers, some silent communication going on between them. 'I was told to get you back to America by any means, immediately, and that's what I intend to do.'

Saul shook his head. 'No, Lucas, surely you understand that the mission has changed now? I never said by any means.'

Lucas gave the older man a resigned look. 'Not you, Saul. I'm not acting under your orders, nor are we intending to take your pay cheque so don't worry about that. I'm under a direct order from the US Secretary of State for Defence, our deployment signed off by his British counterpart.'

'What?'

'The hell you are!' Will and Trace both shot to their feet and took defensive positions around their brother and father. The aggression in the room rose to the red zone.

116

'Be reasonable. Special Agent Victor Benedict is too much of a security risk to go running off after a bit of historical gold, even if it does tarnish his woman's name. Once they're in the US, they can try to clear her, or be given new identities, whatever works best. We can't hang around in hostile territory. He has to go back, and he has to go back tonight. There's a helicopter on standby in Kabul.'

'No.' Victor's tone cut through the room.

Lucas' expression turned sour. 'You have no choice. This is bigger than you, Benedict. You realize by running off that you've risked the safety of all savants? The US and British governments were going to break off cooperation with us, seeing how their most trusted asset went AWOL. They have given us one chance to show we're not all like you, that we can bring our own back into line.'

'I'm so sorry, Victor. I didn't know,' said Saul. 'I didn't sense anything from them.'

Victor squeezed his father's arm. 'It's not your fault, Dad. This is my world, not yours. Governments don't play fair.'

'I think I should mention at this point, so we all know where we stand, that if any of you in this room doesn't obey a direct order from the President and the British Prime Minister and give us your full cooperation, then you will be facing charges of aiding a fugitive.' Lucas nodded to his brothers to fan out. 'Don't push this further than it need go, Benedict. Don't make your family responsible for your mistake. You have to face a disciplinary board. Leave it at that. Don't escalate it to a jail sentence.'

I hugged my arms to myself, outside the circle of posturing males. There were three Robinsons against four Benedicts but somehow I didn't think superior numbers were going to carry the day. We'd not yet seen the Robinsons in action; they had earned a reputation for achieving their mission objectives.

The blanket ban on letting anything leak from them made total sense now; the Robinsons had been planning all along to double-cross us, and as soon as I had shown up on the team they had to go radio-silent.

'Have you got a fix on Dr Nawabi yet?' Lucas asked Scott, who had positioned himself closest to Victor.

'Yes. I've the coordinates. The telepathic link between them is very strong.'

The cold fury in Victor's eyes was terrifying. 'You will not touch my soulfinder.'

'You hardly want to leave her here,' said Scott. 'We're planning to bring her out on the same flight. We assume that's what you would prefer? If you cooperate the visas issues will all be sorted. She can stay with you.'

'She has a life and family here. I've promised her she'll have a free choice where we live.' Victor's words were spat at Lucas.

'You can't always get what you want.' Lucas moved his hand to his sidearm. 'Don't try it.'

Victor closed his eyes and waves of mind-strike poured from him, huge breakers like a sea-swell. He was attempting to disable the Robinsons in one go so he could slip away, not too worried if he gave them a severe mental bashing. But it wasn't working. Lucas wasn't even breaking into a sweat. Instead, he drew his gun and levelled it at Victor. I hadn't even known until then that he had come armed. I noticed now that Scott also had a weapon.

'Your powers don't work on us, Benedict. None of them will so don't waste your energy trying.'

Victor broke off. 'That's not possible.'

'It is if you have someone on your team impervious to savant attacks. That's my little brother, Hal, if you hadn't realized, the only one we know of his kind. Send anything his

118

way and it just vanishes. He's the ultimate camouflage and forcefield rolled into one.'

Hal? The 'aw, shucks, you're all freaks' boy? It had all been an act to hide their ultimate secret.

'You're a savant?' I asked him hoarsely, feeling acutely betrayed.

Hal gave me an uneasy look and tried to brush my arm but I stepped out of reach. 'No, flower, I'm a not-savant. I told you.'

'Don't you dare call me flower.' Anger bubbled; I wanted to slap their oh-so-honest faces for leading us into this situation. 'The three of you should be ashamed of yourselves. We came with you in good faith. You've been lying to us.'

Hal scowled. 'Didn't you listen, Summer? Victor betrayed us first. We're putting his mistake right.'

I shook my head and moved as far from him as possible, joining the Benedicts. I couldn't believe I'd been purring under his hands just an hour ago, thinking there might be some kind of relationship between us. I had been an utter fool. 'Team player, Hal? You're certainly a player, I can say that much for you.'

Will put his arm around me. 'We're so sorry we got you in to this.'

'It's OK.' But it wasn't OK. I'd bargained away my chance to leave home in order to help Victor, only to find I was just a decorative addition to a well-thought-out plan to trap him. His employers knew he'd come if he thought his family was at risk; it was the only bait alluring enough to get him away from the side of his soulfinder. I felt furious for us all. I had to do something or I'd explode—and my feelings had to be but a pale echo of what Victor was experiencing.

'Summer, be reasonable,' pleaded Hal.

I ignored him. 'You know something, I'm not leaving.

Atoosa and her family don't deserve that. There are three of you and five of us. What's to stop us just walking out of here?'

'Loyalty to your country?' suggested Scott, not liking the turn this discussion was taking.

I'd worked out that none of the Robinsons were prepared to hurt me, though I wouldn't put it past them to use force on the Benedicts, so it was up to me to exploit this one small factor in our favour. I just had to get them so angry that Hal dropped his savant-nulling shield. He may not be a regular kind of savant but I knew from my experience with my mother than any kind of mental shield would collapse when emotion got in the way of control.

Watch for our chance, I told the Benedicts, making sure my message channelled only to them. *I'm taking down the camouflage.*

Be careful! warned Victor.

Don't worry. They won't shoot me. At least I hoped not. 'My country, Scott? That's rich coming from mercenaries who hire themselves out to the highest bidder.'

'Mercenaries!' Hal's fists clenched. 'We're soldiers.'

He didn't like that, did he? 'You made a serious error when you sold out to the FBI. Crystal Benedict could have found your soulfinders for you; now she's more likely to send you into a swamp. Try using your GPS super power to get out of that, Scott. Two lonely little savants living out their miserable existences with only their bank accounts to comfort them. Oh yeah, and their non-savant sidekick—Robin to his Batmen brothers.'

'Shut up, Summer,' hissed Hal.

Time to get right up into his grid. 'What have I said that's not true, Hal? You told me you were straightforward. You even flirted with me to make me forget my suspicions about not being able to mind-shadow you, didn't you? You made me like you, all that tea and chocolate, flower and princess pet names. So we can add heartless love rat to your other titles.'

'Shut up!' His face was flushed now; he was close to yelling at me, which was just what I wanted.

'Shall I recap?' I mockingly counted them out on my fingers. 'I think you're a mercenary, a player, a traitor and a heartless—'

'Shut the hell up!' He had lost it, making a grab for me, but I didn't give him a chance. I slammed my power into his head and took over.

We both froze.

'Summer?' He sounded bewildered.

'Oh my God. No, no, no.' This couldn't be happening. It was like being inside the most beautiful crystal maze, rainbows flashing everywhere I looked, warmth, humour, everything I wanted. It was home.

The mood in the room changed again as everyone realized something else had gone seriously wrong.

'What's is it?' asked Lucas, shaking his brother. 'Hal, snap out of it.'

I had to do it; the Robinsons had forced me to this point. But it was wrong too, so wrong, like taking a black marker pen to the Mona Lisa. *Block your brothers.* I sent the command to Hal, scrawling all over his fabulous mind. *Run!* I ordered the Benedicts, stumbling out of the French windows.

I didn't look behind but I knew that Hal was wrestling his brothers, preventing them from reaching the doors and following us. I held Hal there as long as I dared, tears streaming down my face. I could hardly see where I was going, guided only by Will as we followed Victor into the labyrinth of streets on the evacuation route he had already planned. He'd stashed a car in an alleyway. Jumping into the driving seat, he was pulling away even as Saul closed the rear door behind the last of us.

I curled up into Will's lap, sobbing.

'Tell us what happened, Summer,' Will said gently. Victor was driving so as not to attract attention, which meant that the car was moving painfully slowly away from the disaster zone we'd just fled. It wasn't doing justice to my racing heart. I wanted to plunge my foot down hard on the accelerator and drive over a cliff. 'What did you do?'

I gulped then forced myself to sit up, scrubbing my sleeve across my cheeks. 'I took over Hal. I can get past his defences when he loses control. They'd forgotten I can work on non-savant minds too.'

'We got that bit. What is it that you're not telling us?'

'They say Hal's not a savant, but that's not really true. He's just a rare form, the opposite. He absorbs all our mental energy, except mine.'

'How do you know this?' asked Saul, but I think they already suspected.

'Because when I got into his mind I discovered that I am his soulfinder.'

Chapter 10

Silence met my announcement. Victor started to drive a little faster, risking attention from the local police.

'That's not good,' said Trace, shaking his head.

'I'm sorry, sweetheart,' said Saul, shooting Trace a warning look. 'But don't worry—we'll sort this out. Maybe if you go back? Talk to him?'

I felt something wither inside me. Hope? 'I don't want to go back.'

'If you look at it from their point of view—'

'Please, Saul, not now.' I knew what he was going to say, that sometimes doing the right thing felt wrong and the wrong thing right. Neither team could be sure which was which with so many crossed loyalties. What I couldn't stomach was the idea that Hal had been playing me, getting me to lower my barriers so that he and his brothers could more effectively trick us as to their intentions. He had destroyed my trust.

'Dad, Summer's right.' Victor took a side road off the main one he had been following, wheels lurching in and out of potholes. 'We haven't got time to take her back right now as they know where Atoosa is. We have to save my soulfinder first before we deal with the Robinsons.' He slowed as we came to what looked like a goat-shed. 'Stay here while I get her.'

The clicking sounds of the cooling engine sounded very loud as we waited in silence. I rubbed my arms, remembering how Hal had been caressing them but a short while ago. Had he really not known he was a savant? Had that been the truth or yet another lie? Technically, he may not have spoken any to me but his whole behaviour had been one big pretence. Suddenly it all seemed very different—his attempt to keep me off the team had probably been motivated by knowing that would mean he had to keep shields up twenty-four seven, then the care and teasing had all been cheese leading to the baited trap.

'Don't, Summer.' Saul took my hands in his. I realized I'd been leaving scratch marks on the skin, not even noticing the pain, such was the inner agony.

'My life is so crap.' I didn't normally admit to private thoughts but I was sitting wide open. 'I don't get the good breaks, only the bad ones.'

'It might not be so bad.' Saul pulled my head to his chest in a fatherly fashion. I could feel his warm breath touch my hair. 'Karla and I, we didn't start out so well. She thought I betrayed her when I took a decision she disagreed with, and I was angry that she didn't support me. We forgave each other in time, but it was difficult for a while.'

'I didn't know that, Dad,' said Trace softly.

'Me neither. You and Mom seem so much a team,' added Will.

'Oh we are now.' Saul smiled wistfully, lost in reminiscence. 'But all of you will have to learn that relationships aren't made by love at first sight. You both fell on your feet with Diamond and Margot but still there's the happily-ever-after to hammer out—that's what matters. That's the true test of character.'

Victor returned leading a woman by the hand. She was wearing a full burka so we couldn't even see her eyes. He opened the rear door. Will climbed over into the back to make room on the seat. 'Dad, this is Atoosa. We have to move now, so we'll do the rest of the introductions while on the road.'

Saul shifted up so I was in the middle, Atoosa next to me.

'I can't tell you how pleased I am to meet you, my dear girl,' he said to her.

'Thank you, Mr Benedict.' Atoosa's voice was pitched low, an alto if she sang. I was reminded that under the folds of cloth was a doctor of archaeology, a sophisticated career woman.

'Please, call me Saul, or Dad if you like. All my daughters-in-law do, including the ones who aren't yet officially hitched.'

Despite our predicament, I had to feel a little glint of pleasure at meeting her. The last piece of the Benedict family had finally slid into place. Victor was no longer alone. They all knew that what happened from here on was far less important than that solid fact. Victor turned onto the highway and continued driving north. He was glowing with pride and satisfaction; to him our crisis was something to conquer, a challenge like Hercules performing his labours, proving his strength to his new life partner, not the complete mess-up it was for me.

'Where are we heading, Vick?' asked Trace, who was riding in the passenger seat. 'Do you need me to navigate?'

'No, thanks, Trace. Atoosa is familiar with the roads and is directing me.'

I liked this little hint that they were already working as a team. I had always worried that Victor might overwhelm his soulfinder but that didn't seem to be the case here.

'We know the Robinsons are hot on our heels but we've a couple of tricks still up our sleeve,' Victor continued. 'We've found someone with a small plane who is prepped to pick us up from an airfield near Balkh. It's used mainly for tourist flights over the historical ruins so if we get there quick enough we should be able to get out before the authorities stop us.'

'None of us have our passports, Victor,' cautioned Saul.

'Did I mention that the pilot is Atoosa's brother? He won't be interested in passports.'

'Which one?' I asked.

'The oldest, Ramesh. Javid's coming too. It's Atoosa's uncle's plane but he's too far away in the Panjshir valley to get back in time to help us. Fortunately, Ramesh knows how to fly and has done runs over the border for their uncle. I asked Atoosa to contact Ramesh once we got in the car. He got permission from the uncle and they've just reached the airfield and are preparing the plane.'

As the guys were discussing our plans up the front, I felt a slim, cool hand take mine.

'Victor told me,' Atoosa whispered. 'I'm sorry I am the reason you are in this situation with your soulfinder.'

I immediately felt surrounded by her calming air, warm where Victor was a little too cool. It was a good match. 'It's OK, really. Don't blame yourself.' Hal's betrayal shouldn't hurt so much as it did. I had already resolved that I couldn't live the savant life with my background; when I got back, I was going to commit myself completely to a normal existence, forget the mind powers, switch them off as far as I was able to do so. Hal would've been a terrible distraction, someone to pull me back into that world. Besides, he was clearly aiming to be Action Man and thought of me as Barbie. Any child could tell you that they didn't live happily in the same doll's house even if I had briefly flirted with the idea.

'We don't want you to suffer for our mistakes. Victor says he should have told his family his plans, not just disappear like he did. But he could sense my distress even over all those miles and it sent him a little crazy.'

'I'll be OK. I'll handle it.'

She glanced out the window, saying goodbye to the homeland she might never be able to return to if her name wasn't cleared. 'Javid likes you. He was hoping you would be his soulfinder.'

'How do you know this?'

'Because we're all talking again now I needn't hide where I am. We're almost there. You'd better put this on.' She pulled a scarf from the little bag she was clutching.

'Thanks.' I was wearing T-shirt, pyjama bottoms and slippers, the least suitable clothing for fleeing the country. It was just as well we hadn't been stopped at a roadblock, though with Victor in the driving seat that might not have been luck. I spread the scarf out to its full extent so it swathed as much of my upper body as possible.

'Is the airfield clear?' asked Victor.

'Yes, only friendlies,' confirmed Will.

Victor swung on to the tarmac and parked by the side of a hangar in front of which sat a white, single-engine plane.

Will got out first and checked the surroundings a final time. 'OK, gang, go straight up the steps and into the cabin. We're outta here.'

'Won't the Afghans try to stop us?' asked Saul.

Atoosa gave a little laugh. 'Not here, Mr Benedict . . . er . . . Saul. Uncle pays them to turn a blind eye. He is very creative with his import-export business. You really don't want to know the details. This won't be so odd for them, believe me.'

I followed her into the plane. She exchanged brief affectionate greetings with her brothers before buckling up in a seat near the front.

'There's a car coming towards us at high speed,' warned Trace, who was keeping watch at the still open cabin door.

'I don't sense anything, no kind of threat,' said Will, pausing by me on the top step. 'Could it be just passing by?'

Watching the headlights fast approaching, I couldn't feel the people in the vehicle either. The penny dropped. 'Close the door! It's them. If you don't sense danger it's because Hal's got his shield back up.'

127

'Get this bird in the air, Ramesh,' said Victor, buckling in the co-pilot seat as we scrambled for places. Ramesh's dove was perched on the headrest, taking us all in with interested dark eyes. Ramesh flipped some switches and started taxi-ing to the runway.

Javid took the seat next to mine. 'Are you all right, princess?' His dark eyes were full of concern.

I swallowed. He'd picked up the silly nickname from Hal. Why couldn't he be my Aladdin? That would've been easier in the long run as I didn't feel so susceptible to him, just liked him in the ordinary way. Instead I was left with the genie, who could twist and turn my feelings like a confectioner playing with hot spun sugar. 'I'm OK. Would you mind calling me Summer?'

'No problem, Summer. I'm sorry about what happened.'

Atoosa had already briefed her brothers, which made it a little easier. At least Javid wasn't still hoping for more between us. We could part as friends.

The plane picked up speed. Out of my window I saw a white SUV screech to halt near our abandoned car. Too late, boys. 'Do you know where we're going?' The nose lifted, then the rear wheels. We were on our way.

'There's an airfield in Uzbekistan Uncle uses. We'll take you there.'

And then what? I was stuck in Central Asia in just my pyjamas. It was almost funny.

Javid pressed a finger lightly into my cheek, trying to get me to smile. 'Don't look so sad. We got away. Atoosa's soulfinder will have plan. He is very resourceful, she says.'

Victor was also a rogue agent as far as his government was concerned and we had all put ourselves at risk of arrest if we managed to get back to our home countries. It finally struck me that it was more than just the beginning of the school year

I was missing; I might also miss out on the rest of my teenage years as I'd be spending them in prison. That hadn't been part of the deal I'd made to come to Victor's aid.

'Hey, don't cry. Don't be sad.'

'I'm not crying.'

'Then why are there tears on your face?'

OK, I had to admit to the weeping but not for the reasons Javid thought. 'I'm not sad. I'm furious. I don't do this kind of thing, Javid. I do not run out in the middle of the night, take planes illegally across borders, and throw my future up in the air.'

He looked at me as if I'd gone a little mad, because I was clearly doing all those things.

I shook my head, trying to express myself better. 'This isn't me. I'm not like this. I keep things steady—under control.'

Javid glanced round the cabin, at his sister talking quietly to Saul, at Will and Trace checking a map. 'Then maybe, Summer, you aren't who you thought you were?'

I must have slept for a while because when I next roused I found Atoosa next to me, head resting against my shoulder in the dimmed light of the cabin. Javid had moved upfront to be with his brother. Her veil had slipped and I had a moment to study her face, smooth, olive-toned skin, long dark hair loose, dusky lashes, heart-shaped face. From her slim hands to tiny feet, everything about her was delicate. She was really quite pretty looked at like this and I suspected she would be beautiful when her eyes were open and expression animated. She had to be worth this mess, didn't she? I tried to imagine the last few days from her point of view: she had been sitting in what must have been grim conditions in jail, thinking that her life was effectively over, when a complete stranger walked in and said he would bust her out. What had that been like?

129

Victor stretched over the narrow aisle and tucked the blanket closer around his soulfinder. 'You're awake, Summer?' he asked me softly.

I nodded.

'She's a miracle, isn't she?'

His miracle—that was how the soulfinder connection worked at best. 'She's lovely.'

He leaned back against his headrest and smiled. It was going to take me a while to get used to this new smiling version of Victor. 'You should've seen her face when I found her. I'd made some urgent suggestions to her guards that they really wanted to let me in and allow me to leave with her, so when the moment came I simply opened the door and told her it was time to go. It was all something of a half-baked plan to be honest, but I was desperate.'

'Did she know then who you were?'

'No. She thought I was just another official come to question her.' He scratched at his beard; with that covering most of his face he did look as if he could be a local. 'She asked to see my credentials so I showed her.' He reached out and stroked her hand. Atoosa's eyes flickered open and she lifted her head from my shoulder.

'Are we nearly there yet?' she murmured.

'Sorry, sweetheart. I didn't mean to wake you. I was just telling Summer about how we met.'

She gave a hum of laughter. 'I felt like you dropped the pyramid of Giza on my head.'

Victor quirked a brow at me. 'One thing I'm learning about my soulfinder, she's not very romantic.'

Atoosa squeezed his fingers. 'But it's true. I was sitting on my bunk, fretting that I was going to face an even longer prison sentence and harsher discipline because the crown had turned up in Delhi, and next you came in, announced I had to leave

130

and then you topped it all by making telepathic connection. It was a good thing that I was sitting down already.'

'What did it feel like—other than flattening?' I asked.

'Truly wonderful, the first good thing that has happened to me for two years.' She smiled into his eyes, her dark brown ones locked on to his grey. 'His mind is a labyrinth, my Victor's, but there's always the Ariadne thread running through to show me the way.'

'Only for you, my love.' Victor kissed her fingertips. 'Only someone good at puzzles could understand me.'

She laughed.

'I'm pleased for you both.' I swallowed against the choked feeling in my chest. It felt horribly like envy.

'I only hope Victor can solve the tangle I am in, but thank you, thank you, everyone, for coming for me.'

'Hey, Vick, can I borrow you a moment?' Trace called his brother to the back of the plane. I could sense a buzz of concern from him, not our old worries but a new one.

'Sure.' With a final kiss to his soulfinder's cheek, Victor made his way down the narrow gap between the seats.

Unable to go back to sleep now, I yawned and stretched my cramped limbs. 'Dr Nawabi, will you tell me more about this crown that caused all the trouble?'

'Please, call me Atoosa. I allow all my rescuers to use my first name.' Her eyes twinkled.

'Atoosa.'

'As for the crown, it's an amazing piece. How much do you know about our history, Summer?'

'Not much, I'm afraid, only the last couple of centuries of fighting against various imperial powers, the Great Game between Russia and Britain, then the Soviet Invasion, and now the newer troubles with the Taliban and other militant groups.'

She nodded, in full professorial mode now. 'You are better informed than many in the West. What you might not know is that we have always been on the crossroads of cultures. Before Islam reached us, there was a civilization in this area called the Parthians—I'm talking about the first century AD, time of the Roman Empire in Europe, long before the Prophet. Part of the Parthian burial practice was to entomb certain high-position individuals, princes and princesses, in mounds with their most precious artefacts around them. We know very little about their beliefs but this usually suggests an investment for some idea of an afterlife.'

My mind conjured up images of these hoards of gold hidden among the soaring mountains of the Hindu Kush— definitely the stuff of Arabian Nights tales. 'But you can't take it with you when you die, they say.'

'Not in the view of the Parthians. They were giving it a good try. The gold crown belonged to a female ruler; it was by far the best of the finds and the centrepiece of my exhibition. It has been such a long time since Mazar-e-Sharif enjoyed sufficient peace to have a cultural experience of such a high calibre that I got carried away. I thought only of the joy it would bring my people showing them the gold that had been thought worthy of special exhibitions in the West; I did not realize it was going to bring my family and me such misery.'

'And do you have any idea who took it—I mean, have any suspicions?' I remembered her colleague at the museum, Dr Abdullah, but didn't want to mention him. It had just been a feeling, nothing concrete in his thought patterns that had tipped me off.

She raised her palms in a helpless gesture. 'No. The security was top notch; I made sure of that when I hired a reputable firm from Kabul. This was not an opportunistic theft but a planned robbery. I would not be surprised to find one of the security guards was bribed, but I thought I'd seen to that by ensuring two were always on duty at any one time. They were questioned but the prosecutor claimed they were innocent.'

'A conspiracy then. I was just wondering, you mentioned that the crown is the symbol of a female ruler: could it have been taken as an anti-feminist gesture? Could some conservative cleric have organized the theft to make you look bad?'

Atoosa frowned. 'I know of no such man, but it is true there are many in the country who would like us to return to a medieval society and do not understand the value of our cultural history. It is possible, but then these conservatives are not people I know so that makes them even harder to identify and catch.'

'No, I don't suppose they would be the kind of circles you would mix in.'

Victor returned to his seat. From his grim expression he was the bearer of bad news.

'What's happened now?' I asked.

He gave me a meaningful look. It was bad. 'Atoosa, I think we might have made a breakthrough in the case.'

Her eyes lit up then as quickly dimmed when she saw his face. 'Really? What do you know?'

'You remember I said that my oldest brother Trace has the ability to follow objects, see where they've been, what they've been touching?'

'Yes, you told me that.' Her quick mind was already putting the pieces together, her eyes pleading with him not to say it.

'I'm sorry, darling, but he found traces of the crown in the hold at the back of the plane. He wasn't even looking for it but while searching for some clothes for us, he opened a box and discovered a black cloth. He examined it with his gift. The trail is unmistakable: it had been wrapped around the crown to protect it during transport. You didn't use this plane to move the pieces for the exhibition, did you?'

'No, of course not. It's my uncle's plane.' She closed her eyes. 'My *uncle's* plane. You've already guessed that Uncle's a smuggler.'

'I don't suppose there is any chance he might not have known what he was carrying?' I asked quietly.

She shook her head. 'He's not usually for hire; he runs his own business. I thought it was mainly contraband from China, fake designer goods and other luxuries. Alcohol occasionally. He likes a single malt whiskey. I'm not sure if he deals in opium but he's always sworn not.' She thumped her knees, a sudden rush of anger blowing away her sadness. 'But he was one of my staunchest defenders—paid for my lawyer—held my mother's hand at the trial! Uncle Maiwand wouldn't do this.'

Victor was obviously reading her inner thought contradicting this statement, as I was. I caught a glimpse of an oh-so-sympathetic dark-haired man, making frantic promises that he would get her out of her sentence. In her heart of hearts she thought that this was exactly the kind of thing her enterprising uncle might get up to. He wouldn't be above moving some stolen antiques across the border. 'I'm sorry, sweetheart, so sorry. I know it feels like the worst kind of betrayal but we don't know that he intended you to be blamed for the theft. Trace's ability doesn't give motive, just facts. What that tells us is that your uncle did have the crown for a while and, what's more, now Trace has picked up the trail he can tell us where it has gone.'

'So where is it?' she asked bleakly.

'It is in what feels to Trace like a private collection from the glass case around it; velvet display stand. He's only getting the very shadowiest of impressions at this distance but he thinks the room has domestic furnishings, so not a museum.'

'Yes, but where?'

'Far from here. Singapore, or maybe Indonesia. He'll have to check again when we land.'

Atoosa sighed, pressing the back of his hand to her cheek. 'So I guess that's where we're going next, isn't it?'

Victor nodded. 'That's where the trail leads. But I was thinking that Trace, Will, and I should go on our own.' He wasn't looking directly at her now, trying to avoid her eye. 'It might be too dangerous to risk you both.'

She dropped his hand. 'Victor Benedict, you are not leaving me in Uzbekistan! That's not safe either.'

I'm pleased she said it before I could.

He looked a little sheepish, an unfamiliar expression on him. 'I wasn't going to abandon you; Trace and I thought we could leave our father with you.'

'And what if these Robinsons catch up with us when we're there? It's not so very far from Mazar-e-Sharif and you said they seemed to have some way of locating me thanks to the powers of one of them.'

'Yeah, Scott Robinson.' Victor rubbed his beard. 'But I'm banking on the fact that I'm their mission. I'm expecting them to come after me, not you.'

'Yet we found out tonight that Summer is the soulfinder to one of them; their mission will have changed. Once they've had time to think what that means, they'll be after her as well as me, as I can lead them to you. They'll think of me as a bargaining chip if nothing else. You said they were ruthless. We'd be sitting ducks.' She folded her arms, having blown all his counter arguments out of the water.

He laughed softly. 'I've been matched with a tigress. I think I like it.'

'So we are all going to Singapore?'

He cupped her chin and brushed her cheek with his thumb. 'Yes, we're all going.'

'Sorry to butt in, but how?' I asked, gesturing to my pyjamas. 'We've no luggage, no documents.'

'Don't worry, Summer, I still have a few favours I can call in,' said Victor. 'We'll get what we need the other side of the border and catch an onward flight before the Robinsons work out our direction of travel.'

Naturally he had a plan. 'Sorry. I'm not used to travelling with a super spy.' I'm sure there were many people around the world who owed Victor and many he could trick to do what he wanted. I needn't have asked.

'Ex-super spy,' he corrected. 'I'm not sure the FBI will forgive me and I for one won't forgive them for siccing the Robinsons on us.'

Chapter 11

After saying an affectionate goodbye to Javid and Ramesh in Uzbekistan, we emerged from Singapore's Changi airport twenty-four hours later looking slightly more prepared for international travel than we had on leaving Mazar. Thanks to Victor's persuasive powers and Javid's bargaining skills we had purchased replacement clothes in the local Uzbek town to tide us over a few days. I'd gone back to western clothes—skirt and T-shirt—with some relief, though the 'I Love Yorkshire Beer' slogan on the top left a lot to be desired. Perhaps a serviceman had sold it on locally while on a tour of duty, otherwise I couldn't imagine how it got there. Good fake documents weren't available so we had had to rely on Victor persuading the various officials at airline desks that they had seen our passports and that, yes, everything was in order. He got Yves to send over the details and scans of our original documents so at least the real information tallied with what they were entering on their computers. With the American authorities after us, I'd expected us to be stopped at each connecting flight as we made our way east but so far no one had caught up with us.

'Victor, I've been worrying that the Robinsons will know where we are when we come up on airline computers,' said Saul as we were waved through the final immigration check and emerged into the super-modern concourse of the arrivals' hall.

'They'll know anyway, Dad, thanks to Scott's GPS powers. I've heard he can attach his gift to a target like a homing

137

beacon so he'll've latched on to my signal when we fled.'
Victor dismissed the first few taxi drivers who came touting
for business until he found one whose thoughts he approved.
'They aren't the best in the business for no reason. The only
chance we have is to keep moving so quickly we are always a
step ahead. Take us to the Golden Grove Hotel.'

Passing briefly out into the wet heat of the early afternoon,
we piled into the driver's air-conditioned minibus and headed
off into the busy roads of the city. Gazing out of the window,
Singapore struck me as an extraordinary country. I already
knew it was a city on a peninsula located between Malaysia
and the islands of Indonesia, a port and travel hub. Ever since
I could remember I'd heard about it in my Chinese great-
grandmother's tales—she lived here all her life—and later I
sought out more information from twentieth-century British
writers, but the modern city that confronted me through the
windows of the taxi was a long way from the literary colonial
world that I carried in my head. Now it was all skyscrapers,
neat parks with elderly people practising Tai Chi, housing
developments of low-rise flats, roads busy with a population
drawn from all corners of Asia. Pedestrians were almost all
connected to some kind of digital device as we were in London.
Afghanistan had been a rare break from technology: only every
other person had been on the phone. A visitor from an alien
planet would find our behaviour very odd, set apart from all
other species on Earth as we rarely surveyed our surroundings
as any other creature with survival on their mind did. Even
before the phone, I'd have been the type to always have my
nose in a book—not much different if you think about it—eyes
fixed on a window giving access to other human-constructed
worlds. We had always looked for ways of avoiding reality it
seemed. Now I had neither, no phone or book to distract me
from puzzling over the crumpled pieces of my heart.

The taxi drew up under the white carport of a top-of-the-range hotel in the city centre. The tower block rose up at least twenty floors, reflective glass mirroring the buildings opposite and the sky above. Victor was clearly not going for low key. Maybe he was thinking more of impressing his soulfinder as so far they had pursued their romance in jail and in a goat-shed?

'Will they have room?' I asked him.

'They'll make room.' A muscle in Victor's cheek twitched.

'You'll do your . . .' I waved my finger in the air to indicate mind control. Normally us savants with mind powers followed an unwritten code not to over-use it.

'No need. I know the manager. He's a savant and he, well, let's just say he owes me. He'll keep our visit off the books.' I caught a flash from him of images involving a Chinese Triad gang and threats to a member of the manager's family, then Victor mowing down the bad guys with a scary mind-strike and rescuing the daughter. I'd forgotten how cool Victor could be.

'Yes, I bet he will.'

'He's got rooms ready for us so we'll bypass reception and go straight on up. Atoosa, you are sharing with Summer.' He passed us swipe cards from an envelope the bell boy had handed him. 'Room five-oh-six. Fifth floor. Next to ours. Let's go.'

He hustled us quickly through the public areas. I had just enough time to glimpse the wonderful palm tree garden in the atrium and a pool outside. I felt a twist of longing that I could be here on holiday, Hal massaging my shoulders as I stretched out on one of those recliners.

No, not with Hal. With someone—anyone—else.

Atoosa swiped the key in the slot and entered our room first.

'Which bed do you want?' she asked.

'I don't mind. By the window?'

'Go ahead.' She put her small bag down on the queen-sized one nearest the door. 'At last: a soft mattress! I can't tell you how I've dreamt of this moment.'

I poked my head into the en suite. 'They've a Jacuzzi bath.'

'Oh my word, I'm in paradise!'

'You get dibs on the bath then. I'll just take a quick shower and leave you to soak.' I unpacked my few toiletries on the sink unit. 'You know that the guys think they're going to cut us out of the next part of the investigation?'

She gave an unladylike snort. 'Then they can think again. I'm a puzzle solver—all I need is the information and I can put this together. I've already worked out how I think my uncle came to be caught up in this.'

'Yes?' I held off running the shower, more interested in hearing her deductions.

'You've not met him, but despite what you've heard, he's not a bad man, more accident-prone and too naive.'

'Not good qualities for a smuggler.'

'Maybe naive is the wrong word?' She wriggled her toes on the white rug, savouring the luxury. 'Better would be "overly optimistic". I can see him getting in too deep with a contact in this part of the world and having his arm twisted to supply the goods. The exhibition was all over the news at the time. If someone had the crown on their list for acquisition, that would have been the moment I would have picked to try for it.'

'So do you think your uncle actually did the theft?'

She shook her head. 'Unlikely. He probably had no idea that I was to be the scapegoat. I can see him being the pilot of the getaway vehicle but not breaking into the museum. There will be others involved, perhaps some insiders?'

I had to ask. 'What about Dr Abdullah?'

'Him? I didn't realize you even knew he existed!' Atoosa

flopped back on the bed and groaned with pleasure as she flailed her arms on the silky spread. 'I admit I don't particularly like my colleague but I can't see him having connections to international crime.' She rolled over to her side and propped her head on one arm. 'The best I can say about him is that he is a scholar. He is about museums and archaeology, no expensive tastes or he wouldn't be trying to pursue a career in that sector in our country. There is next to no money in it.'

'More reason to steal then?'

'But he's genuinely committed to our history. It would be like a father selling off a child if he arranged the theft—not unheard of but against everything I know about his character.'

'Hal and I saw him briefly at the museum. I caught from his thoughts that he rather relished your disgrace. That's why I mentioned him.'

'That I can believe. He felt threatened by me. Now hurry up in that shower. That bath is calling my name.'

'All right, all right!' I laughed and closed the bathroom door. It was nice sharing a room with her. I was beginning to feel she could be like the big sister I didn't have.

My own shower finished and leaving Atoosa to soak, I knocked on the door to the other room. Saul answered, a cup of coffee in one hand. The guys were behind him poring over a map of the area, Trace holding his head as if his eyes were paining him, sure sign he was straining his gift to the utmost.

'Everything OK, Summer?'

'Fine but I was wondering, Atoosa and I have really weird clothes.' The market in Uzbekistan had only stocked an eclectic mix of hand-me-downs. Apart from my 'I Love Yorkshire Beer' T-shirt, all the underwear was huge. I could fit three of me in one of the pairs of knickers, but I didn't want to go into that detail in front of Saul. 'I know we're in a hurry but do you think it safe for me to go and shop for us both in the mall downstairs?'

'If one of us comes with you. We've time for a quick visit as Victor says we won't go out till after dark.' He looked over his shoulder. 'Hey, boys, anyone up to escort Summer to the mall?' As if he'd asked for volunteers for kidney donation, his sons all ducked their heads and suddenly looked very busy. He quirked his lips in a wry smile. 'Looks like that'll be me.'

'And, er, money?'

'Yves has wired me some. We're OK, at least I think we're OK? You don't have designer tastes, I hope?'

'I'll try not to bankrupt you.'

We took the lift down to the mall. I asked the question that had been burning away inside me. 'Did Victor say how long he thought it would be before the Robinsons catch up with us?'

Saul gave me a shrewd look. 'We had just finished talking about that when you knocked. He thinks later tonight at the earliest. The American Embassy will already have had eyes on us soon after we landed but as it is a savant matter we think they'll wait until the Robinsons get here to try recapture us. They're too worried about Victor's powers to try on their own. With good reason. My boy is spoiling for a fight. Now I know where Zed gets it from.'

'And they get it from . . . ?'

'Karla.' Saul chuckled. 'But I have to admit I've been known to lose my cool when I'm angry enough.'

'You? No, you are calm. Your mind is like a reflective pool, not a ripple.'

'You've looked?'

I could feel a blush rise in my cheeks. 'Only a brush across the surface so I can recognize you. I've not intruded, I promise. It's how I see people.' I had a little mental file of mind signatures for each of my friends and family. Saul was a mountain pool; Victor a stormy sea; Trace a highway through

142

a forest, focused on his goal; Will a playing field, open and friendly; and so on. Hal had been what? A blank. That should have told me everything right there.

'Maybe you sensed my calm because I meditate. Otherwise my mind would be a mess, I can tell you. My father was a volatile, sometimes violent, man and I've been battling that inheritance ever since. But I learned early on that we can change patterns if we put enough work into it; we don't have to repeat the mistakes of earlier generations.'

I realized he had now subtly shifted to talking about my situation. Before I could reply, the lift doors opened and we walked out into the fountain courtyard a level below reception. We were surrounded by boutiques and cafes set amongst an indoor garden.

'Can I buy you a drink before we hit the shops?' Saul asked. I think he was just trying to delay what he anticipated being a painful experience of shopping. He didn't know me that well then.

'Thanks. I'd love one of those coconut juices.' I pointed to a bar set amid palm trees where a couple of schoolgirls my age were drinking straight out of a coconut shell using a straw.

Saul ordered at the counter while I chose a table screened by the pot plants. The people in the mall were all brightly dressed, like flocks of tropical birds perched on the balconies and gathered on the marble pavements. It reminded me of the Nawabis' courtyard. I wondered how Javid was getting on. Three older Chinese ladies passed wearing jewel-coloured silk jackets, just like the one in my favourite picture of my great-grandmother. She had died two years ago and I probably still had relatives in Singapore if I but knew more about that side of the family. Dad hadn't thought to tell me, not imagining I'd end up this far from the UK.

'I thought that looked so good I ordered one for myself.' Saul put the two ridiculously large shells down in front of me. 'Cheers!'

Smiling, I bumped my coconut against his. As he seemed ready to talk, perhaps I should take advantage of being alone with him? 'Saul, if I were your real daughter, what would you advise me to do in my situation? You know, with Hal?'

He rubbed his chin, not rushing to answer. 'Honey, I'd love to have had a daughter like you.' He gave me an amused look. 'As you might guess, Karla and I kept hoping, but we only seem to produce boys.'

They had done the female world a big favour. Who wouldn't want a Benedict as a soulfinder? 'You've got daughters-in-law now.'

'And that's a huge joy to us both. But what I'm trying to say is that, I've come to care just as much as if you really were my little girl. Not all bonds are blood ties.'

'Oh.' I looked down, embarrassed.

'My boys feel the same way too. Don't think we haven't noticed how you always put others first. You've sacrificed your own interests again and again, even to the extent of running out on the first encounter with your soulfinder. How could we not love you for that, choosing us over him?'

Memory of that moment was like biting down on a sore tooth. 'I'm not so noble—I didn't want to stay. He lied to me.'

'He was undercover. Is that the same thing?'

I rested my forehead wearily on my hand. 'I don't know. I thought he liked me but he was using me.'

Saul discarded the little paper parasol that had been tucked in the top of the shell and swirled the straw. 'Could he not have been doing both? You're very likeable.'

That was sweet of him to say so but I was totally the wrong fit for Hal. He needed some Amazonian girl to mud-wrestle, not a girl like me who worried about matching her accessories and was ridiculously well read. I counted those as my few good points but I doubted he'd see them that way.

'But you know about my mother?'

Saul nodded. 'That's not your fault.'

'No, but I do carry *that* with me.' I revolved my hand in the air, gesturing to all the horrible vampire rot that infected me. 'According to the Savant Net, I'm not supposed to have a family, am I?'

Saul sipped his drink. 'That was the old policy, it's true, but we've moved on in our attitudes to mental illness. Your poor father, I can't imagine what his life has been like.'

I felt immediately defensive of the real victims of this situation. At least Dad and I could have a semi-normal life. 'And there's my brother and mother, they don't have a great time either.'

'Of course they don't, and it's them I feel most sorry for. But I was wondering, savant partnerships are about balance. Have you not asked if there might be some way that a blend of your gift and Hal Robinson's could neutralize the worst of the problems? And maybe your brother's soulfinder, if we can find her, can do the same for him? In retrospect, when I look at the bad in the world, very often I find there is some mercy at work under it all, some good that can be drawn out of it.'

'But my father and my mother? What mercy was there for them?' I didn't even start on the list of global atrocities that countered this argument.

He sighed. 'I didn't say it was a perfect world. I'm just talking about what I've seen among savants.'

We lapsed into silence as we finished our drinks.

'Thank you for talking to me,' I said at last. 'My dad doesn't really do that. We just bargain and cope with crises.'

'That's because he's too close to you, not able to see straight.

It's often easier to talk to someone outside the situation. But let me say one more thing: you have to remember that we are all here for you; you don't have to do this alone.'

'Don't I?' I could feel tears in my eyes. 'I rather think I might have to.'

'Summer, don't you dare try it. You'll have all of us Benedicts, and Misty and Angel on your case if you do. You can't think we're so cruel as to abandon you.'

I closed my eyes, feeling the tears slip down my cheeks. What was happening to me? I'd not cried so much in years. 'But I want to keep you all away from my mother. She's toxic.'

'Don't call her that, Summer. It's not fair to her or to you. Next you'll be telling me you feel tainted.'

'Well I do,' I whispered.

'Honey, your mother is ill and she needs treatment. And do you really think one little vampire savant is a match for my family? You and your father have struggled on your own for too long; don't you think it's time you accepted help?'

Right now my mother's condition seemed less pressing than what I'd left behind in Afghanistan. I wanted my own happy ending, of course I did. I wanted what Misty had with Alex or Angel with Marcus, but instead I got two-faced Hal and an unexploded bomb of a genetic inheritance. 'But who is going to help me with my soulfinder?'

Saul shook his head. 'Another thing I've learned from my years watching my family, when it comes to soulfinders, best not to get between them. It's like slipping in that gap between an ocean liner and the dockside—major chance of being crushed. We'll support you but you're going to have to work that one out with him.'

I hadn't expected Saul to have a magic wand but I suppose I had been hoping he'd have more answers. 'Then I'll have to see him again?'

'You've plenty of time for that. Let's remove the little issue of an international arrest warrant and being on the run for the rest of our lives first, OK? Get ourselves into smoother waters.'

'Good point.'

We finished our drinks and started on my shopping list. I surprised Saul with my no-nonsense approach. Thanks to an upbringing with Dad, I was used to high-end stores in the West End and knew that assistants would go the extra mile for commission. You didn't have to waste time going from store to store, you could just pick a large one and present a list of what was required and sizes. They could then do the running. We had a clutch of bags and a single bill to pay in under thirty minutes. Saul admitted it was a record. His wife took a less direct approach to purchases.

'I can take longer if you like,' I said. 'Just today I wasn't in the mood for browsing.'

'If only Karla had days like that. I'll have to get you to train her,' he said with a twinkle in his eyes that showed he wasn't completely joking.

I dumped the bags on my bed and joined the others in the other room, our temporary mission control. Atoosa was already there, sitting next to Victor in front of the map. She was murmuring softly to him while he nodded his head, his hand absentmindedly stroking the long length of her hair as it snaked on her slender back.

'What are you looking at?' I asked.

'Yves drew a blank with the auction house. He thinks it was a fake posting to get Atoosa into more trouble. And Trace is having trouble pinning down the end of the trail,' Will explained, nodding to his brother who was now stretched out on a bed, flannel wrapped round some ice from the minibar on his forehead. He was asleep. 'He's taking a break.'

'What's the problem?'

'It keeps moving. It shouldn't as the surroundings remain the same.'

'That's weird. Is the trail dying out or something?'

Atoosa suddenly clapped her hands. 'I've got it! He's not wrong about the moving but we are thinking about this the wrong way. A yacht. I'll stake what's left of my reputation that this collector is keeping it on a boat to avoid scrutiny.' She stabbed a finger at a large marina, home to luxury vessels. 'One reading was near here, yes? We thought it was the hotel but it could have been in the hotel harbour. Then it moved further down the coast. We've got to look out to sea to find it.'

Will shook his brother awake. 'Trace, Atoosa solved it. You're not going mad, bro. It's on a boat.'

Revived by the news, Trace sat up and chucked the flannel in the direction of the bathroom where it landed in the sink. 'Thank God for that. I was making my brain curdle trying to pin it down.'

'So what now?' asked Atoosa.

Victor took her hand and kissed it. 'Thanks to my clever soulfinder, we go find out which yacht's movements match my brother's coordinates for the crown's location. I'll take the coastguard. The others will scout out whichever marina it ends up in tonight. We're almost there, I can feel it. Once we have a name I can call in some favours and get a raid on the yacht. With the crown recovered, we will be well on the way to clearing your name.'

'Don't you mean, *we* will take the coastguard? I'm not staying here.' Atoosa poked him with her finger.

'But the Robinsons won't be allowed to get to you. I've told the manager to keep them out and they have no jurisdiction in this country to demand entry.'

'I'm not afraid of them, Victor. This is my mess and I want

to solve it. I spent eighteen months in jail thinking about doing this.'

Victor's face took on a priceless harried expression. Here was the one person he could not bulldoze. 'But Atoosa, darling, we're not sure what we're facing. This collector is bound to have security, he'll be dangerous.'

She pulled her hand free and crossed her arms. 'So?'

'I don't want to risk you.'

'I'm old enough to take my own decisions about danger—exact same age as you in fact. I'm coming.'

Victor sighed, knowing when to make a tactical retreat. 'I draw the line at taking Summer out there. She's only seventeen.'

'True.' The argument between soulfinders settled, Saul stepped in, looking at me with an apologetic expression. 'I made a solemn promise to her father we'd keep her out of danger as far as possible and I'm not doing well on that to date. There's no need for you to come tonight, Summer. We won't need to mind-shadow anyone as we're following the crown not a person.' He turned back to Victor. 'I guess one of us will have to stay back with her?'

I didn't like the suggestion that I required babysitting and to be honest I didn't fancy the idea of poking around marinas either—too tired by my hopeless situation, too jet-lagged. I had nothing to offer this part of the mission so the least I could do was make their life as simple as possible. 'No need for that. If you ask the manager to make sure no one disturbs me I'll just have an early night. You can tell me all about the excitement tomorrow.'

Victor nodded. 'Thanks, Summer. I want to split Will and my dad between the two teams so that's really helpful. Here's the manager's channel.' Victor gave me the telepathic direction, allowing me to sense the way in which he contacted his friend. It was as good as a phone number to a savant.

'Got it, but tell him I probably won't have to use it.'

'Fine.'

'What about the Robinsons?' asked Will. 'What if they say "hang jurisdiction" and kick down the door anyway?'

Victor folded up the map. 'I'd imagine they'd be more interested in following us to the coast.'

'But Hal?' Will glanced at me but I looked away.

Victor put the map in his backpack. 'Tactically, they'll have to stick together as without him we'll be able to sense them.' He shouldered it, the signal for the others to start preparing for their expedition. 'No, I think it an acceptable risk. Besides, they won't want to harm Summer even if they do come here first. She's precious to them as a soulfinder. They'll want to know what we are up to and I'm fine with Summer telling them. We've nothing to hide. All we wanted was more time. We'll have to go back to face the music eventually and I don't care if it's the Robinsons that escort us, as long as we've got our answers.'

Back in our room, I wished Atoosa good luck and double-locked the door after her. Having had no time to eat yet, Saul had told me to order room service so I flicked through the menu. Pizza would do. I called down with my selection then collapsed back on the bed. My mind briefly shadowed my friends. They were all fine, heading out as they said to the two destinations, port authorities and the hotel marina Trace had last sensed. I thought about the time difference between here and the UK, wondering if it was OK to phone home. I didn't have a mobile yet but the bedside table had a landline. Did my dad and my friends know what had happened? The Benedicts had been updating Yves and he had been passing on the news to the others. I couldn't imagine Phoenix keeping the news from her best friend Sky and she would certainly tell Misty and Angel. Yes, they would know. I fingered the dial then laughed. Oh my gosh, I didn't even know their numbers! I'd always used my contacts to call them. I knew my home phone, of course, but I had no desire to talk to Dad about what was going on. He would probably say something along the lines of 'I told you so'. With no computer in the room, I'd have to think about risking a trip down to the lobby to use the internet.

There came a knock at the door. Had to be my pizza. I checked the spyhole and saw the cheerful face of a Chinese porter with a trolley. I opened to let him in.

Hal stepped into view, a big bunch of flowers in his arm. 'Surprise!'

Chapter 12

I wasn't ready for this.

'I told you, babe, I wouldn't forget our one-month anniversary. Thanks, Deng.' He handed the waiter a tip. 'You've been great. As I said, my girlfriend is a sucker for the romantic touch.'

The waiter's smile faltered when he saw my expression. He may have been gullible but he wasn't an idiot. 'Miss, did I do the wrong thing? I can call security, OK?'

To do what? My brain scrambled to catch up like the last puny recruit over the obstacle course. Hal and I needed to talk so we might as well do it now. At least if he were occupied with me there was a chance his brothers were at hand and not chasing after the others. I could buy Victor the time he wanted. 'No, it's fine. I was just a little shocked.'

The waiter's smile returned and he pushed the trolley inside the room and received a second tip that I already had waiting. 'Enjoy your meal, Miss.'

Hal did a quick check of the room, verifying that I was alone.

'Thanks.' I followed the waiter to the corridor.

'And happy anniversary.'

'Um, yeah.' I closed the door behind him. I turned and looked across the full stretch of the room to see Hal at the window, arms crossed, stance mirroring mine. Why did he have to be so . . . so desirable? Call me shallow, but it would be much easier to turn my back on him if I didn't feel this tug towards him from my very core.

I had to keep my distance or I'd do something stupid, like hit him or weep in his arms, both impulses wrestling to be first through the gate. 'Well, you're here now, so say what you want, then you can get out. I was planning an early night.' Having him in the same room was like pricking myself with drawing pins, tiny bursts of pain all over my body.

'*Say what I want?*' I could feel his fury even at twenty paces, ironically standard distance for a duel. He chucked the flowers on the coffee table, making me jump. 'OK, I want to know how you took over my brain. I'm supposed to be immune to savants. You shouldn't be able to touch me with your power.'

This seemed off the point. I was expecting him to go straight in with the soulfinder revelation but he was hung up on my brief command-and-control phase in his head. 'I told you what I could do. Your brothers were pointing guns at us; I had to take drastic action. *That* part shouldn't have been a surprise.' Was he going to mention the main issue or would I?

'That's not good enough, Summer. I need to know—we have to understand how you do it. Right now we think you're a real and present danger to our team's effectiveness.' He got out his phone and placed a call. 'It worked as you anticipated. I'm in the room. No, she's alone. No, no, she's not attacked me; my mind is holding up fine. Yeah, I won't let her hurt me. See you in a moment then.'

So his brothers were here and they were on their way up and Hal was treating me like a lion cornered in a cage, to be held off with a chair and whip. I would've laughed if I hadn't felt so fragile. But that was good news, wasn't it? If they thought I was a big deal, I'd be distracting them from Victor's business.

Trying not to betray that my knees had turned to jelly,

that the lion was really a pussy cat, I went to the trolley and lifted the lid. 'That looks good. Mind if I eat while you get on with this little interrogation of yours? Maybe you can delay bringing out the thumbscrews until after I've dined.'

He looked very much as if he did mind but to say so would sound petty. He shrugged. I lifted a slice of pizza onto a plate and took a napkin. Now I had started going through the motions of eating I felt ridiculous. Taking a knife and fork, I sat down at the desk and carved off the point of my Fiorentina, no longer sure I could stomach it.

'You eat pizza with a knife and fork?' Hal couldn't help himself. 'And you're sitting there in an "I Love Yorkshire Beer" T-shirt?'

Somehow the normality of his mocking helped me swallow that first mouthful. 'As you know by now, I'm full of surprises. Your brothers are joining this little party I take it?'

'They're just finding a route past hotel security. Benedict has this place locked down pretty tight.'

'But you got through.'

'They were told to stop soldiers, not Romeos bearing flowers.' He smirked, far too pleased with himself.

'You should put them in water. You wouldn't want to waste the fortune you must have spent on them in the lobby.' I chewed resolutely at my pizza. Never had it tasted more like cardboard.

He moved the flowers to the bin where they landed with a thunk. 'Don't worry—I'll bill them on the company accounts.'

'Of course you will. You wouldn't actually waste your own money on your soulfinder now would you?' I carved a new piece, nearly cracking the plate with my onslaught. 'I can't see you finding any romance in the savant cosmic marriage of true minds.' He said nothing. 'That was another literary reference by the way. Shakespeare sonnet. No need for you to Yahoo it.'

Hal shook his head. 'You can be really nasty, can't you? I didn't get that about you, thinking you were as sweet as you seemed, but Lucas called it right.'

This sudden turn into real vitriol shook me deeply. I'd never been called nasty, not once in my life. Where was this bitterness coming from? Maybe the Shakespeare dig was a bit catty but not cruel. 'What have I done to deserve that?'

'You know what you did.'

'No, actually, I don't. Enlighten me.'

He adopted an it's-so-obvious tone. 'I'm not a savant so I don't have a soulfinder. Luc said that only someone who is prepared to go really low would plant that connection in my head to confuse me. Then you violated every human right I have by taking me over and making me block my brothers.'

And him barging into my room totally respected my rights, did it? 'You think I made it up?' I gave up my pretence of eating and put my hands to my head. 'So let me get this straight: you believe I invented our connection?'

'We know you did.'

'Why exactly? I mean, I'm sure you're someone's type,' I gave him a look that strongly indicated that I wasn't that girl, 'but really, you and me? Who would have dreamt up that nightmare?'

'Trust me: I wasn't flattered. You were just playing your best card for the escape. We were never going to shoot you.' He lifted the lid on the pizza box then put it down with a grimace without taking a slice. 'I didn't think you'd try to carry on with the lie. That's lame even for you. Give it up. It worked once but don't add insult to injury. You are in so much trouble, Summer. I don't think you even realize the half of it.'

There came a knock at the door. Hal warned me with a look to stay seated as he crossed to check the spyhole. 'Come on in, guys. At least there's pizza—sort of.'

155

His two brothers entered, incongruously wearing suits and ties and carrying computer bags advertising a conference for accountants taking place in the hotel. Lucas had even gone as far as to have the Clark Kent touch of thick, black-rimmed glasses. Victor had said they were no threat to me, that they would think I was precious. I think he had got that wrong as they were looking at me as if I were as desirable as a set of falsified company books they'd been asked to audit.

'Miss Whelan,' Lucas said curtly, putting down the satchel and taking off the glasses.

So I was Miss Whelan now, was I? Two could play at that game. I knew plenty about the armour provided by steely politeness. 'Mr Robinson, Mr Robinson and Mr Robinson, how kind of you to call by.' I perched on the edge of the desk, back to the wall.

'Where's Benedict and the rest of his family?' asked Lucas, opening the pizza box and taking a slice.

Scott followed him to the trolley. 'Geez, what's all this green stuff on it? That's just wrong.'

'Spinach.' I felt a little glow of vindictive pleasure.

'I warned you what's she's like. Made-in-Chelsea can't even order decent pizza,' Hal said, but, like his brothers, that didn't stop him stealing my supper.

Angel had once tried to tell me how liking for a soulfinder could very quickly mutate into something close to hate. I wished she were here so I could tell her I was rapidly heading that way and desperately needed her backup. She'd plunge straight in, cutting Hal down to size for me aided by any nearby water appliances, thanks to her gift for manipulating the stuff. Misty would hold her coat and cheer her on. I missed my friends desperately. I wished I had their courage to take on people; I was far more used to smoothing the way. Time to find my inner tough girl.

'Obviously, it's lovely to catch up with you all but I'm tired and really not up to visitors.' I gestured to the exit. 'Don't let the door hit you on the way out.'

Lucas scowled and settled in the armchair by the window. 'We're not leaving until we've done with you. And then you'll be on the first plane back to the UK. Your father has been informed of the charges.'

The gloves were well and truly off, weren't they?

'Let me get this right. We're in Singapore, correct? You have no more jurisdiction in this part of the world than Mickey Mouse.'

'We have savant friends in the government.'

'I'm sure you do. And when they knock on my door with proof that they have the authority to do so, then I'll take notice. I don't have to listen to you and I have every right to chuck you out of this room.' I toyed with the idea of summoning the manager but failed to anticipate how that would go. Lucas could though, and doubtless had some way of keeping him out.

'Summer, that's not fair.' So Scott had been delegated to play good cop to the two bad ones, had he? 'Let's sort this out in a friendly fashion. We get where you're coming from. We all make mistakes for those we care about.'

I gave a humourless laugh, cold creeping inside my heart as I tried to toughen up against appeals. 'You're saying I'm not being fair? What about three of you teamed up against one of me? What about the fact that you're eating my pizza? What about Hal insulting me and accusing me of making things up when I haven't?' I flicked Hal a glance but he wasn't moved one iota by my denial. 'You're saying I'm facing charges—something that's potentially going to ruin my life—all for standing by a man who is only trying to save his soulfinder? And you want us to be friendly about this? Do you think I'm stupid?'

Hal chucked his piece of pizza back in the box. 'Yeah, actually. Back in Mazar, you should've trusted us to get the job done.'

I was so tired of this. 'Why? Tell me one good reason why I should've done that.'

'Because we're the good guys here, Summer, not Victor Benedict,' said Scott. 'We're the ones putting the interests of other savants first.'

They thought they were right and weren't going to allow for my point of view. It was a waste of energy to defend my choice. Being tough was exhausting. I slid down off the desk to sit on the floor, then found I could easily scoot backwards so I was under it—not something I'd done since I was a child but just then my instinct to hide was stronger than dignity. I couldn't be bothered with this argument; what I really wanted to do was curl up and sleep for a year—a hundred years—and maybe this would all be sorted.

This move clearly wasn't in their interrogation technique handbook. 'What are you doing under there?' asked Lucas irritably.

Annoying them hopefully. The longer I stalled, the better.

'Summer?' Scott knelt down to peer in at me.

I gathered my knees to my chest, arms linked around them. 'Aren't you gone yet?'

'We really need to know where Benedict is.'

'He's out proving his soulfinder's innocence, exactly as he told you he would. Can't your GPS locate him?'

'Yes, but he keeps moving. I need to know where he will be, what the real plan is, not where he is now.'

'Get Lucas to anticipate. I'm not doing your job for you.'

'How did you get inside my head?' Hal had joined our little party crouching on the beige carpet.

I couldn't look at him. 'It's what I do, I told you.'

'But savant powers don't work on me.'

'You are a savant, I told you that. And it appears you can't keep your soulfinder out.'

'Not that again.'

'Yes that again.'

'Please, Summer, we know he's not a savant,' said Scott. 'Stop this.'

'How do you know?'

'Because he's not. He doesn't do telepathy for a start.'

'He does with me. We talked that way once.'

Hal stalked away. 'She's lying. She did that, I told you. She made it feel so wonderful then blindsided me. It was a classic honey trap.'

Scott hadn't moved but was studying me. 'Wait a moment, Hal. I think she really believes what she's saying.'

'No, she's making *you* believe she believes what she's saying. The mind-manipulators do that, you've always warned me, that's why they're dangerous. Look at her vampire family. Who knows how many landmines someone with a skill set like hers can plant in a brain?'

'Hal, shut up.' Lucas intervened this time. 'I know you're hurt but it's not right to attack her for her mother. You don't understand what it means.'

'Yeah, because I'm not a fricking savant and I don't get all this sick stuff your lot can do.' He kicked the waste bin, flowers shedding petals on the golden brown rug by the window. 'Look, this mission is getting old. Can we get our answers and get out of here?'

'You know, I liked him better when he gave me chocolate,' I said to Scott. 'Now? Not so much.'

'You really are his soulfinder?' asked Scott.

'Tragically, yes.'

'That kinda changes the game, doesn't it? Lucas?'

Lucas uncrossed his legs and leant forward to get a better look at me in my burrow. 'I'm not convinced. Prove it.'

'You know something? I can't be bothered.' I rested my head against the wall, eyes half shut.

'See!' Hal threw his hand up as if that was all the evidence he required. 'She's lying.'

Like hell I am. I enjoyed the horrified look on his face when he realized I'd got inside his head again. I could feel him rushing around trying to slam doors to stop my entry but he didn't get that I was already past all defences. It was much easier to evade his barriers as I'd got his mind signature on my last visit. To a savant like me that was like having the safe combination.

Get out!

I'm going. Now tell your brothers you don't do telepathy. I left as quickly as I had come.

Hal's brown eyes blazed with fury. 'She did it again! Talked inside my head!'

Lucas exchanged a look with Scott. 'And you replied?'

'He told me to get out,' I said wearily. 'I obliged, more than I can say for you invading my room.'

'OK this mission is more and more resembling a slow car crash.' Lucas seized Hal and shook him by the shoulders. His face cracked into a wide grin that made him seem much more attractive than the man-of-steel act he'd adopted before. 'Damn it, bro, you're one of us after all and we didn't know. That's great.' He slapped him hard on the back in that strange male bonding thing men do.

'Except for the fact we've alienated his soulfinder. I'm definitely getting hate vibes from under the furniture.' Scott stood up and hugged Hal. 'Welcome to the crazy gang.' He pulled the flowers out of the bin. Quite a few of them were bent. 'I think you'd better rethink your strategy here.' He shoved them into Hal's arms.

Hal looked so confused I almost felt sorry for him. 'Stop joking. But you've always said . . . This isn't funny.'

'No it's not. And we're not.'

Lucas got down on his knees and held out a hand to me. 'Sorry, Summer. I really didn't think he was one. I thought you were hurting him on purpose.'

I didn't want to come out yet so ignored the hand. 'It's OK. I understand. You were protecting your brother. If we're all friends now, can you just go?' I'd stalled long enough. 'Victor said it was fine to tell you that he's going to the coastguard's office. The crown Atoosa was blamed for stealing is on a yacht in one of the marinas and he's trying to get the name of the vessel.'

He rocked back on his heels, taking in this sudden rush of information. 'Have you told him we're here?'

'Not yet. He knew you were on your way.'

'And he still left you on your own?'

'None of them think you would harm me. I'm not the mission.'

Scott crouched beside Lucas. 'Summer, sweetheart, I'd say you have just been promoted to that coveted number one spot. Welcome to the Robinson family.'

'Oddly, I've no desire to join it today. Just go please.'

Scott gave Lucas a wry look. 'Her eagerness to be with us is almost embarrassing.'

Lucas stood up. 'The Benedicts' room is next door, right?' He swiped the key that Saul had left for me on the bedside table. 'I've got some calls to make. Come on, Scott.' He turned to Hal, who was still occupying the window end of the room like the last man standing on the battlements. 'Don't be a jerk. Deal.' With that crisp order, he walked out of the room, Scott following but not before he swiped another piece of pizza with a wink at me.

Hiding under the furniture wasn't a long-term solution to my predicament and the more I delayed the harder it would be to emerge. I crawled out, legs going through a painful little episode of pins and needles as I shook out cramped muscles. Hal didn't say anything but I could feel his eyes on me.

I was the first to speak. 'So?'

'So what?'

'Haven't you got anything you want to say to me?'

'Have you?'

I reminded myself he had just had his world turned upside down, that he was still adjusting, but it was impossible not to feel angry. With savant brothers he had to have some inkling what this meant. 'You're not happy with this?'

'Are you?'

If he even acted a little pleased that it was me, I'd tell him that I had liked him a little, that I was sorry for taking over his head, but none of that could pass my lips in the presence of this hostility. 'No, I'm not happy.' My voice cracked. I was going to cry and that would be the last straw. 'Look, I . . . need to use the bathroom.' I hurried inside and locked the door. My arms were shaking as I leant over the sink. 'Control, poise, Summer.' It was how I coped with my mother. Hal was just another form of that, a drain on my emotions. I needed to put on my armour. I ran a basin of water and splashed my face. I had to reason my way out of this. OK, I had a soulfinder who wasn't ready to be one. I'd already decided that I would turn my back on savant life before I even suspected his existence. None of that had changed. Hal hadn't spent all his life waiting for me to come along. If I told him that he was off the hook, and that we'd just forget about it when we got home, then it wouldn't be a big disappointment to him. In fact, it would probably be a relief. I should look on the connection as useful: I doubted the Robinsons would be eager to see me charged with anything now they knew. I'd go out there and have a polite conversation telling him how I wouldn't make any demands. I'd let him get back to his life.

Drying my face I smelt an odd scent in the air. Not the towels; it was coming in under the door.

'Hal?' I opened the door to come face to face with a stranger wearing a gas mask. I screamed but the cry faltered as more of the gas got caught in my lungs. I coughed and doubled over, dropping onto my knees. *Victor. Help.*

Chapter 13

I knew at once that I wasn't coming out of a natural sleep. My arms and legs felt like sacks of concrete, my head ached, throat dry. Even raising my lids was a task equivalent to lifting an Olympic weight above my head. My bed was rocking, adding to the disorientation.

'Summer?' A hand brushed my forehead then tapped my cheeks firmly.

'Wha—?'

'You've got to return to the land of the living. We're in trouble.' It was Hal. Of course, if I were going to wake up to find myself in hell, he'd be there with me.

I opened my eyes and his silhouette appeared blearily between me and the small window behind him. 'Where—?'

'We're on a yacht.'

'A yacht?' I struggled to sit upright. He put his arm under mine and helped hoist me up so the wall could steady me. A blue-grey horizon undulated in the thick glass. Sickness churned in my stomach.

'Yeah—the big fancy kind. We were knocked out by some kind of sleeping gas and brought here when we were both unconscious. I feel as sick as a dog; you?'

I nodded. 'Your brothers?' Glancing around the bare cabin I could see that we were alone.

'I don't know where they are but if we were taken here, I'd guess they were too, or maybe left knocked out back at the hotel.' Little worry lines bracketed the bridge of his nose. I wished I could smooth them away but what could I say? 'They had to be put out of action. No way would they let anyone just walk off with us. Here, have some water.' He held a glass to my lips and I gulped down a few grateful mouthfuls.

'Who did this, do you think?'

He took the glass and put it back on the ledge. 'Not our side.'

'Definitely not mine.'

'So it has to be mixed up with what you told us about Victor's soulfinder. Weren't they tracking a yacht? Can you contact him or one of the others? See if they know what's going on?'

Could I? My mind felt like mush. I rubbed my temples. *Victor?*

Nothing. Just the hiss of emptiness. I wasn't being blocked; I just couldn't find him. 'Where are we?'

Hal shrugged. 'No idea. Can't see anything from the window, just ocean.'

'What I meant was how far out to sea do you think we are? There's a limit to my range.'

'You need my brother to tell you that. Judging by the light it could've been hours. It seems to be nearly dusk so we've lost a day.'

I pushed my gift a little further, hoping Victor was feeling out for me, holding up his part of the bridge. *Victor?*

Summer? He was very far away, I could tell that from the faintness of his voice, but fortunately we were both strong telepaths. *Thank God you're alive! Where are you?* I could feel his shock and distress humming down our link. The normally implacable Victor had most definitely lost his cool, which was all the more alarming.

With Hal on a yacht. We don't know where. The other

165

Robinsons could be here too but we haven't seen anyone else yet. We were attacked in the hotel room.

We got that much. They sent the whole floor, including the guards, to sleep by putting the gas through the air conditioning. I had no idea the Robinsons were with you but a waiter said something about a guy with flowers.

That was Hal. The brothers followed him.

I guess Lucas' anticipation is no use if it only kicks in while he's succumbing to unconsciousness. They got you all when you were out cold.

Who are 'they'?

Men working for Ivan Chong, otherwise known to law enforcement as Mr Singapore. He's one of the savant gang lords we didn't get in that raid in London.

I had heard about that operation from Phoenix and Sky. They had been there when Victor took down the international network of savants who used their gifts for organized crime. Phoenix had been under the thumb of a creepy guy who called himself the Seer; he'd ended up behind bars with the rest of the ringleaders.

Chong dropped off the radar to regroup after we smashed the ring. Now he's resurfaced and it's safe to assume he was behind the theft. We think you have to be on his ocean-going yacht, but it left harbour before we could get the team together to raid it. We had no idea he'd snatched you until too late.

Why take us?

We think he believes you are us. Someone tipped him off that we'd arrived—he must have informants at the airport. He knew more about us than we did about him, we think, thanks to Atoosa's Uncle Maiwand. He's gone missing too. Javid said he got on a plane saying he was going to follow us and make sure Atoosa was safe. The family isn't too pleased to learn he was playing a double game.

No, I'm sure they're not. I remembered with great fondness the colourful courtyard and close family—horrible to think of Maiwand betraying all that.

The only way I can make sense of them taking you rather than lying in wait for us is that they were under the impression the Robinsons are us Benedicts, and that you're Atoosa. They were in our rooms so they saw what they expected to see.

Well, that added a nice twist to an already complicated situation.

And when he finds out he's caught the wrong fish, what do we do?

Stall for time. Don't tell him anything unless you have to. We're putting together a rescue party.

You'll have to find us first.

Are you wearing the same T-shirt?

I hadn't expected to feel grateful for my decision to keep a clean set for the following day, wearing 'I Love Yorkshire Beer' for bed. *Yes.*

Trace will use that. He's picked up the trail for it in the bag you carried. Keep it with you. And Summer?

Yes.

We messed up. It's pretty clear now that we're dealing with a savant crime, not an ordinary collector's theft. Chong is a mind-miner, uses his skills to run his criminal empire in this part of Asia. Be on your guard.

I shivered. Mind miners were almost as popular as savant vampires. Miners looked on and enjoyed others suffering, while vampires sucked the emotions dry in order to feel something themselves. *I will.*

We're coming for you.

I don't doubt it.

And I didn't. If there was one thing I knew about Victor it was that he would move heaven and earth to rescue me, and even the Robinsons, whom he had no reason to love.

'Found Victor?' Hal hovered by the window, fist clenched on the sill as if he had a mind to smash the glass.

'Yes.' I quickly recapped what I had learnt.

'So we wait for the Benedicts to ride to our rescue? Wow, ironic.' Hal gave a hollow laugh. 'Can you see if my brothers are OK, please?'

Suddenly so polite. 'I'll try.' I spread out my power looking for their mind signatures but drew a blank. I could feel many others around us, busy in kitchens, storerooms, engine room, cleaning cabins. Seeking a little further, I felt a malign presence pulsing away at the heart of all the activity, curled up on his hoard of gold. I couldn't afford to let him know I was there. That particular dragon came with a nasty bite.

'I don't think they're on board. I'll get Victor to look for them on land.' I sent a quick message to that effect but sensed Victor's alarm which he quickly damped down. They hadn't been killed and dumped, had they? I couldn't speak my fear because if Hal hadn't already thought of that possibility he didn't need me to suggest it.

'What's a mind miner? Another of your savant creepy skills?' Hal asked, fortunately heading off in another direction with his questions.

'Someone who can burrow through your memories and use them against you. You should be immune though, so don't worry.' I hugged my knees to my chest.

'What about you?'

I shrugged. 'Not met one before. We'll have to see. It's going to be the savant equivalent of an arm wrestle but in the mind: who's stronger, him or me.'

'Doesn't sound good.' Hal rolled his shoulders. 'Look, Summer, I want to apologize.'

Another of Hal's sorries. Would this end up with him being rude too? 'For what?'

'For not protecting you. We let these guys get the jump on us. If we hadn't split up, we wouldn't have been so vulnerable.'

'I doubt even staying together could've done anything against that gas.'

'Maybe, but we exposed our throat by not keeping our protocols intact.'

'What protocols?'

'We stick together. Lucas calls the shots, Scott aims us against the target and I provide the covering fire by not allowing anything through.'

I rubbed at a black streak on my arm. Where had I picked that up? 'And can't you accept that that is a savant skill right there? We all have some level of shielding.'

'But I'm really not like you. My skill isn't something I do consciously. Powers just don't work on me and if I put myself in front of my brothers, they get the same protection.'

He really struggled to see himself in this new light, I could feel it even if I couldn't read him so easily as I could others. 'So you've no control over it?'

'Not that I know. As for the savant thing, my brothers thought that not being able to do telepathy was more important. They say it's how you know each other.'

You can do it too, with me at least.

Yeah, so it seems. 'But it's taking me a while to adjust to the new intel you brought us.'

He reverted to speech, not at ease with the odd sense of talking to someone inside his head. At least I could quiet his fears on one score.

'I was going to say to you, before all this.' I waved at the cabin prison. 'You needn't adjust too much. I'd already taken the decision that my home situation makes mixing with other savants almost impossible. My mother is too much of a threat.'

His dark eyes settled on my face properly for the first time since we'd woken. It felt like touching a live wire, a jolt of intense need. Mine? His? I couldn't tell. 'You're planning on leaving just as you dragged me into that world?'

I nodded.

'Hey, princess, that just isn't fair.' He crossed the distance between us and sat beside me on the bunk. 'You can't leave me alone with all these people doing bizarre stuff with their powers. I had enough just coping with my brothers. I need backup.'

'I wouldn't be good for you.'

He nudged my shoulder. 'I thought it was a done deal. That was the only sweet part for me.'

'You could've fooled me.'

The door banged open. A stern-faced guard stood in the door with a semi-automatic rifle cradled in his arms. He was the size of a concrete pillar and about as friendly. 'You're to come with me.'

Hal stood up and offered me a hand off the bunk. Silently, we followed our escort along a corridor. The pillar stopped outside another cabin.

'The girl is to go in there.'

Hal's grip on my hand tightened. 'I'm not leaving her.'

The guard's answer was to club Hal in the chest with the butt of the rifle, forcing him away from me.

'Stop it!' I shouted as he raised the gun for a second blow.

'Keep back . . . Summer,' Hal panted. 'Don't give him an excuse to hurt you.'

'It's OK, Hal,' I said quickly, ignoring his order as I got between Hal and the rifle. 'Let's do as the man says.' *We'll keep in touch this way, OK?*

Clutching his ribs, Hal nodded reluctantly. I opened the door to the cabin and went inside. *It's just another bedroom but more luxurious and there are clothes laid out on the quilt.*

170

The guard paused in the doorway. 'You've ten minutes to change for dinner. Come on.' This last was directed at Hal as he was pushed further down the corridor.

You OK? I asked anxiously.

Yeah. I'm in the next cabin down with Meathead here. I'm to change too. Damn.

What's wrong? I rifled through the clothes. There was a pretty tunic and loose trousers made from light pink silk spread out for me. Tiny birds were embroidered on the cuffs and hems. With a V-neck it was going to look really odd to wear my T-shirt underneath. I'd have to take that off and hide it.

There's a whole dinner jacket deal here. I'm guessing our bad guy has watched too many spy films. He's expecting cool Federal Agent, Victor Benedict, not a seventeen-year-old squaddie. I'm going to look ridiculous.

Do they fit? I dipped into the bathroom and did a quick wash, stripping off my old clothes and putting on the new.

Not too bad. Do you know how to tie a bowtie?

I pulled a face at my reflection, imagining the scene next door. *Of course.*

Then I need you.

In a moment. I brushed my hair, slipping the hairband on my wrist in case I wanted it later. I then rolled up the T-shirt and tucked it in my waistband, hoping the long line of the tunic would hide what I was smuggling in with me. It didn't feel very secure. I'd try to transfer it to Hal's pocket when I had a chance.

The guard didn't bother to knock, just opened the door and gestured me to join him in the corridor. Hal stood beside him, wearing a top-of-the-range suit a little too big for him, bowtie hanging loose. His eyes brightened on seeing me.

'Look at you: the princess is back.'

'And you—all ready for prom.'

'Yeah, all we need is the stretch limo out of here.'

'Ever thought of modelling?' I gave the guard a 'wait a moment' look as my fingers quickly went about tying the bow. 'You'd be a shoo-in.'

'Yeah, I can really see that on my CV. Right up there with desert survival training.' He dipped his head closer once I finished the tie. 'You holding up OK?'

'I'm hoping that if they wanted us dead then they'd have killed us by now.'

He swallowed. 'Like my brothers?'

So he had thought of that. *Victor's looking for them. We don't know what's been done with them. Let's not borrow trouble.*

He pulled me into a hug. It felt wonderful just for a moment to be held. 'Sorry, but I can't stop wondering. They're, you know, everything to me.'

'I understand.' I embraced him, trying to transfer all my support through the pressure of my arms. 'I'll search for them as soon as I get back near enough to Singapore to do a scan for mind signatures.' *Keep this safe for me.* I pushed the T-shirt into his pocket. *Trace is using it to track us.*

A shove from the guard told us that he'd lost patience.

Hal held up his hands, distracting the guy from my fumbling in his pocket. 'OK, OK, keep your shirt on, mate.'

Cheeky.

Yeah, that's me.

We started walking, taking a flight of stairs up to the higher levels of the yacht.

The guard stopped at a set of double doors. He jerked his gun in their direction. 'In there.'

'I don't think he graduated *summa cum laude* from butler school, do you?' I murmured.

Hal shot me a grin, then made sure he went through the

doors first. He reached back and took my hand. 'It's OK. We're not being made to walk the plank quite yet.'

We entered into a lounge area, windows showing an almost three-sixty-degrees view of the sea. A cluster of small green islands like something out of *Robinson Crusoe* could be glimpsed to starboard as the sun set, flooding the room with golden light. The sunbeams caught an object sitting in the middle of the room on a plinth, protected by a glass case. Light dazzled on little disks, like golden dewdrops suspended from twisted wire. The Bactrian gold crown.

'Beautiful isn't it, Dr Nawabi? I hope it is worth your time in prison? You can leave us, Weiner.' As the guard backed out, the speaker appeared at the top of the spiral staircase set in one corner. We turned to face him. Shiny white shoes, weightlifter legs: he was generously built and on the short side. He had squeezed himself inside a white dinner jacket, and now his face was glowing with a smile I'd last seen on the many statues of the laughing Buddha in the curio stores in the mall. A glass of amber liquid on ice rattled in his right hand. 'My name is Ivan Chong, but you can call me Ivan, Atoosa. You don't mind if I call you Atoosa? Such a lovely name with a fine historic pedigree.' He didn't wait for my answer as he began the final turn. 'Forgive the forceful invitation. I have always found your Victor Benedict to be most unreasonable about mixing with what he views as the wrong sort, as no doubt you are learning.' Reaching the floor, he caught his first proper sight of us. 'That's not Victor—and you're not Atoosa. Who the devil are you?'

Chapter 14

A second man followed the laughing Buddha down the stairs.

'Where's my niece?' The tumbler in the man's hand slipped from his grasp and smashed on the floor below, denting the pretence that this was all some bizarre social call. 'What have you done with her, Ivan?' From his fading good looks and imperious nose I could trace a resemblance to Javid. Uncle Maiwand.

'I haven't done anything to her it seems. And I don't like your tone.' Ivan was still smiling but in the manner of a great white shark about to take a bite out of Maiwand's leg.

Maiwand flinched. 'I'm sorry, Mr Chong. I forgot myself for a moment.'

Hal put his arm around my shoulders. 'There seems to be some mistake. You weren't expecting us and we weren't expecting to be here. We're just a couple of students caught up in something we don't understand. Why not put us ashore and we'll forget it ever happened? We'll get on with our gap year.'

Ivan Chong advanced towards us, finger wagging at us. 'No, no, I think I understand the puzzle now. You must be Will Benedict and this, this has to be the girl Maiwand said is your sister, Summer Benedict.' He turned to Atoosa's uncle. 'What a joke: I wanted the Federal Agent and the academic. My idiot guards took the wrong members of the family, but no matter. There are some openings that still need filling.'

'But you really don't want the mini-me versions if you were wanting our . . . er . . . brother and Dr Nawabi,' Hal said reasonably, slipping into an American accent. We had to hope that, as neither of the men were native speakers, they wouldn't notice our mistakes. 'We don't want any trouble so we're happy to make our own way home from any port.' *He's not going to let us go, is he?*

No. But he doesn't know much about us if he isn't even sure what we look like or how old Will is. He might not even know our powers. Good accent by the way. I'm scared to say anything.

Chong ignored Hal's offer and walked to the crown. 'I was going to ask Dr Nawabi to tell me more about this piece's history. A beautiful lure for my trap, it is a shame she can't be here to admire it. Lovely though, isn't it?'

'Yes, but it belongs in a museum,' said Hal.

Chong gave a belly laugh. 'How very Indiana Jones of you, young man. I loved that film when I was growing up, though you might not be surprised to find I always rooted for the bad guys. So misunderstood.'

'Not by God. Punished them, didn't He, for touching something sacred? Melted, struck by lightning, turned to ash—yeah, I always cheered at that bit.'

Chong's smile died. 'I thought you were supposed to be able to sense danger. Saying things like that will only make this situation more dangerous for you.'

Better dial back the taunts, Hal. He knows about Will's gift already. We should assume he knows about mine, I warned him.

But not mine. For the good reason I didn't know about it.

Unless Maiwand told him about what happened in Mazar. They might be able to work it out for themselves.

Yeah, then we're stuffed.

Chong signalled to a maid who had hurried in to clear up the broken glass. 'Be quick then leave us.' She swept up nervously then scuttled out. 'I guess then that Dr Nawabi is out somewhere with her soulfinder? No matter, we'll just have to trade you for her when the time comes.' He was looking at Hal as he said that, not me. 'Having your sister here is an unexpected bonus. I'd considered acquiring her, decided it might be too complicated, and, look, she fell into my lap!' He sipped his drink, savouring the taste, smiling benignly at the company.

'I'm sorry but I don't understand what's going on here.' Hal shifted to keep Chong in his sightline and me slightly behind him. 'Clearly, you've got the wrong people. We've no interest in the crown. If you free us, we'll say nothing.'

Chong lowered himself down on to a white leather sofa, balancing his tumbler on the arm. 'This isn't about the crown. That is just,' he fluttered his fingers in the air, 'icing.'

What does he mean? Hal asked.

I really don't know. I was relaying everything Chong said to Victor, hoping he would have more clue than us. I could feel the silent tension at the other end of the telepathic link as the Benedicts watched us swim with the sharks. That wasn't helping. And why wasn't Chong blocking me? He had to guess now that I was a strong telepath and would surely have someone on his savant staff team who could stop telepathy? It wasn't an uncommon gift.

I agree, his security is weirdly lax, but keep us in the loop, replied Victor, catching my doubts. *Better to have the information while you can get it to us. That window might close any moment.*

'Maiwand, fix our guests a drink. Sit down, sit down.' Chong gestured to the sofa opposite his.

Atoosa's uncle didn't ask what we wanted, just handed over two Cokes over ice in tall glasses. He had poured himself a fresh drink too.

'You're a long way from Afghanistan,' I murmured as I accepted the drink, trying to figure out his part in all this.

His light brown eyes went from my face to the window behind me and the splendour of the sunset. 'We're all a long way from home, Miss Benedict. Please remember that.'

'The Benedicts have been a thorn in my side for a long while, did you know that?' Chong said conversationally. 'I met your father, the mighty Saul Benedict, when I was doing a Masters in Business Studies at Harvard—must've been back in the 80s. I didn't like him then, and still don't like him now. I would be doing the world a favour if I reduced your number.'

We're gonna have to tell him who we really are if he's got a vendetta against the Benedicts, cautioned Hal.

Wait to see where he goes with this. I'm working on getting his mind signature. I'd decided that the quickest way out of this was to take Chong over if I could.

'As far as I know Dad doesn't have a quarrel with you,' Hal said.

Chong sniffed. 'Will Benedict. According to Maiwand's information from his family, you're someone who senses danger like your father—not an interesting skill, as I often told Saul, but it has its uses. I don't think you pose much risk to someone like me. I'm content to trade you.'

'As you said, we aren't a threat to you, sir.' Hal put his drink down on the coffee table untouched.

'But your sister, now she's much more interesting. I thought there were only sons in the family.' Chong swirled his Scotch. 'But Maiwand swears she's one of you, was introduced to his family as such, and she is said to have powerful mind control skills.' *Who are you really, my dear?*

Taken by surprise at his sudden shift to attack, I grabbed my temples, only having just enough time to break the link to Victor before Chong found it. That gave Chong the second he needed to get in. He was as strong as I was, maybe stronger, and now he was rooting through my memories.

My mother's first assault on me when I was five, leaving me blank-faced in a playground as she danced off with her stolen emotions. Skipping rope dropped at my feet like a white snake. Dad running home with me, howling in remorse as I lay inert in his arms.

Again, when I was seven, when she'd slipped into my bedroom one evening while Dad was at work, Winnie-the-Pooh nightlight not protecting me as he had promised, her grip on my wrist until driven off by my brother's screams.

That led Chong to Winter, an angry boy of ten, battering me with a plastic ruler for snooping in his head, bad voices screaming after a nightmare about our mother. Chong lingered here, enjoying the violence. I could feel the blows all over again, raining down on my back as the mind-miner got to work.

Mother draining me of everything but shame in front of my friends as I curled up in a corner of the kitchen.

Then Chong was gone. There was nothing but Hal. My breath sawed in my chest.

Sorry, took me a little while to work out what he was doing and how to get in front of you. Still not sure how I did it.

I opened my eyes and discovered that I'd tipped the Coke all over the white fur rug at my feet. I was chilled to the bone with those memories, the pain still zinging around my body like a pinball flipped in a machine by a pro. Hal gave me a searching look, worried for me. I took a breath and squeezed his hand, signal that I would survive, but not again please.

Chong was smiling at me in his sickeningly jolly manner. 'Interesting. How did you do that?'

'Do what?' I wanted to curl into Hal but we were playing brother and sister and I didn't want to tip Chong off. He'd found out far too much already.

'Never mind, Miss *Whelan*. Not Benedict after all. You have a most interesting family of your own. We've more time to discover your skills as I've decided I won't get rid of you. I'll have to run some more tests, though, as I sensed I only saw the tip of the iceberg of your skills. Can you really take people over?'

I shrugged, trying to hide my alarm. If he'd seen that then he'd be boosting his shields, making any mental arm wrestle we might get into much more difficult for me. At least he hadn't seen from my memories that Hal was also an imposter.

'I bet you can. That's jolly good! You can fill the last opening—you're just what I need.' Chong slapped his thigh, belly quivering with laughter. 'Dr Nawabi and you will make a splendid addition to my staff of savants. I do like to surround myself with the best and most beautiful.' He gestured to the cabinets on the walls. I hadn't had time to register them before but they were filled with exquisite artworks, icons and paintings, bronze statues and ceramics. 'I should have known not to push my luck by trying to recruit any Benedicts but I did hope Victor would come over to my side for his soulfinder. However, Saul was always too tediously inflexible and I expect his sons are the same. I know that having you and Atoosa here, though, will keep them in line.'

He was definitely counting his chickens before they were hatched. No way would Victor let Atoosa walk into the dragon's den. 'And why would we stay?' I asked, fearing I could guess the answer.

'Quite simply because otherwise I'll kill the people that I'm holding hostage, the two we took from the hotel room next door. Trace and Will Benedict, wasn't it?' His face clouded as he realized the further mistakes in the equation. 'But Will's here. Who have we got, then, in the warehouse?' He dug out a mobile from his inside pocket and called a number. 'Lao, send photos of your guests please. There have been some distressing mistakes made; I'm afraid you'll have to punish those responsible on your team. No, not kill. I suggest,' he drummed his fingers on his belly, 'how about a fingernail for each mistaken identity? Hah! Yes, yes, very good joke.'

The man was a monster but we already knew that.

You're not staying here with this clown, said Hal.

Hardly a clown. I'd cracked the code and Chong's mind was leaking information to me, a swarm of images and sick stuff I really could do without. His thoughts kept returning to an island. His home? No, it meant something to him but I couldn't tell what. *I can see his thoughts now. He's killed many times. There's a disconnection in his brain, no sense of morality.*

You've got his signature?

Yes.

Can you take him over?

You want me to try?

What are the risks?

When I do, it's a complete merging. He could take me over if he proves stronger.

I could feel Hal's revulsion. Our link was growing the more we talked telepathically. *In that case, we'll keep that option in the locker until there's no choice.*

So what do we do?

It looks like we're going to have dinner with Bozo the clown and dear Uncle Maiwand.

A trio of servants entered from the far end of the living area and placed covered dishes out on a table already set for four. Chong hoisted himself from his low seat and held out a hand to me. His murky grey eyes were the colour of the sea on a foggy day, predatory in expression despite the laughter lines crinkling the corners. I sensed he only laughed at things that made others shudder.

'Miss Whelan, if you would sit on my right.' When I didn't rush to take his fingers, he wiggled them like pale slugs in my face. I could see the images of retribution in his mind so accepted his helping hand. 'From England, are you?' He led me to the table. I could feel Hal right at my back, desperate to intervene but, like a basketball player knowing how to block an opponent, Chong wasn't giving him the opportunity. 'A real English young lady?'

'I'm a mixture.'

'Aren't we all? My mother was American, my father Korean, Singapore their adopted home.'

'Were they soulfinders?' I wondered how much I could get him to tell us about himself. If his manner was any guide to his character, he was an egomaniac and they usually liked talking about their favourite subject. Know your enemy seemed wise advice right now.

'Of course.'

'And your own soulfinder? Where is she?' Perhaps she could be a good influence on him if Crystal could find her, someone who could plead on our behalf?

He stiffened. 'I'm afraid she died, Miss Whelan.' He handed me to my chair then a waiter took over to tuck it in behind me.

'Oh, I'm sorry.' I really meant that.

Chong sat down and shook out his napkin with a snap before spreading it on his lap. 'You should ask Saul Benedict about her. I'm sure he'll remember. After all, she was best friends with his wife.'

I caught a glimpse of a laughing round-faced girl with long red hair and freckles, a teenage giggler dressed in the peasant blouse and rah-rah skirt of the eighties, a green lawn, Harvard. If she had lived, would this man beside me have taken a benign route in life, his humour genuine and not undercut by bitterness? Could they have produced a family of giggling, chubby little babies? There was a disconnect in his brain, yes, but did it date from the time he lost her or had it always been there? I should never forget that being a soulfinder was curse as well as blessing.

'However, I think now that Annie-May was too good for this world,' continued Chong. Thanks to the leaking images in his mind, I saw the same girl lying on a bed, wasted by disease, but smiling bravely at him. His inner pain was intense, still piercing his heart after decades, no healing or softening. 'She didn't have the toughness we savants need to survive. Do you have that toughness, Miss Whelan?'

I thought it unfair to brand the girl who died as not tough enough. Cancer wasn't a battle to be won but a test to be endured, no fault the outcome. 'I don't know, sir. I guess any of us can fall ill—or have an accident.' I hope he hadn't noticed my mistake in betraying I'd seen how she died. He didn't need to know I could read him.

'True. Life is fragile. That's why I like to preserve these beautiful things from the past. If I keep them safe, then they will survive another few centuries.'

From the way he looked at me I could tell that he collected people as well as things and unfortunately I now featured on his list of must-haves.

'A ship doesn't seem that safe to me,' said Hal, taking a seat opposite me.

'I assure you we are equipped with the most up-to-date flotation devices.' Chong picked up a set of chopsticks and plucked a king prawn from a dish in front of him and scooped up some rice in a little lacquer bowl. 'If there is a catastrophic accident this room will seal itself and wait until it can be raised from the seabed.'

'Like the *Titanic*?' Hal couldn't resist the jibes, or was it more calculated than that? Was he trying to deflect Chong's attention from me? He winked at me. Of course he was.

Chong frowned, another dissonance making itself felt. 'You

don't sound quite right for an American, Will. Now why is that?'

Hal's eyes flicked to the window. 'Spent too long studying in the UK, I suppose.'

'No, no, there's something odd about you.' Hal had certainly achieved attracting Chong's attention but not in a way we wished. 'The word is that you and your brothers were raised in some place in Colorado; but there was surprisingly little information on the Benedict family when I checked. And believe me, that was my first priority after Maiwand told me that Victor had sprung his niece from jail.

'I knew getting Dr Nawabi into trouble would eventually bring Victor to me,' continued Chong. 'I hadn't realized it would drag so many of you into my net.' He turned to me. 'Why aren't you eating?'

I took up my chopsticks and selected some vegetables from the dish nearest me.

'I don't suppose you have a fork?' asked Hal, looking at his with dismay. Like a magician producing a scarf from a sleeve, a waiter placed a fork by his plate and removed the sticks. 'Thanks.'

'No, definitely not American.' Chong pointed his chopsticks at Maiwand. 'Who is he?'

I could feel the perspiration trickling down my spine. Javid and Ramesh had no reason not to tell their uncle about our escape. We'd used his plane after all.

Maiwand cleared his throat and cast a quick look at Hal and me. 'Javid said that the Benedicts had come with some cousins from England. He must be one of them.'

Hal, he didn't betray us and he could've done. He knows what happened in Mazar.

Hal's eyes met mine as he speared an oyster mushroom. *He's playing his own game then.*

183

He must be another of Chong's unwillingly collected items. Chong's got some hold over him to get his cooperation, like he has us.

'Cousin are you?' Chong sniffed. 'Yes, you don't have anything of Saul or Karla about you. Why did you lie to me?'

I prayed Hal would come up with a good excuse as I couldn't think of one right then.

'Because I'm not a savant, sir.'

Maiwand poured himself another drink. He wasn't eating I noticed. 'I remember now: my youngest nephew Javid has a gift for sensing other savant's powers. He told me about this one.' Maiwand dismissed Hal with a jerk of the head. 'Only his older brothers got the gift; he was left out of the genetic inheritance, taking after his non-savant parents.'

'So why didn't you say?' Chong asked with a benign smile as he arranged some cashew nuts on the edge of his plate.

Hal looked down, pretending a bashfulness that didn't suit him. 'It's a little embarrassing to admit, surrounded by so many of you savants. I didn't know what you would think.'

Chong's eyes narrowed. He was trying to get inside Hal's head, I could sense that from where I was sitting. We had to stop him meeting the blankness and guessing Hal's secret.

'That looks good.' I reached for the bamboo basket of steamed dumplings, knocking over the water carafe and shooting water into Hal's lap. He leapt up and swore.

'Summer! Watch what you're doing!' He flapped the napkin at the spreading puddle getting in the way of the waiter who had hastened over to clear up. *Clever girl.*

'Sorry. I'm not normally this clumsy.' *Anytime, Mr Robinson.* 'I'll have to go and change.'

My distraction had produced the desired result; Chong was no longer concentrating on Hal. 'I fear you must be tired, Miss Whelan.'

184

Getting knocked out by gas attack does that to a girl. 'Yes, I am, a little.'

'And I need to look after my treasures better. We'll cut short our dinner and resume our conversation tomorrow when you are fully recovered. By then I hope Miss Nawabi will be able to join us and our non-savant guest here will be happily on his way home. You see, I don't want any of you to be unnecessarily disturbed about your change in circumstances. From what I glimpsed of your memories, I'm saving you from a difficult situation at home. You'll not have to deal with your mother or brother again. All I ask in return is you play your part faithfully in my organization and everyone will be, how can I say this tactfully? Alive. Yes, everyone will be alive.' He chuckled like a favourite uncle making a slightly scandalous joke at the Christmas dinner table, then signalled to the waiters to clear the table. 'Until tomorrow, Miss Whelan.' He ignored Hal, having lost interest in him completely now he was convinced he was neither a savant nor a Benedict.

'Goodnight.'

Yeah goodnight, you jerk. Hal took my hand. *Let's get out of here. He's making me feel like throwing up all over his shiny shoes.*

Back in the room where we first woke up, we were finally able to breathe more easily.

'Do you think this place is bugged?' I asked.

Hal ran his fingers over the fixtures and fittings. 'Could be, but why bother when your guests can talk telepathically? I'd have a bug for that if such a thing exists.'

'I haven't sensed a listener.'

'Not got one in his collection then? Bit of an oversight.'

'That's what I thought. I'm worried it's part of Chong's plan that I tell Victor all this. What do you think he's really up to? I mean all that stuff about collecting me and Atoosa, sounds crazy.'

'The world is full of crazy people.'

'But it just doesn't seem worth it. A very expensive and inefficient way of recruiting staff.'

'Unless he has a particular job he needs you for. He's cherry-picking skills.'

'He mentioned he knew he'd net Victor if he went for Atoosa. Any idea how that could be?'

'You're the mind reader.'

'Gee, thanks. Getting past the "I'm-your-new-best-friend" smiles and close to his mind is like wading through a sewer under Disneyland. I saw an island in his head but I'm not sure what that has to do with Atoosa and me.'

'It's one puzzle after another, isn't it? And I really don't like the way he looks at you.'

'I know. Of all my crappy life choices, being part of his collection appeals least.'

I hadn't meant to distract us but that comment raised the ghost of our unfinished business. Hal cleared his throat. 'It's gone all wrong for us, hasn't it?'

'I can say I've had better weeks.'

'Summer, I know I behaved badly at the hotel but I want to explain.'

'Go ahead.' I curled up on the bunk.

'I've been furious with you for days because I thought you were inventing the soulfinder link only to take it away. That hurt. A lot.'

If we were going to talk about it, I'd prefer to do it without him looming over me.

'Why don't you come and sit next to me?' I patted the spot on the bunk. He sat down and I let my head rest against his shoulder, a gesture of camaraderie. Peace was breaking out between us, thanks to our mutual enemy. Another irony. 'Why did it matter? I didn't think you even liked me.'

'That's just not true. There's a lot to like about you. You're beautiful, obviously.'

'Really?' It came out as a very uncool squeak. 'You think I'm pretty?'

'Not pretty: beautiful. Summer, you take a guy's breath away. Surely you've worked that out?' He shifted to face me.

'Er, no?'

'Just as well or you'd be unbearable.' He brushed my nose. 'But I've also found I like teasing you and making sure you look after yourself.'

'I do look after myself!'

'You get distracted and forget to eat. An army marches on its stomach.' He settled back so I rested against him, arm around my shoulders.

'Listen to you, quoting Napoleon.'

'I'm quoting my mother actually.' The little circles he was stroking on my arm were driving me crazy.

'I think she might've got it from someone else.'

'Whatever.' He grimaced. 'I'm not so sure about the brainy thing you do but I can learn to appreciate it.'

'Sorry. I'm an incurable know-it-all.'

'Hopefully not incurable. And we've proved you don't know it all, not even a decent fraction of what you should.'

My pride was pricked. 'When?'

'Snake in my boot? Nicholas Cage's popcorn movies?'

'Oh, OK. I didn't watch a lot of children's films when I was younger.'

'Yeah, you were probably watching *Pride and Prejudice* and the Proms.'

How did he know that? I was hopeless, wasn't I? Raised to live in the wrong century by a traditional father.

187

'But I suppose what I really like is that you're such a girl and make no apology for it.' He picked up my hand and nibbled on a nail-polished fingertip.

I lifted my head. 'Why should I?'

'Ssh.' He pressed my head gently back down. 'I'm trying to tell you that I feel, you know, something for you.'

'So eloquent.'

'I'm a squaddie, not a poet, so get over it.'

'I'm over it, honest.' I nudged him to go on. To hear so many lovely things from him was the last thing I expected from this conversation and I didn't want to stop now.

'And despite the false trail laid by the pink suitcase and coordinated nail polish, you have inner steel—a different kind of strength from my brothers and me but I respect that.'

'Thank you.'

He closed his eyes, head back against the wall, a big smile on his face. 'I started by not wanting to give you a chance, but then by the time we reached Mazar I was completely stupid about you. The way you had a snooty little comeback for my insults—major turn on. I wanted to punch Javid when I thought he might be the one for you.'

'You hid that well.'

'Humour—my deflection. Punching innocent civilians isn't best practice for a soldier, and definitely frowned upon in the Geneva Convention.' He kissed my knuckles. Every touch made my body shiver with little quakes of delight. 'I hope you don't mind that part of me? You called me a mercenary, but this is my life.'

I'd long since stopped thinking about him as a mercenary. That had been unfair of me, said to make him lose control. 'Hal, does it matter what I like and what I don't?'

'It does to me.'

'Well then, you and your brothers do an important job and I can appreciate that.'

'Anything else?'

'I liked you when you gave me a massage and the chocolate was a nice touch.'

He snorted. 'Did I mention you were high maintenance?'

'But it went sour when I realized you only did it to make me unsuspicious.'

His fingers started a gentle squeeze of my arm just below the short sleeve of my tunic. 'So she's not so smart after all. Summer, I didn't need to do that. Lucas said he didn't see any of you guessing that we were following a different set of orders as you all played with a straight bat. Victor would've been more suspicious as he is as twisty as they come, but he wasn't there until the end. No, that wasn't the mission; I did those things because I couldn't help myself.' His hand lifted to massage my nape. 'Does this soulfinder deal come with a physical connection between the two people, because I think we've got that in spades and I'm kinda finding it hard to keep my hands off you.'

'I . . . I think that maybe it does. Do you mind?'

'Not at this exact moment, no.' He tipped my chin up and pressed his lips lightly to mine as if testing the fit. 'Hmm, yes, definitely something there.' He replaced his lips with his thumb, rubbing the spot he'd just touched. 'Soft, like petals.'

I lifted my hand to trace the edge of his jaw, pleasantly rough under my fingertips.

A rueful smile curved his lips. 'I need a shave but somehow they forgot to send for my valet along with the suit.'

'I like it. It reminds me you're such a guy.'

'Such a girl, such a guy: see, we're the perfect match.' The twinkle was back in his eyes. I'd missed that.

I laughed softly. 'If it were only that easy.'

'The way I see it, you need me to look after you, help you

189

relax and stop you being taken advantage of by your friends and even your family.'

'What do you mean?' He wasn't thinking we'd actually continue with this soulfinder relationship, was he?

'For a start, you should never've come on this mission. You've no training.' He interrupted me before I could protest. 'I don't mean you're not capable but you didn't sign up for danger, not like my brothers and I did.'

'Being born a savant signs you up whether you like it or not.'

'Then that's clear enough: my new mission is to keep you safe. He's not collecting you.' He turned his eyes to the door. 'Whatever Chong sends through there, I'll protect you, I promise.'

I laced my hand with his so they rested on his thigh. 'And I'll protect you too.'

Chocolate brown eyes dipped to mine. 'You will?'

'Uh-huh. Someone told me we're a team.'

He smiled and rested his head against the wall behind us. 'This is so bizarre. This should be the worst moment of my life, discovering I'm a savant and then being knocked out and locked up, but instead I'm kinda singing inside.'

I hugged his waist. 'I know. We're in the middle of a disaster but it feels good, like I'm finally digging out from under the rubble.'

'I'll be right there to help with the heavy lifting.'

I sighed, letting myself savour his unique scent for a little while, just an edge of musk under whatever soap he used to shower yesterday. We probably both needed another one but I didn't find the odour unpleasant, which surprised me. I'd always been a little too finicky about cleaning up, according to Misty. She'd approve of the sign I was relaxing my standards. Joining the human race, she'd call it.

'What are you thinking?' His fingers were combing strands

190

of my hair straight. I'd bundled it up into a high ponytail for the meal but that had collapsed to the back of my head.

'That I like the way you smell.'

'Princess, don't say things like that to a guy, not unless you want him to go crazy.'

'Maybe I want you to go crazy.'

'Summer,' he groaned. Pushing me back on the pillow and leaning over me he settled for another kiss, this one serious. Could I allow myself a stolen moment of closeness? I'd have to separate from him eventually but just now I had every excuse to throw caution away. My hands roamed his back, griping the material of his shirt, then stroking it smooth. I found a soft little patch of hair at his nape, the rest was cut short and as velvety as it looked. He'd proceeded to my neck, nuzzling there, edge of his tongue tracing the oh-so-sensitive bones of my throat, followed by nipping kisses. 'You smell so good too. Tell me to stop.'

The words wouldn't come immediately but finally I dragged them kicking and screaming from my conscience. 'You'd better stop.' I had to remember I couldn't keep him. I'd told him that already.

He sighed. 'You're not doing your "I've got messed up genes" thing are you?'

I nodded.

'Jumping the gun, aren't we? We're both just seventeen. Plenty of time to iron out the wrinkles.'

'You have to think ahead. A soulfinder deal is for life.'

'Yeah.' He brushed my fingertips against his lips. 'But forward planning for so many years isn't my style. I'm more a go-with-the-moment guy. This feels good now. That's what matters.'

'I expect that's what my dad told himself. Sorry.' I eased my hand away and slipped off the bunk.

'We're gonna have to work on that martyrdom complex of yours,' he said grumpily. I couldn't blame him as I was feeling edgy myself, having led him into the starting gates then pulled up at the first fence.

'That was my fault. I can only say I'm sorry again.'

He got off the bunk and snagged me in an embrace. 'Stop beating yourself up. I know where you're coming from. You warned me and I listened. And we've bigger problems than that right now so no final decisions, OK? We need to work together and having a row about a kiss or two is not going to help.'

'So we don't kiss?' I traced a figure of eight on his shirt. He looked incredibly hot with his bow tie loose, jacket unbuttoned, a whole bundle of my fantasies in a very nice wrapping.

'No, we kiss but don't argue about it.' And he made good on his promise. I gave in because I really wanted to. I was protesting too much. Dad was right. The pull between soulfinders did make you reckless. Lock us up in a confined space and we could hardly be expected to be sensible. Chong had another thing to pay for when all this was over.

Chapter·15

We were both asleep, spooned together on the same bunk, when they broke into our cabin. The lights flared on and Weiner stood at the threshold with three men.

'You, come,' he gestured to Hal.

We sprang up, my hand locked in his.

'Come where?' I asked.

'He's leaving. You're staying.'

'I'm not going without Summer,' said Hal.

Weiner's answer was to kick at the spot where our hands were held. Pain shot up my arm, fingers numbed. Lunging between us, Weiner grabbed me by the hair, unsheathed a knife and hauled me against his chest. 'You will go,' he told Hal.

If the threat had been against him, Hal would've fought but he couldn't risk me.

Summer, what do you want me to do?

My ability allowed me only to take over one mind at a time so I didn't fancy our odds if it came to a struggle in this confined space. *Do as he says.*

'Summer, I'm sorry.'

'I know: you've got to go.' I wished I wasn't shaking so hard. I hated that Weiner knew how scared I felt with his knife at my cheek.

Hal put up his hands to show he didn't mean trouble, grabbed his jacket, then walked to the door.

'Good decision.' Weiner released my hair and shoved me towards the bunk.

The men left, the key turning in the lock behind them. This felt like the worst moment yet, not knowing what they were going to do to Hal. Chong had talked about trading him but no way would Victor allow Atoosa to exchange herself for a Robinson. Hal wouldn't want her to either. I crawled across the rumpled covers to the window. A small boat was heading away from the yacht. I could see Hal sitting in the middle of two guards. No sign of Weiner.

Have they said where they're taking you?

No, princess. You're not to worry about me, OK?

Do you still have the T-shirt in your pocket?

Oh hell, Summer, I should've left that with you! I'm sorry, I didn't have time to think of it.

No, no, it's OK. I want you to have it.

A soft hum through the floor indicated that the yacht's engines had restarted after several hours of being moored. *We're moving away.*

His boat was getting smaller and smaller, now just a faint light on the horizon. *You're good at this telepathy thing, right? It'll be miles and miles before you and I can't talk any more?*

Yes.

Keep strong.

Oh Hal.

It's OK, flower: I'm a big boy. Save your worry for yourself. Don't anger them. Do what you have to do to survive.

A couple hours after dawn I was summoned to share breakfast with Chong on deck. Clean clothes had been provided: navy shorts, a white T-shirt with an anchor on the back, white socks and plimsolls. Crew clothing I guessed. I looked like I was about to climb the rigging, not sip coffee and eat croissants.

As I walked towards the breakfast table, Weiner at my back, I tried checking in with Hal. We'd last spoken at about four when he had reported being left on a beach, he wasn't sure where. There had been a cool box with a bottle of water waiting for him and he was hoping he would be able to walk to a village when it grew light, but we both feared this was highly unlikely. They wouldn't leave him such an easy escape. This time though, with the sun well up, I couldn't reach him. I tried Victor, last spoken to when I'd told him they'd separated us. Now there was the same sense of cotton wool filling the space between us. Chong had his telepathic dampener active this morning. Whatever he had wanted to achieve by letting me speak to Victor yesterday must have been done.

'Summer, I must say you don't look very rested,' said Chong pointing to a chair beside him.

I sat down. What else could I do? 'Odd that. I would've thought having a friend taken forcibly in the middle of the night was the secret for a good night's sleep.'

Smiling indulgently at my sarcasm, Chong helped himself from a selection of Chinese breakfast dumplings. 'Take a look at the photos on your plate and tell me who they are.'

I lifted the napkin. Scott and Lucas, both tied up with their hands over their head, squinting in the harsh light of a torch in the face. I swallowed against the bile that rose in my throat.

'They're the cousins Maiwand mentioned. Are they OK?' Of course they weren't OK, but I meant are they alive?

Chong smiled blandly at me, eyes dead. 'I did some more research after dinner last night and discovered that the Robinsons are no relation of Saul Benedict.'

I straightened my cutlery.

'That is why Maiwand Nawabi can't join us this morning. He is feeling the aftereffects of lying to me. It is really not a good idea, so I'll try again. Who are they?'

I briefly touched his mind. Maiwand had been beaten up and was in his cabin nursing his bruises and a cracked rib. This had all happened shortly after Hal had been taken away in the night. Chong knew exactly who the Robinsons were already so I wouldn't be betraying them.

'I'm not sure, but I think they might be military.' I poured myself some tea and added a splash of milk, all so I didn't have to look at him. 'Mr Benedict hired them.'

'Are they savants?'

'Yes, I believe they are.'

'Their gifts?'

'Something to do with fighting and finding things.' I took a piece of toast and spread butter to every corner. 'I'm sorry but I've only known them a few days. I was only here because Mr Benedict asked me to help find Victor.' I concentrated hard on the truth of that statement rather than all the things I was leaving out. Like soulfinders.

'That's all you know? Will you prove it by letting me see your memories?'

I raised my eyes. 'I'd really prefer it if you didn't. I don't like what you do with my memories.' We held each other's gaze for a breathless few seconds.

Chong was the first to look away. 'Could I get in now you are shielded against me? How powerful are you, I wonder?'

'I'm nothing special.'

'No, that's where you're wrong. I think you might be very special indeed.' He looked at his watch. 'If you'll excuse me, I have to make a call on the satellite phone.' He got up from the table and went inside.

At least with him gone and only two guards watching me, I could manage some breakfast. I repeatedly tried telepathy but to no avail. The shutters were down and I was cut off from the world beyond the boat. I gazed bleakly out at the expanse of turquoise sea surrounding us. The yacht was making rapid progress thanks to the fair conditions, porpoises following us, seagulls wheeling overhead. A stiff breeze tugged at my hair, whipping it into salty strands. It could have been an advert for upmarket sailing holidays in different circumstances. At least I wasn't completely powerless, even if I was trapped. Touching on the many minds on board, I had a clear sense of purpose and of anticipation. This was no pleasure cruise; the crew knew we were heading somewhere important and they were expecting a big reward at the end of it. I pushed a little harder at the nearest guard's mind. An island—the same one I'd spotted in Chong's thoughts the night before. I tried for more information but beyond a clear sense of isolation, he knew very little. What were they planning? I caught something more from a chambermaid. She was wondering if they had enough rooms for their expected guests as she counted sheets and towels in the laundry. Who were they? All she had been told was that they were very important and everything must be perfect.

I pulled my thoughts away from her as I felt Chong's presence behind me. He was furious, carrying the mood like bad body odour, but hiding it under a deodorant of a blinding smile. Him being frustrated had to be good news for me, didn't it? He dropped back into his chair, throwing his mobile with some force onto the tablecloth.

'It appears, Summer, that Dr Nawabi won't be joining us after all. That is sad, isn't it?'

'She's not?' I hadn't expected her to walk into the trap.

'I've overestimated the Benedicts' sense of decency. You'll be appalled to hear that the Benedicts have decided to leave that non-savant friend of yours to die rather than send her in exchange for his location.'

'Y . . . you left Hal to die?'

197

'He was marooned on an island with no fresh water but the single bottle I left for him. I made that perfectly clear to the Benedicts. He has another day or two and then he'll be dead but they didn't care. Victor told my agent that there was nothing I could offer that would persuade them to hand over Atoosa.'

It couldn't be true that they'd let Hal die. I wouldn't allow it to be true. 'Please, we have to go back for Hal.'

Chong sat back in his chair to study me. 'Interesting. You care about what happens to him.'

'Of course I care.'

'Then maybe if you're good we'll go back for him in a few days. It might not be too late.' Spirits restored by my distress, he poured himself a coffee. 'You're not to think about him any more. I want you to have a clear mind now you're replacing Dr Nawabi on this mission. You won't have to worry about the other two Robinsons either. They were the wrong bargaining chips and they were tying up resources.'

How could I switch off thinking? Was that what Chong did in his sociopathic brain? 'How can I not worry?'

He picked up the photographs and shredded them. 'It would be too late so therefore pointless. They were killed and disposed of.'

'No.'

'I never leave any loose ends.'

'Please no.'

'Blame Saul Benedict and his boys, not me. The Benedicts might be more flexible over people they care about than these soldiers. Do they care about you?'

I jumped up and walked to the rail. Would he try to stop me if I threw myself over, not that there was any way to swim to safety?

'I have a person with very strong telekinetic powers. They'll lift you out of the water if you do what you are contemplating.'

My eyes went to him, considering.

'And if you try to take me over, I've given my men orders to shoot you.' Chong was giving all these pieces of information as if we were discussing the weather.

I had to cooperate. If there was even the slightest chance we'd go back and get Hal, I had to do it. 'What do you want me to do, Mr Chong?'

He smiled at that. 'Sit down and I'll tell you.'

I took my seat.

I couldn't do it, could I? Fretting, I paced my cabin, imagining Hal lying on a beach, gasping under a tropical sun, desperate for water. He had my T-shirt but would that be enough for him to be found in time? I'd grieved for his brothers for over a day and a half; I owed it to Hal and to them to take whatever chance I had to make sure he at least survived.

My brothers mean everything to me, Hal had said.

Oh Hal. I'm so sorry.

Come on, Summer, there's no choice. Chong had promised we'd go back for him; I'd dipped into his mind and found that he half-meant this. If it proved convenient, we'd circle back. He had decided that Hal was useful again as a way of controlling me. All I had to do to save him was commit a terrible crime.

There came a knock at the door. A crew member opened it, behaving like the stage manager summoning an actress to the stage.

'Five minutes, miss.'

'OK.' I checked my outfit for the last time. I was dressed all in black. Even patches of pale skin had been covered so as not to shine in the security lights. I didn't recognize myself in the mirror. What was I doing? This was madness. Would Hal think the price of his survival too high and tell me to back out? If I was part of this, I'd be responsible for what happened next

199

and the body count might be very much higher than just his brothers. What was the right choice? Save Hal or thousands of people I didn't know?

'Miss?' My escort was back.

'Coming.'

I arrived on deck to join the rest of the team going to the island. That lay to port, a flicker of lights from buildings higher up the cliff and a floodlit port at sea level, so tiny it looked like a toy from here. There was no moon, just a spray of stars across the expanse of the night sky like a spill of glitter on a children's craft table. A warm breeze whipped the sea into choppy peaks. A dark grey landing craft was moored alongside the yacht, barely visible except for the bouncing tip of the cigarette being smoked by the pilot.

Chong was there to see us off. He of course wasn't planning to be present for the dangerous insertion, intending to come along when we'd cleared all obstacles from his path. 'Good evening, gentlemen, lady. You all understand your parts?'

'Yes, sir,' my teammates replied smartly.

'I want no mistakes, no deviation from the plan. This island was once an American sea base before turned to its present purpose, so the defences are considerable. Expect anything and everything to be thrown at you.' He paused, waiting for the murmurs of agreement. 'Maiwand will disrupt communications and mask your entry. Lee will lift the chain across the harbour entrance. Keller will extinguish the lights. Weiner and his team will take out any armed guards. In the absence of our own puzzle solver, Miss Whelan will find a mind among the guards able to unravel the encryptions to the top security area. The signal that you have got in safely will be when Manfred, Bristow and Wu drop the telepathic shield. Weiner, if Miss Whelan shows any reluctance, get rid of her and force someone else at gunpoint to get your team inside.'

'Yes, sir.' Weiner seemed quite eager to get started on that part of his orders. I'd have to make sure I didn't give him any excuse.

'Now, go. I want this done. If you complete the takeover in under thirty minutes, I'll double your bonus.'

That lit a fire under the team as Chong knew it would. They jostled for a place to go over the side. Remembering that I was being watched for reluctance, I stuck close to Weiner and followed him down the ladder to the smaller boat, then took a seat on my own near the front. Maiwand joined me a few moments later. He was moving with great difficulty, hand clutched to his side.

'You look like you should be in bed,' I muttered.

'You look like you should be in England.' He gave me a sympathetic grimace.

I could sense his reluctance. He did not have very strong shields masking his emotions which must make him easy prey for Chong. 'How did you get caught up in all this?' The boat rocked as Weiner took delivery of a crate of arms from above.

'I got into debt. You really do not want to cross a man like Chong. He knows where I live, who my family are, he wouldn't hesitate to take it out on them.'

I'd guessed it was something like that. 'So you're working off the debt. Any luck with that yet?'

'You don't ever pay off this kind of debt, you just keep one step ahead of being thought disposable.'

I could see how that worked. In Chong's mind, I was already part of the special group of people he kept onside by always holding out another threat or another promise. There was no endgame for him unless it was a bullet in a person he no longer required. 'I'm sorry.'

'So am I.' Maiwand shook his head, clearing his thoughts. 'Excuse me, I have to concentrate.'

As the boat got underway, he closed his eyes. A low-pitched hum started to emanate from him. He directed it to bounce off one of the high cliffs of the volcanic island so it returned at the perfect pitch to cancel out the wavelength of the engines. This took a lot of skill and practice to get it just right. He'd explained to us in our briefing earlier how his power worked. Sound was a wave, so if you sent another in the opposite direction to disrupt it they would effectively kill each other. It was the technology behind the most expensive noise-cancelling headphones. He could also use the same technique at different frequencies to mess with radio signals. If the three telepathic blockers responsible for the cotton wool muffling around our operation were like the pawns in this operation, he was the first back row piece, the rook on this dangerous chessboard.

The knight went next: Joseph Lee, a thin man with short grey hair, one of the most powerful telekinesis experts I had met. His appearance of fragility was a great lie as he could lift many times his own body weight. His role was to help us pass the thick metal chain that formed a gate across the narrow opening to the harbour, but the timing had to be perfect as the harbour walls were intermittently swept by search lights. Waiting for the latest one to pass, he lifted the chain out of the water, seaweed dripping from the links, so that our low-lying vessel could squeeze underneath, just like guessing the right time to go under a skipping rope. Maiwand immediately countered the noise of it splashing back down behind us.

Next up was Helmut Keller, a taciturn German man with a noticeable burn down the side of his face—a side effect, he had admitted to us, from his early experiments with his power. He could manipulate heat, magnifying it or extinguishing it, whatever the situation called for. On this operation his role was to burn out the generator by taking its normal energy and ramping it up until it went into emergency shut down. But to do this he had to be actually touching the machine, so the pilot put him ashore at the far end of the dock near the little power plant for the island. Keller slid off into the shadows to get to work, ducking behind some fuel tanks decorated with the American flag.

Weiner poked me with the stock of his gun. It was time for me to locate a mind that could take us through the secondary levels of security. I was only dimly aware of the lights snapping out and the armed members of our team invading the watchtowers to take out the guards. I concentrated on the control room at the centre of the harbour complex, reasoning that it was most likely to have someone with an overview of the software controlling the onward gates and locked doors. I touched briefly on three or four heads, dismissing them quickly when I saw that they only dealt with the outer ring. They were busy fretting about the power cut, gathering emergency lights and trying to raise their colleagues in the watchtowers on the radio. They knew something was happening but had not yet worked out how close we are.

'Not found what you're looking for?' asked Maiwand softly.

I shook my head, an edge of panic creeping into my search. Failure would be interpreted as reluctance, giving Weiner the excuse to shoot me he so dearly wanted.

Maiwand took my hand and held it. 'You need the boss. If he is like most senior managers I know, he wouldn't put himself on nightshift. Find someone who's asleep.'

I switched my scan to the staff quarters situated a little further up the hill. Reading someone when they're asleep is very difficult, but fortunately our other activities had prompted some conscientious underling to go for his chief. I caught my target just as he was waking up, bleary thoughts a strange mixture of annoyance and alarm. He knew he was running one of the most hazardous places in the world but he hadn't yet caught on that the danger was about to get much worse.

Weiner came back to the boat, wiping his knife on his trouser leg. 'Got a target?'

'Yes.'

'Come on then.' He reached down and took my hand. I thought he meant to steady me as I climbed up but instead he lifted me in one smooth move from the boat on to the dock. 'You have fifteen minutes.'

Before they lost their bonus, he meant.

An alarm started wailing in the distance. Finally someone had realized something was seriously wrong. Weiner and I ran along the dockside, past the control room with its emergency lanterns, to the staff quarters, which were in a low-level apartment building. Weiner kicked the door in and pushed me inside.

'You go first. They won't shoot a girl on sight.'

I followed my sense of the senior man to the third door along the corridor. It stood part open.

'The generator's down, sir. We can't reach any of the guards on the radio. It's possible the power cut has affected the equipment but that's unlikely. I think this is savant work.' A man dressed in a beige and brown uniform was reporting to another who was still in his dressing gown. With buzz-cut black hair, a dark complexion and military bearing, the chief made an impressive figure despite the disadvantage of his nightwear.

'Have you sent the SOS?' He had a low-toned rumbling voice.

'Immediately, as per procedure.'

'Then gather the remaining guards. We have to assume we are under attack by hostile forces. What? Who are you?'

I'd been spotted. Both men turned to look at me standing

hesitantly in the doorway. I had a bizarre feeling that I looked like some troublemaker interrupting the head teacher in a conference with a member of staff. I didn't give them time to reassess why I might be here. I broke into the senior man's mind and took over. I quickly gathered the information I needed: Charlie Rotji, lieutenant colonel, originally from Nigeria, now working for an international force under UN auspices.

Tell him there is no situation. It's all a drill.

'On second thoughts, Winston, stand down,' said Rotji quite calmly now. 'My friend has reminded me that we had scheduled a surprise test of our security arrangements.'

'Your friend? No, that's not right. What is she doing here?' Winston wasn't buying it.

'She's taking over,' said Weiner, coming in behind me and pointing his gun at them both.

My brain was occupied in sorting through Rotji's mind. He, like all the people seconded to the island, was a savant; in his case a strong gift for healing so no immediate threat to me. I burrowed a bit deeper, wishing I could apologize but I had to find out the secrets he was trying to hide from me. Unlike my mother's sick mind, which was fairly easy to control because she was so weak-willed, this mindscape of a healthy savant tried to resist me by throwing up barriers in my path. He wasn't going to break easily. My own control was fracturing as he pushed back.

'Seven minutes and counting,' said Weiner.

'Give me a moment.' Sweat was dripping down my spine. It was like wrestling with an octopus: the moment I thought I had Rotji under control, another arm would wriggle free.

'He knows how to get through?'

I nodded, teeth gritted against resistance.

'Then I kill you and make him open the doors.' He lifted the gun to aim at my back.

My conscience whispered that perhaps I should let him do it. I already knew that Rotji wouldn't give up his secrets even under threat, so the second ring of barriers would defeat this raiding party and Chong would have failed.

But then there would be no chance to return for Hal.

Pausing in my struggle, I called Weiner's bluff—if bluff it was. 'Go on then. Shoot me.'

Unexpectedly my challenge caused Rotji to drop his last defences against me. *You would die?* I could feel him probing for an answer. Taking over like I do is always potentially a two-way street so I let him glimpse the stakes, my dilemma.

You must resist. You can't let them get in there.

I'm so sorry. I can't do that. There was a slim chance Victor's team might find Hal but, if not, I had to get back to him the next day at the latest before he died of thirst. I pushed on, finally subduing the colonel to my will. 'I'm in.'

Weiner checked his watch. 'Four minutes.' He led us back outside to a set of steel doors in the cliff face. A complex control pad had been bolted into the rock: sensor, screen and keyboard. 'Power back on for the doors.' Weiner gave the last order in a short-wave radio message to Keller, whose job it was to cool the generator and override the emergency shut down. With a hum and a flicker of light, the electricity was restored. 'Three minutes, Miss Whelan. We're counting on you to make the deadline.'

I told him what he could do with his bonus while I set Rotji to work on the control pad. His objections still echoed in the back of my mind, like protestors banging on the reinforced doors of a police van, but I couldn't listen. I followed the sequence I found in Rotji's mind. First the eye scan. Rotji leant down to allow the sensor to take the image and match it to computer records. The first of three lights went green. The next was a ten digit code on the computer screen. I made

Rotji tap those in. It was his own personal code, changed after every use and valid for only one entry. Whoever had designed this system had defended well against mind readers who could pick out familiar passwords. Even Atoosa would have had a challenge cracking the pattern. The second light went green. Now for the final part of the puzzle, the cryptic test that Atoosa had been expected to solve. The screen flashed up a series of pictures that should lead to a word only the person trying to enter should be able to guess, but they only had twenty seconds to work out the connections. The clues were a New York skyline, a smiling elderly woman, a river, and a cat's collar. Though Rotji was desperately trying not to think of the answer I could see it clearly and typed it in for him. Mississippi, the name of his neighbour's cat when he had done a stint at the UN headquarters. The third light went green.

With a hiss of hydraulic hinges, the vault door began to open. 'Drop the damper on telepathy,' ordered Weiner, talking into his radio.

Immediately I was assailed by a clamour of voices in my head, all screaming at once. It was impossible to hear if Victor or Hal were among them in the bedlam. Releasing Rotji from my control, I slammed up my defences to shut out the din.

Then one voice overrode the clamour. It was Chong, making the equivalent of a savant public service broadcast.

Dear colleagues, please do not be disturbed. The voices stilled. *I have just effected your release and will be joining you shortly. Those who wish to take my offer of a voyage out of here please make yourselves known to me or one of my men. Those who can arrange their own transport, you'll be welcome to use the island facilities, which will soon become available to you.*

Rotji was staring at me in horror, ignoring Weiner and his rifle or the arrival of the rest of the team. 'What have you done?' he asked me.

I just shook my head, blinking back tears. We both knew exactly what I had done. I'd traded my honour for the slight chance of saving Hal. I reached out to find a distant Victor at the other end of the link, many hundreds of miles away to make my confession. *I'm so sorry, Victor. I just broke your enemies out of jail.*

Chapter 16

I didn't have time to say any more as Weiner dragged me along the tunnel, right into the heart of the island prison camp. Chong must have given him instructions not to let me out of his sight because Weiner didn't lock me up in the basement of the staff quarters with Colonel Rotji and the other guards they had captured. I think I had to be in shock because my brain wasn't functioning well. Or maybe there was someone close by with the gift for making my worst nightmare seem ten times as bad? I hadn't worked out what kind of savant Weiner was but I wouldn't be surprised if he was having this effect on me. Either way, I wasn't making much use of the break in the telepathic block.

We reached the end of the tunnel. Please, no, I didn't want to be here or see this.

Summer, speak to us. Are you OK? That felt like Hal but I was too scared to hold up my end of the telepathic bridge and I had such terrible news to tell him.

I'm sorry.

The final door was a simple heavy bolt. If you had got this far, the designers of the prison had reasoned, then you were meant to be there. Weiner slid back the bolt and heaved the door open. A crowd of uniformed inmates blocked our way, all dressed in orange tunics and baggy trousers. With hands stretched out, clawing towards us, it was like a sequence from a zombie horror movie. Their desperation had stripped them of any dignity.

'Is it true?' one asked. 'Are we free?'

'Let me out!' ordered another. The demands and shouts in various languages rose in volume, people pushing and shoving each other to get to the front.

'Gentlemen.' Weiner held up his gun and fired a burst into the air, subduing them. 'Yes, it is true, and yes, you are free to go. Please step back. Mr Chong will be with you momentarily.'

'Ivan Chong really did it, did he? Well, I'll be damned.' A man shouldered others out of his path and offered his hand to Weiner. 'Jim Doors, pleased to meet you.'

'Mr New York?' The criminal savants had always referred to each other by the city in which they principally operated.

'That's right, son.'

Weiner actually smiled. 'I always admired your work, sir.'

'After this, name any position in my organization and it'll be yours. Who's the girl? Another of Ivan's operatives?' He turned a genial face to me. Despite being dressed in prison uniform, Doors managed to look a little better groomed than the other savant prisoners, clean-shaven and hair neatly cut. Here was someone prison hadn't changed. He was still the cut-throat businessman under the charm, ready to pick up his criminal activities from the point where the Benedicts had forced him to give up.

Weiner pushed me forward. 'She's not important. Useful now as bait as Mr Chong will explain.'

The leader of the American savant criminal network gave me a pitying smile and patted my cheek. 'Bad luck, kid. You remind me of my daughters. At least I can now look forward to seeing them soon.'

I didn't reply, my mind worrying over this new information from Weiner. Bait? In what way was I that? Oh God. The answer came to me in a horrible slide into a septic tank of realization.

Victor, are you still there?

Yes. You must stay in touch, Summer. We know where you are. We're all coming for you.

No, no, that's exactly what you mustn't do! Chong is using me to bring you here. Anyway you've got to save Hal first. Oh, and oh God, I'm so sorry I forgot to say, his brothers were killed. This is all my fault.

Calm down. Hal's here, sitting right next to me, a bit sunburnt but no worse. He had been through survival training, remember? He'd made himself a dew trap and was spearing fish by the time we arrived last night, a real Robinson Crusoe. He could've lived there for a month with no problem. And he had the T-shirt as the distress beacon. I thought you knew we were following it?

The huge wave of relief would have brought me to my knees if Weiner hadn't been holding my arm. Hal was safe, so everything else was bearable. *Yes, but I wasn't sure anyone would get there in time. Hal, I'm so sorry about your brothers.*

I could feel Hal's presence in my mind now, much stronger. *Don't be. I know they can be a pain but I'm rather pleased they survived myself.*

What?

Did you really think some gang lord's thugs would get the better of the Robinsons?

But I saw the photographs!

Which ones? The ones of them looking like rabbits hanging outside a butcher's shop or the ones where they kicked gangster butt?

Don't joke about that. It wasn't funny.

His tone sobered. *No, I'm sure it wasn't. They're just mad they got caught with their trousers down so I'm giving them stick about it. It's a brother thing.*

So Chong lied to me. I remembered now that I hadn't pressed to find out why he was so angry at breakfast the day before. It hadn't been just Victor's refusal to hand over Atoosa. That hadn't really been a surprise to him. The bad news had been that he'd lost his two hostages and marooned another so he had less hold over me than I knew. *I fell for it.*

Princess, we're going to have to do something about that believing-the-bad-guy thing of yours. Of course he lied to you. It's what the bad guy does.

But I mean I didn't see it.

Yeah, I guess you can be excused because you were a little upset at the time, though, weren't you? What with seeing your soulfinder dragged off and dumped and everything. I've a newsflash for you, you're not perfect. You're human.

And I've just made a huge mistake. I helped break these people out.

And if you refused, you'd already be dead. You did what you had to do to survive, just as I ordered. None of us are mad at you.

The crowd was getting more insistent in their demands for information. Weiner shoved me over to a concrete bench at the side of the exercise yard in the middle of the barracks so he could be free to deal with them. 'Wait there.' He plunged back into their midst, answering as many of them as he could.

This was a horrible place. A barren square of volcanic soil that had been pressed into service as an army camp and now prison. The cone of the extinct volcano loomed above us like the last rotten tooth in a whale's jawbone. There was little or no vegetation bar some tough grasses and spiny plants growing in cracks. There was no need of a further fence as the sheer sides of the island plunged straight down on to rocks. Even if you did manage some kind of Spider-Man act and get down, how could you get a boat close enough to pick you up? A hot tropical breeze blew even at night, promising an unbearably sultry day to come. The only living creatures that liked it were seabirds nesting on the cliff ledges, their screaming a constant background during daylight. Even the most dominant savant must have felt his wings were well and truly clipped by being sent here.

Uncertain how best to behave to avoid any attention, I stood behind the seat, hoping my black clothes would make me disappear in the shadows. It wasn't long, however, before someone bumped into me from behind. I felt their clammy hand on my arm and a mind trying to invade mine. Acting fast before he could take hold, I kicked him in the kneecap and ripped my wrist free.

'Back off!'

My assailant cringed. He acted like a feral dog scavenging at the margins while the wolf pack gathered around Weiner. I knew him instantly from Phoenix's description. Prison had not been kind to the Seer, a.k.a. Kevin Smith.

'Wow, orange really isn't your colour, Kevin,' I said. Pasty-faced and carrying too much weight, he looked like a walking heart attack. The uniform wasn't helping.

He flinched at the name but didn't correct me and demand his stupid title. 'You've got to get me out of here!' he pleaded in his wheezy voice. 'They'll kill me—kill all of those that they don't want. They've already said there are only twenty berths on the yacht.' He was looking at the men I'd termed the wolf pack. They were rapidly sorting themselves out into leaders and followers as if Weiner was some chemical dropped into their petri dish that set off a chain reaction.

'I can't get anybody out of anywhere. You'll have to look out for yourself.'

'But I've got no allies here, no friends.' He was breathing heavily now, sweat beading on his forehead. He mopped it with a sleeve. 'Come on, little girl, be nice to a harmless old man.' He was trying to invade my brain again. Phoenix had warned me about her old enemy: he could plant suggestions like landmines in your head. Put one foot wrong and you could find yourself doing something completely against your will.

But this time Kevin Smith was up against a much stronger mind controller. I shoved him out, adding a mental slap to the process. 'Try to invade me again and I'll take over your mind so that you'll be dancing to someone else's tune for a change. I'm betting you wouldn't like that.'

His little eyes darted in all directions looking for another way out. 'No, no, but please, you must do something. I'm not joking that they'll kill me. They hate me.'

'They're not that keen on me either.' I could well understand how Smith had become the target of bullying seeing how it was on his turf in a Soho jazz club that most of the men were arrested. I'd never stopped to ask what had happened to them. Conventional jails unable to hold savants, Victor and his colleagues in international law enforcement must have sent them here to be kept well away from the ordinary prison population. Who would have thought anyone would go to the immense trouble of breaking them out? With no love lost among thieves, criminal rivals who were still at large were expected to have welcomed the clearer playing field. Victor hadn't factored in Chong's ambition to get the kudos from being the one to free them. It was a dangerous gamble Chong was taking, thrusting his hand into the vipers' nest to lift his potential rivals to freedom.

As if my thought had conjured him, Chong himself arrived at that moment, driven through the tunnel in a white golf cart, Maiwand at the wheel. His appearance was greeted with spontaneous applause and whistles. Dressed in a silk shirt and beige slacks, he stood out among the men, underlining the difference between inmate and free agent.

'He's the one you've got to get on your side if you want protection,' I said, nodding towards Chong.

Smith looked between Chong and me, weighing his chances. 'I think I'll stick with you.'

I gave a hollow laugh. 'Bad choice.'

'You're strong and you don't want to kill me. That seems a good enough reason.'

'Just give me time. I remember what you did to my friend Phoenix.'

Something flickered in Smith's eyes, a little of the old cunning Seer. 'Dear Phoenix. How is she? I was always like a father to her.'

He was appalling. 'That's not how she remembers it.' I didn't want to talk to this repellant individual but he could give me useful intelligence to pass on to Victor. 'Who're those men talking to Mr Chong?'

Smith glanced over once then moved to stand behind me in what looked like a practised survival technique of run and hide. 'Daniel Kelly and his vampire son, Sean. They used to run Las Vegas until the Benedicts took them down.'

Sky had told me about them: a mafia style family who had kidnapped her to get revenge on Zed and his brothers. Daniel Kelly could falsify memories to devastating effect. A famous businessman before his fall, he now had a real tan, rather than the orange one with which he had entered prison. I wouldn't have recognized his son though: Sean looked older and much harder than his photo. 'The news just keeps on getting better and better.' *Victor, I really think you need to reconsider the wisdom of putting all the people that hate you in the same place.*

Not my choice, believe me. Governments would only pay for one savant-proof prison.

Not so savant-proof after all. Are you getting all this? I'd been relaying what I was seeing as best as I could.

Yeah. I would say hi to Kevin for old time's sake but it's better you don't let anyone know how far your telepathy stretches.

215

You're close?

I'd prefer it if you don't know the details, Summer. Some of those guys can take apart a mind in a few seconds and, if they gang up on you, I'm not sure your shields will hold.

Thanks for that thought.

I'm sorry, but you need to know. Keep as low a profile as possible.

Smith was still watching the cluster around Chong. 'Daniel Kelly talks a lot but it's Sean you have to watch. He's had us all at each other's throats so he can suck up the emotions. Tao, Mr Beijing, killed the Russian over it.'

'Didn't anyone do anything?'

'The guards wouldn't touch the vampire, though they removed Tao and handed him over to the Chinese authorities. I guess that was the end of him. Mr New York, Jim Doors, tried to rein Sean in but Kelly senior encouraged his boy. Those two are bitter rivals.'

I could see that now: Daniel Kelly was on one side of Chong, Doors on the other, both trying to ingratiate themselves with the man who broke them out.

'The moment they're free of here, expect the fur to fly.'

That moment didn't seem very distant as they were already jostling each other, months of prison rivalry kept under control by the presence of guards, escaping like steam from an overheated car radiator.

Chong held up his hand, one of his sickeningly jolly smiles on his face. 'Friends, friends, please, there's no need for this. We all have our own separate spheres of interest beyond these walls. There is no need to fight now.'

'You haven't had to live with this schmuck for a year and a half!' shouted Doors, forgetting to turn on his usual charm. 'His son has been feeding off us like a damned parasite.'

Chong shook his head. 'I know, I know. You have all

suffered. But please grant me more sense than to spring you from jail without planning for the aftermath. I thought you would all need a reminder why we have more in common than what separates us. We need each other if we are to go ahead with what we planned.'

'What did they plan?' I asked Smith.

He gave me an odd wistful smile, the expression of a man who knew that the ship had sailed for him. 'An international organization of savants to corner the world market in crime.'

Chong's announcement had caused a momentary pause in the argument. 'I suppose you think you're the man for the job of leading it?' said Daniel Kelly.

'Correct.' Chong beamed at him as if he were a particularly able pupil in his class. 'I'm not saying I'd take over control. I see my role more as coordinator of our activities so we can keep peace amongst ourselves and remember who is our real enemy.'

'For a cut of our business, I've no doubt.'

'For a little token of your appreciation. Nothing you can't afford. If I don't earn my place then you don't pay me. Simple.'

Doors folded his arms. 'Simple? How are you going to prove you're worth it?'

My heart leapt into my mouth as Chong pointed me out. 'See Miss Whelan over there, hiding so modestly in the shadows? I'm afraid she's rather a reluctant guest at this reunion. Knowing their white knight complex, the Benedicts will be hurrying to her rescue even as we speak, because I've said I'll kill her most painfully if they aren't here by tomorrow night with the ransom. I've kept the dampening field down so she is probably telling them everything we say. I think it's about time we reestablished communication blackout.'

I kept my expression as bland as possible but I couldn't disguise the fact that I was shaking. I sat down on the bench

217

and pretended I couldn't hear him. The dampening field was back up. I was cut off from Victor and Hal.

'The Benedicts are coming? Are you mad? In what way is that good news?' demanded Kelly.

'Only half of them. Victor, Trace, Will and the father, Saul, are the only ones close enough to get here in time to meet my deadline to save her. Take them down and you kill off the family as an effective fighting force.'

'But they've friends in high places, especially that Fed. They won't be alone.'

'Give me more credit than that. I've made Victor a pariah. A colleague of mine foresaw that a particular museum piece would be his downfall so I arranged for it to be stolen. It turned out that it brought his soulfinder along with it too, a nice bonus for me. No one in the American government dare help a rogue agent and I'm not giving him enough time to get back into their good graces.'

'You sure this'll work?' asked Doors.

'This is the only time we'll catch them so exposed. They were cut off from all help the moment they left Afghanistan and have been on the run since. My informants say there is still a recapture order out against them. The last thing the authorities will be doing is helping them.'

I hugged to myself the thought that he didn't know about the Robinsons' military connections or their continued part in this. Victor wasn't as alone as Chong thought, though even I could see the odds were hugely against them with only the seven of them against this group. That was not enough to win a battle, even if the Robinsons were the elite of their kind.

'Don't you relish the idea of the Benedicts against all of us?' continued Chong, realizing he hadn't yet won everyone over. Too many were eager to get off the rock with no delay. 'Haven't you ever wondered who would come out on top?

If we work together it should be no contest but a massacre. Regard it as my little welcome-home present to all of you.'

'Actually, Dad, what he's set up is seriously cool,' said Sean. 'It's like Batman v Superman, but better.'

The tension between the two groups of savants, those behind Kelly and those behind Doors, visibly reduced at this unexpected perspective on things. They began laughing and exchanging slaps on the back, making jokes about their favourite superheroes.

'OK,' said Doors, 'maybe you might just be worth it, Ivan. How shall we do this?'

'First,' said Chong, 'let me put Miss Whelan somewhere safe. We have a few hours until anyone can get here and I'll know well before they come within striking distance thanks to my team manning the perimeter. That gives us plenty of time to prepare. Think of the fight to come like the ritual slaughter of our enemies before we go out for world domination.' Chong chuckled at his own image.

'I like your style,' admitted Doors.

'Perhaps my honoured colleagues would like to discuss this over dinner on my yacht?'

Seeing Weiner heading for me, Smith slithered away into the shadows. I stood up, not wanting to give Weiner any excuse to get rough. He took my elbow and marched me over to the nearest of the barracks. Bypassing the rooms with bunks and the communal areas, he put me inside a small cell at the far end of the building, one with no windows or furniture. I guessed it had been constructed as an isolation room for when savants got out of hand. Without saying anything, he slammed the door behind me, shooting the bolt on the outside.

It was a horrible place but it was almost a relief to be away from the prisoners. It was too easy out there to feel like a bone thrown among a pack of wild dogs. Emotions scrambled, I slid

219

down the wall to scrunch up as small as possible. What could I do? I reached out to my friends but once again the muffler was in place. Hal, his brothers, and the Benedicts were walking into a trap with their eyes open and there was nothing I could do now to stop them.

Despite my dire situation I must have slept, because when I woke up there was a little natural light seeping under the door rather than the electric light of the night before. I tested the muffler but it was still in place. Feeling out for its limits, I discovered telepathy was possible within the island but the dampening field ringed it from about a mile out. I was reluctantly impressed. All of Chong's telepath experts were at the top of their game and, between the three of them working in shifts, able to keep it active with no break. I got up and stretched cramped limbs. I'd dozed propped up against one corner as far as possible from the drain over the other side. It had a vile smell and I'd been bothered all night by the whine of mosquitos and scuttle of cockroaches. Thanks to a cloudless sky, it was already warm in here and liable to become like an oven as the day progressed. Weiner had not left me any water.

I had to help myself first if I was going to be of any use to my friends. I stretched out my senses to find out where everyone was. I felt the shadow presence of the main players back on the island from their dinner and night on clean sheets at the yacht. They were now organizing their various factions into a coordinated defence. Only one person was lurking alone, keeping away from the action. It was ironic that Phoenix's Seer might be my only ally on this island.

Mr Smith?

Miss Whelan? He wasn't pleased to hear from me but from my glimpse of his thoughts I could tell he was still hedging his bets. If the savant criminals lost the fight against the Benedicts, then being seen to be kind to the hostage would play in his favour.

I'm in the isolation cell but I haven't got any water. Can you bring me some?

You won't try to escape?

Where would I go?

He broke off but a few minutes later the door opened and he appeared in the gap, a plastic bottle in hand. I dashed over to take it and gulped it down.

'Thank you.'

'You'll remember I did this for you, at risk of my own life?'

'I will.'

Satisfied with that he passed me a second bottle then left without closing the door. As we both knew, I couldn't go anywhere and it was needless torture to make me sit in a hot box all day. Chong probably wouldn't approve of me being broiled alive if he knew of Weiner's vindictive spirit. As long as I kept out of Weiner's way, I should be OK. That guy was far too fond of inflicting suffering on others for no reason. I didn't want even to set a toe in a brain like that and hoped it wouldn't come to me having to try and control him.

Sitting in the shade just outside my cell, I reviewed my options. I could either regard myself as a hostage that needed saving or a team member planted inside of the enemy camp. I still had my abilities; the issue was deciding how to use them and not get myself killed. An idea began to form.

I was so lost in thought that I didn't notice immediately that I had attracted some unwanted attention. Sean Kelly had come looking for me. Out of his prison clothes, the twenty-something man was now dressed in polo shirt and knee-length shorts, aviator sunglasses hiding his eyes. His dark hair was slicked back from a high forehead. When Sky had met him, he had been more soft belly than brawn. In prison he had used the empty time to turn a lot of that to muscle, flourishing here like the goldfish eating the others in the tank.

'Miss Whelan, good morning. I see someone has been looking after you,' he said with faux friendly humour. 'I was just coming to check on you.' Without waiting for an introduction he sat down beside me as if we were two mates meeting by chance on the school playing fields. 'You must be feeling very distressed.'

Wouldn't he love me to admit that?

'I'm fine, thanks.' Never show a vampire savant your emotions.

'You must believe you're the lamb thrown among the wolves. You mustn't worry. No one wishes you any harm.'

'I'm sure that's not true.'

He smiled conspiratorially at me. 'Are you talking about Gerhart Weiner? I noticed that he was a little harsh on you yesterday, dragging you from pillar to post. But what do you expect from a distress magnifier, the most sadistic of savants? The only thing he can do with his gift is make life worse for others. Sucks to be him, hey?' He chuckled as if this was the funniest joke.

'I'm sure there are those who would find that a useful ability.'

Sean pulled a face. 'Sadly, in this wicked world, he is much in demand. But I won't let him hurt you. I'd like to be your friend.'

'That's very kind of you, Sean.' Not.

His hand felt for my wrist. 'You see I haven't had a refined emotion to absorb for months. This bunch here are full of the most predictable feelings—anger, greed, murderous rage, some humiliation. No one feels love, hope or shame and I have to admit that they're my favourites, like the very best vintages to a wine connoisseur.'

222

'You like them because you can't feel them yourself?' I was familiar with this pattern.

He squeezed my wrist, trying to force his way inside my shields. 'Exactly. But you've got plenty to spare, I can just tell. Think of it as a donation.'

I sighed and levered his fingers off my skin. 'Forget it, Sean, I was raised by a vampire and she's a good deal better than you at breaking through my shields. You're not getting anything from me.'

Sean snatched back his hand, his chummy act vanishing. 'You might want to think again. I'm your only friend here.'

'You're not my friend, Sean.' *See, Hal, I'm not believing the bad guy.* I sent the message even though there was no hope of it reaching him.

'When you get to the stage of feeling regret, I might consider forgiving you if you share it with me.'

'Not in this lifetime.'

'I'd say your lifetime has just got a hell of a lot shorter.' Sean got up and walked off, prowling for his next victim.

'Jerk,' I muttered, trying to disguise how shaken I felt. He wasn't interested in the plans being made, content to leave that to his father. He was only looking for his breakfast. In a strange way, he was in his element: a captive population to feed off and no checks on his behaviour. My mother would have flourished here too.

The thought brought me up like an emergency stop. My family. I'd been blocking the thought of what my dad was going through but he had to be out of his mind with worry. First he had been told that I was a wanted person for helping a fugitive, then they would have had to tell him about my abduction. We often didn't see eye to eye, that was true, but I never doubted he sincerely loved me, as I did him. I couldn't bear to be yet another burden of worry for him to carry.

And if I survived this, what would he say to Hal as my soulfinder? Where in our life in north London of classical concerts, dinner parties and academic chitchat would my gorgeous rough tough soldier fit? I couldn't keep him, could I?

Stop it, Summer. One life crisis at a time, I chided myself. I needed some of Hal's optimism to carry me through.

Hal, are you there?

I couldn't sense anything, but then I rarely did with him. Even though Victor wanted to keep me in the dark I had to scan for Hal's brain signature. He would come for me, I was sure of that, just as I would have gone for him.

There was nothing at first but then a sudden image burst into my head: Disney's Sleeping Beauty surrounded by a ring of thorns, the prince galloping to the rescue. *Surely even your education didn't miss out on this? I'm banking on at least a kiss at the end of this.* The thought came in Hal's voice but vanished as quickly as it came.

It had to be him, carrying on with his side mission to bring my cultural references into step with most people my age. I tried to connect again but he'd gone, keeping behind the shield. If I carried on scanning I might be able to find him bedded down within the exclusion zone, but maybe I should listen to Victor. Hal had let me know he was there, which was what I wanted to know; the rest I would have to take on trust.

'Please don't do anything stupid,' I whispered.

Chapter 17

Smith brought me some food later in the day, scavenged from the communal table set out in the exercise yard for the less important prisoners. They'd passed the night in their old barracks while the leaders slept on the yacht or in the staff quarters. As I ate the rice and beans, Smith filled me in on some of the headlines.

'Chong has demanded a ransom.'

'I know that much.'

'But not, I'm guessing, that the price is for Victor Benedict to surrender himself in exchange for you.' He watched for my reaction. 'Do you think he'll do that?'

I shrugged. What could I say? I could imagine Victor doing just such a stupidly heroic act if he thought it the only way of getting me to safety. He would hand himself over, wait for me to be clear of danger, then launch the counterattack.

'Chong won't give you up, of course.' Smith brushed off the dust from his orange trousers. He had found a guard's shirt which he'd put on over his T-shirt because no one had included him in the distribution of clean clothes that had gone to the favoured few. 'He's been very impressed by your abilities. He's thinking of using you to break in to some top museums once this is all over.'

'Then he can dream on. I'd never do that.'

Smith shrugged, fanning himself with a floppy grey hat. 'You might with the right persuasion. You'd be surprised what people will do, and he's serious about his collection.'

'He needs to get a life.'

He chuckled as if I'd made a joke. 'That is his life. He and his allies are all drunk on the promise of future criminal success, thinking this showdown with the Benedicts is just an appetizer. Personally I think they're wrong.'

Smith was showing more sense than the others, then. Though still rotten to the core, at least Smith had learned caution from his time in prison. He was a wiser man than the one Victor defeated in London.

'How do you know this about their plans?'

Smith rolled his shoulders, making the seams on the new jacket stretch to breaking point. 'You expect me to reveal my sources?'

I brushed over the surface of his repellant mind. He had got to one of the weaker savants, an enforcer for Jim Doors, and planted a listening bug in his brain. The bodyguard was relaying all important information to Smith without even knowing he was doing it. It reminded me not to underestimate the old Seer. Our interests might coincide for the present but he would throw me to the wolves at the first sign that would benefit him.

'Keep your secrets, Mr Smith. It doesn't matter.'

'The deadline for Victor to surrender himself is dusk. Ah, it looks like they're coming to fetch you. Excuse me.' He hurried off towards the washrooms.

Chong was climbing towards my cell, a multicoloured parasol over his head to shade from the harsh equatorial sun, like some imperial potentate on walkabout. Weiner followed behind, a rifle cradled in his arms.

'Miss Whelan, I hope you've enjoyed your rest?' Chong asked amicably.

'Delightful.' I put aside my plate, which was quickly invaded by ants.

'I need you to come with me. We are expecting a guest.'

I wondered how much to say. I would surely ask what guest if I truly had been kept in isolation all day. 'Who's that?'

Chong mopped his shining brow with a silk handkerchief. 'Don't worry your pretty little head about that. Just do as I say and you should soon be back in your comfortable cabin on my yacht.'

'Can't wait.' His patronizing tone set my teeth on edge but maybe it meant he would underestimate me?

'First I need you to make yourself presentable.' He gestured to my black-on-black ensemble and darkened skin. I'd forgotten I still had camouflage paint on my face too. 'Your own mother wouldn't recognize you like that.' And he needed Victor to be able to see me when he turned up to add to the drama, I could see it in his head. This whole encounter had been scripted for maximum effect.

He conducted me back through the waiting crowd of ex-prisoners. Unlike earlier, when they had formed a desperate cluster, they now sat or stood in neat rows, divided into command units under the lead savants. I hadn't realized how many of them there were. The Benedicts and Robinsons were going to be seriously outnumbered. Chong was going to distribute them around the site, at the harbour, in the staff quarters, here up on the top of the rock. I stole his plans, praying he didn't sense I'd been there and adapt his tactics accordingly. All I needed now was to get the information to my friends.

Hal, I don't know if you can hear me but I estimate there are about seventy savants here. I visualized the layout and the positions of the hostile forces. As before, my telepathic message went nowhere, absorbed by the dampener set up by Chong or bouncing off Hal's shield—I couldn't tell. I continued trying to get out the warning to Victor, then added Saul, Trace and

Will for good measure in case one of them had managed to get within the mile exclusion zone. *Please listen to me: this is one big trap. Go away and get more backup.*

Nothing.

'Miss Whelan, the shower room is yours to use. I promise you no one will interrupt you.' Chong opened the door to one of the barracks. 'You'll find everything you need on the bunk over there.'

I slipped inside and grabbed the bundle of clothes, not taking his word but feeling out to check there were no others present. As he had promised, I was alone. I ducked into the shower room, a grim place with cracked white tiles and the smell of disinfectant. A large spider had spun a web in one corner but as it didn't look interested in me I tried not to freak out about its bulbous body and hairy legs. Normally I am all for equality between the sexes but right then I would've swallowed my pride and asked Hal to remove it for me. Boys do have their uses, aside from the obvious soulfinder thing.

Unless Hal was scared of spiders too. I hadn't had the chance to find out. Clearly that was a deal-breaker. I smiled briefly at the thought of Hal running from the big creepy-crawly. No, I couldn't imagine that.

A miniature shampoo and conditioner plus body wash had been left on top of my bundle like I was staying in some upmarket hotel. I gave a half-hysterical laugh at this odd pampering of the hostage in such a situation. Afraid that someone would come in before I was ready, I quickly showered in tepid water, only then checking what outfit had been selected for me to set the scene. Chong had chosen the pink tunic with the embroidered birds, a totally frivolous garment in this barren environment of dusty volcanic rock. It had been laundered since I last wore it, and it smelled sweet after hours of sweating in my black gear. I kicked those to one side and quickly put on the clean clothes. Combing my hair in the stainless steel wall above the sinks that served as a mirror, I looked completely out of place, a courtier from an Arabian Nights' tale who had walked into a prison-break movie. I even had pearly sandals rather than proper shoes. At least they fitted and didn't have toes that curled up: I had to be grateful for small mercies.

There came a knock on the door. 'Miss Whelan, I have to hurry you. Our guest is almost here.'

Heart lurching horribly, I felt out down the tunnel to the harbour. Sure enough, I could now sense Victor approaching in a small speedboat. He appeared to be alone as I could detect no one else. Looking for a new vantage point, I slipped into one of the minds I could sense—one of the guards on the harbour side—to see what he could see: a tall man at the wheel, hair streaming back in the wind, dark glasses reflecting the setting sun. He looked utterly assured.

Don't do this, Victor. Think of Atoosa.

He ignored my plea. *You OK?*

I'm not OK that you are walking into the lion's den. I quickly sent him the plans I'd picked from Chong's brain. *I might not have got all of them.*

Thank you. I could feel him transmitting these onwards as far as telepathy would allow. The others had to be here somewhere. *It's going to be OK. Trust me.*

Victor, I can read your mind, remember. You're not as sure as you pretend. There are at least seventy of them and they're all gunning for you. Not that many of them had actual guns. As savants they had weapons enough in their powers.

We would rather they focused on me than you, honey.

Chong doesn't intend to let me go. He wants me as some kind of safecracker.

We'll see about that.

'Miss Whelan?' Chong was getting impatient.

'Coming.' Whatever was going to go down now, I couldn't stop. I just had to hope that Victor had more than sacrificing himself as a plan.

I exited the barracks. Weiner came up behind me and pinned my arms behind me in handcuffs.

'Apologies, but it is a necessary precaution,' said Chong. 'Put her in position.'

I hadn't really taken much notice of the changes that had been made to the exercise yard but I now saw that there was a platform erected in the middle like the winner's podium at the Olympics. Weiner scooped me up in a fireman's lift and carried me over to it, only letting go when I was standing on the top.

'I could've walked,' I said, resentful at yet more manhandling.

'Shut up. If you move, I'll shoot you.' Weiner walked off, joining the ring of savants remaining in the exercise ground. At least half of them were now in their battle positions elsewhere.

After a few jokes and remarks about the bait staked out in their midst, the savants turned their attention back to the door leading in from the tunnel.

Victor, I hope you know what you're doing. I sent him a quick image of my predicament. Up here I would have no shelter if anyone started shooting and Weiner wouldn't need much persuading.

Always. He was very close now.

The door opened and Victor stepped through, the oblique beams of the setting sun behind him like an arc light through the tunnel, dazzling us.

'Good evening, gentlemen. I've come to collect something of ours that you've stolen,' he said coolly.

I couldn't see anyone with him. His enemies were going to eat him alive.

230

Mr Chong came forward, flanked by Daniel Kelly and Jim Doors. These two were staring at Victor as though they'd like to tear him apart with their bare hands.

'Mr Benedict,' said Chong with his usual over-friendly smile, 'as you well know, the deal was an exchange.'

'Chong, you can wipe that smile off your face. There was never a deal as you had no intention of letting Summer go free. I'm changing the terms of our negotiation. I'm giving you a choice. Return to the barracks while we free the guards you've locked up and then we can talk. Maybe we can see to making your stay here more bearable. But I'll make this clear: none of you are leaving this island.'

'I think you don't understand who is in charge here, Benedict,' snarled Kelly.

'Oh I think I do.'

Chong was still smiling. 'I don't make deals with disavowed agents. You can't deliver on any of your promises but I can deliver on mine. It's a shame you are so stubborn but you obviously need proof. Say goodbye to Miss Whelan.'

Just as Chong finished speaking, many things happened at once. He gave a nod to Weiner to shoot me. The three Robinsons sprinted from the tunnel.

'Get down!' shouted Hal.

I was already taking a dive off the podium of my own volition. Victor sent out a wave of crippling mind strikes, knocking back both Chong and Weiner. Weiner's bullet went wide, hitting Smith in the leg, who had been lurking at what he thought a safe distance. Lucas tackled Weiner, fighting for the gun. I hit the ground hard, and was immediately pulled up by Hal.

'Run!'

I would've made some comment about stating the obvious if I could spare the breath. I also wanted to hug him. Of course, his ability had kept the fact that Victor had not been alone secret until the last moment. Chong had truly been surprised, trusting too much to what his savant lookouts had told him.

Battle engaged, the savant prisoners took defensive positions as more and more of our side arrived. Uriel, Xav, Zed and Alex sprinted in from the opposite end of the parade ground, climbing harnesses still on, coming up behind the group, who hadn't expected anyone to enter that way. Somehow my friends had scaled the cliffs I thought inaccessible. I hadn't allowed for a Rocky Mountain and Cape Town upbringing. All were experienced climbers. Missiles began flying as those with strong telekinetic gifts swung into action. The glass in the barracks behind us exploded as one of the prisoners drew all the air from the room. Hal threw his body over mine. I didn't protest as he was wearing body armour. But Hal needn't have worried: Zed was there between us and the explosion, using his awesome telekinetic skills to stop the fragments in mid-air, like a swarm of hornets, then redirect them at the man who'd tried to take us out. A lethal hail of shards flew his way. His screams cut off abruptly.

People were going to die here, or at least get seriously injured. I wasn't combat-ready but I was determined it wouldn't be any of my friends if I could help it. 'Let me up: I want to do something.'

Hal got off me, unslung the army rifle from his shoulder and took up position behind a concrete wall. Zed gave me a single nod when he saw that I was OK then sprinted off to rejoin his brothers, who were taking positions around the parade ground to pin down the men in the middle.

'How many did you hide?' I asked as I crouched awkwardly beside Hal, hampered by my hands still cuffed behind me.

'My brothers, all the Benedicts, your friends, just about everyone in Victor's address book. I didn't know I could.' Hal was clearly very pleased to find he could do far more with his ability than he had thought, when he had always considered himself a non-savant.

There was a boom and a fireball rose up from the harbour.

'I think Yves has taken against the men Chong posted down there,' said Hal with a wild grin down at me. 'He's taking back the control room with Trace, Will and Saul. Once the comms are back up, we can bring in air support.'

I was still processing his earlier comment. 'Everyone's here?'

'Yep. Head down.' He took a shot at a group of hostile savants who had also decided the concrete wall would make a good defensive position. I could feel his utter focus. He was loving this, the clarity of fighting for something that was right, knowing he was good at what he did. I, by contrast, felt completely useless, trussed up like a chicken ready for the oven.

A very attractive chicken. He took another shot over the top of our defence. 'Incoming friendly.'

That was all the warning I got before Alex jumped over the barrier.

'Hey, Summer, let me help you with that.' One of Alex's skills was to persuade locks to open, so he made short work of my handcuffs.

'You're here too?' Once my hands were free, I hugged my friend tight.

'Of course. The Robinsons swung the special military flights to collect us all. You OK?' He ruffled my hair, his touch calming me from the high adrenaline of the last few minutes.

'Hands off my girl, Alex.' Hal gave him a scowl.

'If you give me your weapon, you could take over.'

'Don't think I'm not tempted.' Hal took another shot. 'But army regulations don't permit me to hand over my personal firearm.'

'You're not . . . not killing them, are you?' I asked, beginning to shiver as reaction set in.

'Not if we can help it, flower. We've been issued with rubber bullets for riot control. I'm trying to teach them *respect*.' He said it in such a dangerous tone that I felt a shiver down my spine.

A high-pitched note began to sound across the natural amphitheatre of the exercise yard. Peeking over the top of the wall I could see Maiwand standing next to Chong, face screwed up in concentration. The sound was drilling into our brains, threatening to incapacitate us. Telepathy was impossible with that noise drowning everything else out.

'I can take him over—stop him,' I offered, having to shout as I covered my ears. It wouldn't be hard as Maiwand really wanted to defect. I just needed to tip him off that it was safe to do so.

'It's OK. Leave it to Marcus.'

'He's here too?' Just as I spoke a new sound began, a note that seemed to latch on to the high pitch and drag it down to a bearable, then pleasant hum.

'Auto-tuning Marcus style. He's been working on that all night after Atoosa gave us a warning about her uncle's ability,' explained Alex.

I had known Marcus could manipulate music but I'd never thought of its application on a savant battlefield. It then struck me: if their soulfinders were on the island . . .

'Alex, don't tell me Misty and Angel are here?'

'OK, I won't tell you.' He touched my cheek. 'Did you for one second think any of us would leave you to face this alone?'

'I can't believe any of you would let your soulfinders near a battle zone.' The Benedicts were well known for their protective instincts towards women. Alex was easily persuaded to their camp on this.

'They've been told to keep out of the thick of it.' Alex

stopped another incoming missile with a telekinetic counter-blast.

Like that was going to work with my friends.

There was a siren from down in the harbour and a billow of steam. 'And I'd say that was Angel using her awesome water power to put out the fire Yves started,' said Hal. He took two more quick shots and there was a shout from our latest attackers. 'I really like your friends. Only known them a few hours but they are the right kind of crazy.'

I had to laugh. Now I thought about it, Hal was a little like a male version of Angel as far as the derring-do and optimism were concerned. I touched his arm, feelings blazing out like the sun coming from behind clouds. *I love you.*

I couldn't believe it: I'd made Hal blush. *You can't say that kind of thing now, princess. I'm kinda fighting for our lives here.* The rifle barked again.

I think it's the perfect time to say it.

He turned his dark, dark eyes to look at me. *You're mine, right? You're not going to try to save me from yourself—I see that in your head and I'm not going to allow it.*

Well if you put it like that then, yes, I'm yours.

That's good, because when I found out you were stuck on this island with a bunch of criminal nut jobs, I realized that I couldn't live without you and wouldn't be able to go on if you were taken from me. What I'm trying to say is that I think that means I love you too.

'Hal! Shoot!' ordered Alex.

Hal reflexively obeyed the order, forcing Weiner to take cover and give up his bid to take over our position.

'Keep your head in the game, Hal, or you'll get us all killed.' Alex was furious.

Hal wasn't embarrassed, continuing to pick his shots with care. 'Flower and me here were just dealing with the love stuff.'

'Of course you love her. She's Summer. Everyone loves her.'

'Not like I do,' said Hal.

The missiles, that until then had been buzzing constantly in the air, suddenly stopped mid trajectory and fell to the ground.

We wish to call a ceasefire to deal with our injured, said Chong, broadcasting on a savant-wide wavelength. *It is clear that neither side can leave this island without high casualties. We should talk.*

I opened a channel so Hal could listen in too as it seemed I was the only one whose power wasn't absorbed by his anti-savant shields.

Hey, handy. He brushed a speck of dust off my nose. *I knew you'd be useful for something.*

I'll trade for spider removal.

What?

Tell you later.

Why should we make a deal with you? asked Victor.

This is stalemate. You are cut off from your allies down in the harbour as my men hold the tunnel entrance and staff quarters. We can carry on fighting here until half of us are dead but I believe you'd prefer to protect the civilians rather than risk them. And your family. I doubt you'd accept that even one of your brothers could die. That is what is at stake.

Victor broke off for a moment. I could sense a strange desperation from him. Things were not going as planned. I guessed he was consulting with Lucas, who would be aware of the military aspects of our situation. *OK, Chong, a ceasefire. You can take your injured into Barrack Five. We'll take ours to Two.*

Injured? Who was injured? Terrified for my friends, I almost put my head over the parapet to look but Hal hauled me down.

Then we meet in thirty minutes, Chong, continued Victor,

just you and me with a guard each. We'll meet by the podium in
the open so all can see that there's no violation of the ceasefire.

Agreed.

The signal given, Hal got up first, then gave us the all-clear. Alex jumped over the barrier and sprinted to a spot near the entrance to the tunnel. The Benedicts had been trying to gain control of it from the enemy and it was here the fighting had been fiercest. I could see Zed crouched over a body on the floor, Yves at the legs. Together they lifted the casualty from the ground, Alex joining them to help. Swiftly they evacuated into the shelter of the barracks.

Then all who were linked to her felt the cry of the soulseeker as Crystal realized Xav was badly injured. It was like all the atoms in our body suddenly felt a change in the Earth's polarity. She couldn't reach him thanks to the enemy between and was frantic to do so.

Crystal, please! called Victor. If she carried on broadcasting her distress none of us would be fit to do anything.

The sensation broke off abruptly, not because Crystal had regained control but because Phoenix had used her mind-freeze gift on her. *I can hold her for a moment, Victor, but you better be quick!*

Leaving Lucas and Scott to watch that the enemy didn't violate the terms of the ceasefire, I rushed into the barracks to find Xav on a bed, bleeding heavily from a shrapnel slice to the throat. It didn't look good. Uriel was ripping open dressings from his emergency pack.

'Can he heal himself?' I asked, kneeling down beside Zed.

I'd never seen Zed look so distraught. 'No, and he's lost too much blood. I told him to stay back and be our medic but would he listen?'

Oh God, I was going to be the reason why one of the Benedicts died. The guilt was crippling.

Hal squeezed my shoulder. *Not your fault, princess.*

Uriel pressed a new bandage to the wound. 'He's going to bleed out if we don't do something. There's no time to get him to a hospital. We need a healer like yesterday.'

I jumped up. 'I know where to get one. The camp commander—he's strong healer—I saw it in him.'

'But we've not managed to free the guards yet.' Victor rubbed his hands over his face.

'I'll persuade Chong to let him out,' offered Alex. He was standing at the door with Marcus keeping an eye on our enemies.

But I knew exactly what needed to be done. 'No time. I'll get the healer. Hal, can you hide me?'

'Yes.' That was my soulfinder, ready to leap into action without even knowing my plan.

'Technically this might be a breach of the ceasefire,' said Victor, 'but hang that if my brother's life is in the balance. Do it. We'll make sure they're looking the other way.'

Grabbing Hal's hand, I ran outside. The enemy had men guarding the entrance to the tunnel but it was now getting dark and they were trusting their savant senses to spot anyone. Hugging the shadows we made our way to their position.

Keep hold of my hand, said Hal.

I felt his power ripple over me. It was like sliding into a swimming pool, transferring from air to water until I was completely submerged. *They won't sense us?*

Not a thing.

Victor came out of the barracks with Marcus and Alex flanking him. 'Hey, Maiwand, isn't it time you met your niece's soulfinder, you traitor?' he called. 'I want to introduce you to the guy who pulled your fangs with that neat sound trick of his.'

Trusting in Hal, the savant equivalent of an invisibility cloak, I tiptoed around the nearest guard. He was too busy watching Victor's baiting of Maiwand to notice us. We were in the tunnel and out of sight before he knew we'd gone by.

We reached the staff quarters to find two more men on the door. I'd never tried taking over that many. I wasn't sure I could do it.

Then don't. I am more than just a decoration, you know. I'll deal with the one on the left. You take the guy on the right. Hal's utter confidence quieted my jitters.

OK. I can do this.

Of course you can, flower. If you haven't twigged yet, you might just be the most powerful savant here.

If he saw me like that, maybe I should stop doubting myself? With new confidence, I walked into the savant's mind as if all the doors had purposely been left open for me. It helped, of course, that with Hal there my target had no time to defend himself against my sudden appearance. The man Hal was taking care of slumped to the ground after the less subtle intervention of a rifle butt to the head.

He'll be OK? I asked anxiously.

Concentrate on your job, Summer. Stop worrying about the bad guys. And, yeah, he'll be OK. A bit of a headache when he surfaces but I know how to do my job.

I was being a pain second-guessing him, like a back seat driver, one of creation's most annoying individuals. *Sorry.*

I get it. You find it hard to hand over responsibility. I'm gonna have fun teaching you all sorts of way to let it go. He sang the last few words and paused a beat. *Frozen? No? Geez, flower.*

His banter helped calm my nerves. Marching our captive along to the rooms where the former guards were being held, I followed the man's mental map to where the commander was being held. I made him open the door to the room. Charlie Rotji was standing by a barred window, desperately trying to see what was happening. He swung round on our entrance.

'You again!' Rotji tensed, ready to fight me this time.

Go to sleep, I ordered. My captive quietly walked away from me and lay down on the bed.

Hal held up his gun, preventing Rotji from charging us. 'Wait, sir. We're here to release you. We need you.'

'I'm not helping the enemy,' said Rotji bitterly, fists bunched at his side. 'She's working for them.'

'No, she was a hostage under duress. Now she's helping us regain control of the prison. Are you going to waste our time debating or come with us and save a life?'

Summer, you've got to hurry: we're losing Xav! said Uriel.

'Please, sir,' I pleaded, 'I'm so sorry about earlier, but Xav Benedict is dying. If you don't come right now, it'll be too late.'

Rotji shook his head. 'This is a trap.' I'd destroyed whatever faith Rotji might have had in me by taking him over. His pride had taken a severe beating.

Want me to make him come? asked Hal, quite prepared to point the gun at the colonel.

No, I know what to do. 'Look, I know you don't trust me, sir, but I'll prove I'm speaking the truth. You can take me over, look in my mind, full disclosure. I won't get in your way.'

He took a step back, not trusting that this was a genuine offer. 'That's not my gift.'

Summer, Xav's going into shock, said Uriel in despair.

'No, it's mine and I can reverse it if I want—at least I think I can. I've always known a more powerful mind could take mine over when I link with them, so it should follow that I could willingly let someone in to do the same as long as I don't resist.' Not giving him a chance to say no, I dropped all my shields and walked right into his head. *Go on.* I pointed in the direction of my mind.

I have to hand it to Colonel Rotji: once he saw that the door was genuinely open he marched right in. Hal was present too: I could feel him in the background, watching Rotji for the first wrong move. The colonel could have taken control even with Hal there; he could have ordered me to do anything, but he didn't abuse my trust. Instead, he methodically sorted through the information I laid out for him. It was horrible—like undergoing the most intimate strip search. I gritted my teeth for Xav's sake.

'I've seen enough. Thank you. You're a brave girl.' Rotji left my mind, respectfully closing the door behind him.

I swayed, feeling like a doll with the stuffing pulled from it after his departure. So this was how my victims felt when I left them, was it? I'd have to remember to ease my way out in future.

He put on his uniform jacket. 'Take me to my patient.'

'Yes, sir,' said Hal. *Well done, flower.*

241

Chapter 18

'I need another healer.' Rotji had been using his power on Xav for at least five minutes but, aside from a lessening of the blood flow, there was little improvement. 'I can't do this on my own.' He looked up at Xav's brothers, well aware that their hopes were all centred on him.

'You're treating the only other healer here, sir,' said Zed, a muscle in his cheek twitching as he bit down on his emotions.

Rotji rocked back on his heels. 'That's no good. Even if your brother was conscious, part of the gift is that we can't heal ourselves. I'm sorry.'

A chill of despair ran through the shared telepathic link of the Benedicts. Crystal was no longer under Phoenix's mind-freeze but I could feel her in the background, waiting in the control room at the harbour, whispering comfort to her new husband. They'd only been married a month. Saul was with her, hugging her to his chest as he struggled with his own grief.

Victor pressed his temples. 'I'll call for a helicopter evacuation. Maybe if he gets to a hospital ship in time.'

We all knew there wasn't time.

Uriel did not try to hide the tears trickling down his cheeks, hand stroking Xav's hair. 'God, I wondered why Tarryn was adamant we shouldn't come.' His soulfinder foresaw how people were going to die.

No, this was not going to happen! I suddenly realized I was really angry—furious at Chong for dragging me, and by extension my friends, into this predicament where Xav, our joking, healing, life-and-soul-of-the-party guy, was on the point of death. I wasn't prepared to give up yet. 'But the healing energy is there, sitting under your fingertips?'

Rotji nodded.

'Then . . . then what if I take over and use it. Then it's me healing him. Maybe we can trick his body into releasing the energy?'

The colonel frowned. 'Sounds unorthodox. I don't know what it would do to a non-healer to handle that power.'

'What do you mean, sir?' asked Hal.

'Healing energy is like handling fire. Do it wrong and it could kill her.'

Normally I read the leaflets that came with medicine and fretted about the possible side effects before taking them. Today I was tearing all that up. 'Well, we're all looking at the worst case right in front of us, so let's try it.'

'Do it.' Zed framed my face in his hands, pressing his forehead to mine as if he wanted to transfer all his strength to me. 'Please.'

Hal came up behind and pulled me back against his chest, reclaiming me. 'Summer, are you sure?'

'Yes.'

'Then let me be there. If it is protection from a savant gift you need then I'm your guy.'

'You can't block it though, Hal, even if you think it's hurting me.'

'I know, but I'll do my best to shield the bits that matter.'

'My body armour?'

'That's me.'

Kneeling next to Rotji, I tapped his arm to get his attention from the healing he was continuing to try. 'I'm sorry but I might have to visit your mind again to find out what to do.'

243

'Be my guest—this time.' He gave me an encouraging smile.

I quickly entered his head to see how his healing power worked. It was instinctive, like most of our gifts, but not endless. There was an amount of energy he could safely expend before he started damaging his own well-being. I'd have to be careful I didn't end up damaging Xav and undo my attempt to heal him. *Thank you.* I gently withdrew. 'I'm going in.'

'Just do your best, Summer,' said Victor.

I walked into Xav's mind and found it like a building with most of the lights out. Red emergency lights the colour of blood lit the stairwells and passages. There was a white glow coming from under one door at the far end of a long corridor. *See that?* I asked Hal.

Yeah. Looks promising.

The nearer I tried to draw to it, the further off it appeared. *His brain is reacting against me being here.*

Then let's see if I can do this invisibility cloak thing in the mental world as well as the physical.

Give it a go.

I sensed a touch on my shoulder and the cool rippling effect of his gift pouring over me. Waiting a moment before trying to approach the light, this time the corridor stayed put and let me walk down it. I willed the door open and found myself gazing into a white-hot furnace. It was like finding a nuclear reactor in your basement. *Wow.*

That's one strong healer.

Do you think I'll be fried by it? I could feel the danger pouring off it. I wasn't helped by the awareness that both Will and Saul had alerted Victor that I was in severe peril.

I guess there's only one way to find out. Hal wasn't happy that I was doing this but he understood that this was like going into combat for me; I had to do my duty.

All right then. I reached out and pulled some of the energy towards me. It was like trying to carry a block of ice in your bare hands, the cold burning. *I can't keep hold of this.*

In the real world, Hal reached around me and covered my hands with his. *And now?*

I wasn't sure what kind of mental override that provided but it worked. *This feels freaky.* I was carrying what felt like a swarm of buzzing white bees.

So I keep telling you. Us savants are freaky. Hal nuzzled my ear, encouraging me to carry on.

I can't see what I'm doing. Intent on the mental landscape, my eyes were shut and I couldn't risk the lapse in concentration to open them.

Allow me. Hal guided my hands to Xav's throat. I then felt Rotji place his warm palm on top of mine. By contrast mine was freezing cold.

'Push the energy into him,' Rotji said calmly.

I let it go. As it passed through the barrier of my skin to Xav's, my hand began to warm, then to heat.

'Healers learn to control the temperature,' said Rotji. 'You mustn't let it burn you.'

Easy to say but impossible when you were a pathway for a swarm of energy bees. I held on as long as possible. *Hal!*

He was there at once, sliding his hand under mine to give me a rest.

'How am I doing?'

'You're doing great, honey,' said Uriel. 'The wound is closed.'

'We need to replace the blood lost as we don't have transfusion facilities,' said Rotji.

'How?'

'Give his body the energy it needs to speed up production.'

Feeling my hand had cooled sufficiently, Hal slipped his away and I coaxed the bees into Xav, mentally prompting them to find the bone marrow like they were returning to a hive.

Hadn't you better check you've not taken too much? Hal reminded me.

I glanced back down the corridor and saw the furnace was spluttering. 'I have to stop.'

'He needs just a little more to stabilize. Without that we might still lose him.' Rotji was completely empty now, having expended everything he could on this healing.

'But I might end up killing Xav if I take his life force.' I eased my way out of Xav's mind, knowing I had reached the maximum.

'Here, let me.' A new set of hands rested on my head. It was Zed. 'Being the seventh son, I inherited a little of all my brothers' gifts. Find the healing energy in me.' He dropped all his barriers as easily as a guy shucking his clothes for a doctor's examination.

Knowing now what I was looking for, I found his source blazing away in a neat hearth. A little fire compared to Xav's furnace but surely it would be enough? We were so close. *Excuse me while I take over.*

For what you're doing for my brother? I'll have to say, anytime, flower.

Leaving retribution to later for the spread of Hal's pet name, I took all the energy I could from Zed's hearth without putting out the fire, sending that into Xav. We were rewarded by our patient taking a deeper breath.

'Damn,' Xav gasped, 'did someone run over me with a tank?'

Thanks, Zed. I closed the door to his mind.

Believe me, the thanks are entirely the other way round. I could feel Sky high-fiving us both. I realized she had been there too all the time, supporting Zed with an influx of her energy.

I opened my eyes, head spinning. I'd overdone it but it was worth it just to see Xav alert and some colour back in his skin. I pulled myself up by the bedpost but found the floor suddenly rose up to greet me.

I came out of my faint a few minutes later to discover I was lying in the recovery position.

'Back with us?' asked Hal, smoothing my hair off my forehead.

If only I could melt into his chocolate eyes and just stay there. 'Semi.'

'You're lucky, princess, you've got a soulfinder with quick reflexes. You almost did a face plant. As it was, you missed the romantic moment when I caught you and swept you off your feet.'

'You'll have to try again when I'm feeling better. What's going on?'

'Victor's about to meet with Chong. Alex is going with him. Linked to Misty he's going to persuade Chong to tell us the truth.'

I rose up on my elbow. 'I could read his mind for Victor without Chong knowing.'

'Flower, you've done enough. Let the others have a chance to flex their gift muscles.'

I sank back on the pillow. Again he had a point. I wasn't fighting this battle on my own; I had a team with me. 'That flower thing, it's catching on.'

'I know.' Hal grinned.

'Don't think I won't get my own back.'

'I look forward to it.'

Flat on his back on the next bed, Xav raised a hand in my direction. He looked pretty gruesome, like someone who had barely survived a zombie apocalypse. 'Summer, Crystal says anything you want, it's yours.' His voice was rasping but full of the same Xav humour. 'I suggested we name our first baby after you.'

'And what did she say to that?'

'That she already had one big one in the house to look after and wasn't quite ready for motherhood, but I'll work on her.'

I smiled. If Xav was cracking jokes then he really was going to survive, that was if we could get off the island without a battle breaking out again. 'Hal, can we go and see what's happening outside?'

'You recovered enough to get up?'

'If you don't mind stopping another face plant?' I looked up hopefully.

Gathering me to his chest, he lifted me from the bed. 'The things I do for you.'

'Don't believe him, Summer. He loves an opportunity to show off his macho stuff,' called Xav after us.

In the middle of the exercise yard, Victor was facing Chong across the podium. Alex stood behind him, keeping his gaze on Weiner, who had come to the meeting with his gun, not exactly living up to the spirit of a ceasefire.

'So let me get this right: you agree to let us retreat with Summer as long as you are allowed to leave on your yacht with as many of the prisoners who want to sail with you?'

'That's right.' Unbelievably, Chong was still smiling even though he must have realized that his grand gesture had backfired.

'And you give your word that you will not attack us as we leave? We can rejoin the other half of our party at the control room, no tricks, no double agendas?'

'Correct.'

'Alex?' Victor gave him the nod and Alex let Misty fill his mind.

'Mr Chong, are you sure you're not hiding something from us?' Alex asked in his most persuasive tones. Anyone listening would have felt like a cat being stroked by that voice, ready to roll over on his back and purr.

Chong opened his mouth to deny everything and was surprised to find a confession tumbling out. 'There's a second vessel waiting for you, one of my gun-running boats that's equipped with mortars. If we didn't prevail here I was planning to take you all out as you retreat.' He clapped his hand over his mouth.

'You broke the ceasefire,' growled Weiner. 'You used your powers.'

'Not technically a breach as we did not use them to attack,' said Victor. 'Thank you for being so frank with us, Ivan. Now I'll pay you the same compliment. You thought I was a disavowed agent so you'll be disappointed to learn that, thanks to my friends, the Robinsons, this mission has been approved at the highest levels and an American aircraft carrier is coming into range in about,' he looked at his watch, 'ten minutes. Your smuggling pals will find themselves blown out of the water by a computer-guided missile if they take a potshot at us. The island is shortly to be taken over by special forces who have all been trained by myself in ways to deter savant attacks. You're outgunned, outclassed, and outmanoeuvred. I suggest the next words you say are "I surrender" and then hope you can get a good lawyer, as I imagine you'll be joining your allies here in short order.'

With a grunt of fury, Weiner raised his gun but was immediately blasted off his feet by a combination of Zed's kinetic attack and Victor's mind blast.

'I'd say the ceasefire was over,' said Hal. 'Those guys are going to run like rabbits.' He carried me away from the pandemonium that had erupted in the courtyard as it became

249

every man for himself. He put me into the golf cart that had somehow avoided destruction. 'Wanna see?'

'Oh yes.'

His prediction proved correct. The ex-prisoners seized on their last hope: a quick getaway. Pushing and shoving, they bolted for the harbour, gathering members of the other factions as everyone abandoned their posts. We drove down the track to the harbour in their wake. Lucas and Scott followed, picking up any of the prisoners who were thought too unimportant to warrant a place on the yacht. There were quite a few of them, guys who knew when the game was up and had decided coming quietly was the shrewd move now. They were corralled into the barred rooms on the lower floor of the staff quarters, exchanging places with the guards who were now being released.

I watched as Chong's launch, carrying him, Daniel and Sean Kelly and Jim Doors, made it to the side of the yacht. 'They don't really think they are going to outrun an aircraft carrier, do they?'

'I guess they're hoping that was a lie.'

'Was it?'

Hal shrugged. 'No idea. I can't read minds, remember? That's your job.'

'I can't bear the thought that they're going to get away scot-free.'

'Just watch.'

We were joined at the harbourside by our group from the control room. Angel and Misty fell upon me like two puppies on their favourite chew toy. If they had had tails they would have been wagging.

'Summer, you are in so much trouble for going off and having all these adventures without us!' exclaimed Misty.

Angel nodded vigorously. They both looked incredibly

250

cute in their combat gear. 'Yes, you could've at least met your soulfinder when we were there like I did, so you could be suitably embarrassed and confused in our presence. Excuse me a moment.' She touched my arm affectionately and went to join Yves on the harbourside.

'Uh-oh,' murmured Phoenix, joining us. She looked more dangerous than my friends, dressed in stern khaki, hair slicked back, a reminder that she had grown up among a bunch of criminal savants so had an edge we lacked.

Just as she spoke, Yves made a gesture like he was throwing a javelin. The stern of the yacht burst into flame with an echoing boom. With astonishing swiftness, the boat began to slide under the water, tipping so the bow was pointing to the sky. The crew and staff could be seen jumping over the side, swimming for the little boats that had been coming out to them.

Yves wiped his hands ostentatiously and beckoned to Phoenix. 'That felt good.'

She went up on tiptoes and kissed him. 'My gorgeous geek with the powers of a Thor. You are hot!'

He laughed. 'I'm cooking on gas, Phee.'

'Is it my turn?' asked Angel with a far-from-Angelic chuckle.

'Be my guest,' said Yves with a magnanimous wave of his hand, as he got distracted by kissing his wife.

The sea began to churn and a breaker rolled towards the vessel. It swept over the deck extinguishing the flames Yves had started.

'Aw, spoil sport,' muttered Phoenix, breaking away from the kiss.

'She's just thinking of the people in the water,' said Yves. 'Can't have them swimming in burning oil.'

Angel squeezed her hands tight then spread them in a swooshing gesture. Water rushed below decks, hastening the sinking of the yacht. Marcus came running over and picked her up, spinning her in a circle.

'That's my Angel of Destruction!'

'I hope Chong wasn't joking about that room being watertight,' I said as we watched the multi-million pound vessel disappear. 'Or we'll never clear Atoosa's name.'

Looking at my friends gathered on the dockside, I was incredibly touched that everyone who could had come to save me. The only exceptions were Tarryn, who had stayed to look after the expectant Diamond and keep Karla calm while all her boys and her husband were putting themselves at risk, and Margot, who was helping with military logistics and keeping the press away from the story. It was an impressive roll call of soulfinders.

Atoosa approached, hand in hand with Victor. Almost everyone was now gathered on the harbourside apart from Crystal and Saul, who had hurried up the hill to collect Xav in the golf cart.

'Did you say my crown is still on board?' said Atoosa. 'Oh, Victor!'

He kissed her knuckles. 'Don't worry, my love. That's what salvage companies are for.'

Angel patted her arm. 'I can get it back for you if these guys help with the telekinetic heavy lifting.' She gestured to Hal, the Benedict brothers, Marcus and Alex.

'That's what we're reduced to,' said Hal, 'the brawn while you ladies provide the finesse.'

'A glimpse of your future?' And I kissed him, giving Misty and Angel the excuse they were waiting for to whoop and cheer.

Chapter 19

There was a lot to be sorted out once the yacht sank. The aircraft carrier proved not to be a lie spun by Victor. It hovered into view like a floating city, dwarfing the island, and stationed itself just outside the harbour entrance near the site of the sunken yacht. It was a good thing it arrived when it did because there were not enough boats to rescue all the people in the water and it took an efficient navy to round up all the strays. Something about the indisputably huge fact of the ship quelled any further flickers of rebellion. Chong had thought he was taking on just a handful of Benedicts when he had held me to ransom; instead he had found himself taking on the cream of the savant world and the American navy to boot.

Fortunately I did not have to stay with Victor to review with other law enforcement agencies the policy of keeping all these criminal savants in one place. Nor did I have to organize for the salvage of the artefacts once Angel had raised the yacht from the seabed, something Atoosa had volunteered to oversee. The greatest relief was not to have to resolve the tricky issue of what to do with her uncle. I had told Atoosa how Maiwand had been threatened into his predicament but it was clear that he had not made good choices and should have asked for help. Even with the most lenient judge hearing his case, he was facing several years in prison, which surely was only just as Atoosa had spent nearly two years inside a harsh jail thanks to

253

him. The only favour Victor could swing was that it would not be on the island. As a sound manipulator, Maiwand was judged a lesser risk and could live with ordinary prisoners as long as he didn't use his gift. Atoosa and her family would have to decide then what to do about the man who betrayed them, but I guessed that they would be merciful. It was a loving family in that colourful courtyard in Afghanistan, and I could imagine them forgiving him once he'd paid his debt to society.

One forgotten casualty of the battle was Kevin Smith, who had dragged himself off with a bullet in his leg. I only thought of him when Phoenix asked me where he was. In the confusion that followed trying to do a headcount of those left on the island, it was the two of us who found him unconscious and close to death near the cell where I had been held overnight. Phoenix admitted this was the last ending to her story with him that she had imagined: saving his life. He had to be airlifted to the hospital on the aircraft carrier along with other serious cases.

The next two days were a series of partings. First to leave were those heading back to America: Saul, Trace, Uriel, Xav and Crystal, Yves and Phoenix, Zed and Sky. I didn't feel too sad as I knew I'd be seeing them all when we met up at Uriel and Tarryn's wedding later in the autumn. Saul Benedict insisted that now that I had travelled as his daughter, I'd always be one of the family. That started his sons off calling me 'Sis', something I suspected I was going to hear very often in the future. Crystal, Phoenix and Sky invited Misty, Angel and me to stay with them for the girls' night out in Denver before the wedding, something else to look forward to. Line dancing and cowboy boots were mentioned, though I'm not sure if Sky was serious. Angel was already planning to source a pink rhinestone pair and was threatening to get us all matching ones.

I didn't have to say goodbye to the others until we got back to Heathrow. I tried not to think about what it meant to go home to the deal I had with my father. I did very well until I was waiting for my bag on the carousel. Hal had called in a favour from Javid and his family to make sure I was reunited with the infamous pink bag I had abandoned in Mazar.

'You'll be OK?' asked Will. Margot and Kurt were waiting in the arrivals' hall to collect Marcus, Angel and him. They'd warned us not to emerge from customs with them unless we wanted to be part of the paparazzi feeding frenzy. Margot had spread the rumour that Marcus and Angel had disappeared off for a romantic weekend for two in Barcelona to explain their suddenly dropping off the music press radar.

Angel grabbed her silver case off the belt and dumped it on the trolley. 'Want us to come round later?'

'Maybe give it a day or two. I'll come to you.'

She grimaced. 'You'd better or there'll be trouble.'

'I promise.'

'Love you, Summer.'

'Love you too.'

Misty and Alex were next, heading for the coach that would take them back to Cambridge.

'We'll come to London at the weekend. Don't have any more life-changing movements without me!' begged Misty.

'I'll try not to.'

She squeezed me tight, only letting go so that Alex could give me a hug. 'It feels like that bit at the end of *The Lord of the Rings* where people keep leaving,' Misty sniffed.

'But it's only for a few days,' said Alex.

She slapped her forehead. 'That's right. Perspective, Misty, perspective.'

While I was saying my farewells, Hal picked my suitcase up for me and put it next to his holdall on the trolley.

'No need. It's got wheels.' I reached to take it.

'I remember very fondly that it's got wheels.' He whisked the trolley out of my reach.

'Bye, Summer. See you soon!' called Scott, heading off with Lucas to the exit, kit bags on their shoulders.

'Are they leaving you here?'

'Of course.'

'But why?

'I'm coming home with you, that's why.'

'Oh, that's not a good idea. Really not a good idea.'

'I think it's the only idea.' He piloted the trolley like a rally driver through 'Nothing to Declare'. I had to run to keep up with him.

'But my dad will be here to meet me and, oh, it's going to be a whole lot of awkward.'

'I don't do awkward.'

'Well, I do. Often.'

'Hey, Mr Whelan!' Hal was waving to my father like they were best buddies. My dad understandably looked flummoxed.

'What are you doing?' I hissed.

'Starting as I mean to go on.' Hal brought the trolley to a screeching halt at my dad's toecaps. 'Pleased to meet you, sir. My name's Hal Robinson and I'm your daughter's soulfinder.'

'Robinson?' My poor father gazed at him as if he had forgotten how to speak English.

'Yes, I'm also one of the idiots who almost got her arrested for aiding and abetting an AWOL Federal Agent, but she's forgiven me, so I hope you can too.' Hal cocked his head to one side and gave my dad a winning smile.

'Well, I . . .'

'I was also there when she helped save two lives and showed enormous courage in the face of great danger.'

'Danger!' My dad's prepared reprimand for causing him

sleepless nights was crumbling under this onslaught of praise, no doubt exactly as Hal intended.

'And did I mention, I'm her soulfinder, and now she's found me, I'm not letting her go?'

'I . . . I think you did.' Dad jingled the car keys. 'I suppose we'd better get home and discuss this.' Only now did he get to hug me. 'You all right, love?'

'Oddly, I think I am.'

'Does he know?'

'Oh yes.'

Dad patted me once on the back and stepped away from me. 'If you're coming home with us, then I hope you have good shields.'

'The best, sir.'

'Summer's brother is at home too. Winter has been worried about you and wants to see for himself that you are safe, Summer.'

'He does?'

'Don't sound so surprised.' Dad tried to take over the trolley but Hal insisted on piloting it. 'One thing your brother has always been, through everything, is your fiercest protector whenever he could.'

I had recalled Winter driving off my mother from one of her attacks when Chong had mined my mind that once.

'Yes, I remember that now. How could I have forgotten?'

Mother and Winter were sitting together in the living room when we got home, Mrs Bainbridge keeping an eye on them both as she chattered about her infant grandson. I'd not seen Winter for a few months. He was short for a man, about my height, and fragile looking with pale skin and similar green eyes to mine. In fact, I thought him rather beautiful, like a Florentine Renaissance painter's model, not that I'd ever said that to him as any remark of mine was usually taken the wrong way.

Hal let me go in first. *I'll be close by.*

'Hello, Mother. Winter, thank you so much for coming.' I put my handbag down, trying to think how to do this.

Winter came swiftly across the room. I worried for a split second that he might be about to attack me but then I realized he was coming over to touch me, to make sure I really was fine. He held me at arm's length, his version of a hug.

'They didn't hurt you?'

'No, Winter.'

'I was really, really worried for you.'

'I'm sorry that I distressed you.'

'Don't be sorry. You're my little sister. Of course I'm going to worry about you.'

I found tears welling. There was so much our family had forgotten in our constant fire-fighting of my mother's condition; for one, that once upon a time Winter and I had been really close.

Mrs Bainbridge gave me a hug even though my dad was standing right there to remind us she was only staff. 'Good to see you safe and sound, Summer dear.'

'Thank you.' I held the hug for much longer than usual. I was no longer going to be reticent with those people I loved. I'd almost lost them all and knew their value to me now.

'I'll go put on the kettle.' She bustled out. *And who's this tall dark handsome stranger out here in the hallway?*

That's Hal Robinson. He's my soulfinder.

Lucky girl!

From Hal's next emotion, which was surprise, I guessed she had treated him to one of her motherly embraces too.

'Summer.' Mother rose from the sofa and approached. I could sense my father and Winter both tensing, ready to leap to my rescue. 'You seem different?' She brushed her fingers across the back of my hand, part caress, part testing of the emotional waters.

I think this is my signal. Hal came in, looking unapologetically scruffy after hours of travel, unshaven and rumpled.

'Mother, Winter, this is Hal Robinson.'

My mother immediately redirected her steps to him as she was always interested in any new blood in the room. 'Hal, so happy to meet you.'

Dad looked at me. *Are you sure about this?*

Trust me.

'Mrs Whelan, Winter. Summer has told me so much about you.'

'That can't have been good,' said Winter with a self-deprecating laugh.

'What I haven't told you yet is that Hal's my soulfinder,' I announced.

'Really?' My mother's eyes glinted and she gripped his wrist. I could tell she was exerting her full power to sample his emotions.

'Mother!' snapped Winter. 'You're embarrassing us!'

'It's OK. Hal's immune,' I assured him.

Hal patted my mother's hand—actually patted it. 'Mrs Whelan, please sit down. I wanted to talk to you all, not just about Summer and me, but about all this.'

That sounded ominous. *What's going on, Hal?*

Just a hunch. He guided my mother back to her sofa and sat next to her. It was odd for all of us to see someone willingly get close to her without any fear. 'I thought for a long time that I wasn't a savant because gifts don't work on me; I'm a kind of power-canceller. I was talking to Saul Benedict a few days ago—he knows about your family. He told me that soulfinder pairings usually provide the other with what they need. In

259

Summer's case, she needs you to be at peace from the things that torment you, Winter.'

My brother scowled. 'I'm managing. I don't want a stranger coming in here and telling me I need treatment.'

'That's not what I mean, Winter. I am the world's worst speechmaker. Summer's the one who's good at that kind of thing. What I'm trying to say is that I learned when we were healing someone that a savant can transfer their energy into another mind if Summer is in control. I was thinking that if you let her in, I could ring-fence what makes you unhappy, block it off.'

'You could?' Winter looked as if he didn't dare hope. 'You could turn off the voices?'

'Only if you don't want them. I won't do anything you don't want me to do.'

'Wow.' Winter gave a shaky laugh. 'Anything is better than this. I'm up for it.' He pulled me down next to him. 'Do it, Summer. Shut them up.'

I worried now that Hal had promised too much. If this didn't work, Winter might be in a worse place than ever.

Have a little faith, Summer, said Hal.

My dad squeezed my shoulders from behind my chair. 'Please try, darling.' I could tell he was excited that he might, just possibly, get his son back.

I closed my eyes and headed for Winter's familiar brain signature. It was a shock to visit it after so many years of keeping my distance. It was like standing in the middle of a rioting crowd, voices of anyone and everyone who had stood in this locality, ghosts of past arguments, affairs, and mundane conversation melding together until it was impossible to think.

Hal, are you seeing this?

Yes, princess. Let's have a go. Find your brother's gift in all this mess.

I followed my instinct. Winter thought of his power as a deep reservoir that would bubble up and out like a geyser over which he had no control.

Hal reached out and took my hand. *Guide the power where it needs to go.*

I drew on the cool camouflage he had in abundance, letting it pour over the turbulent reservoir. It settled and solidified like ice over a lake. The voices faded then disappeared completely.

Let's see what Winter feels now, suggested Hal.

I gently disengaged. 'How's that?'

Winter was blinking at me like an owl woken in the daylight. 'I can't hear anyone.'

'That's good, isn't it?'

'That's amazing. Oh my God, I can actually hear myself think! Dad, Dad, it's . . . it's just so quiet in here.' He leapt up and ran out of the room. At first I thought he was panicking but he came back a few moments later, beaming. 'I can't hear anyone upstairs either, and there's usually a really horrible voice on the landing, and a screamer in the attic.'

I was crying now. Hal pulled me on to his lap and brushed the tears from my face. He also batted away my mother's hand as she tried to sneak in and steal my happiness.

Winter came over and planted a huge kiss on my forehead and then one on Hal's head for luck. 'How long do you think it will last?'

'I don't know. I guess we'll have to keep it under review. I can check you later and give you a top up if you need it.'

'And, maybe, dear boy,' said Dad, his face ecstatic, 'this will give you the opportunity to learn control over your gift? I'll find some experts who can train you. You never had a chance to learn control.'

'Oh God, I'm just so happy I feel like I'm going to explode!' He turned to our mother. 'You've got to try it, Mother. Please.'

I'd never seen my mother look defensive but she almost curled up into herself. 'There's nothing wrong with me.'

'That's not true, Maeve, and in your heart of hearts you know it.' My dad knelt beside her. 'Once, when I first met you, you still hoped for a cure. You knew it was wrong to live on others, making them feel bad to make yourself feel good.'

'Please, Mother.' I added my voice to the family plea.

'Mrs Whelan, if you don't like it, I promise I'll take my power away and you'll be back to exactly how you are now,' said Hal firmly.

She licked her lips, appearing suddenly very young, the youngest one in the room. 'You promise.'

'Word of honour—and I take my oaths seriously.'

'Well then, all right.'

'Really?' My voice was a squeak.

'Just do it before I change my mind.'

I held my mother's hand, brushing gently so as not to alarm her. I was trembling, and she was too.

I'm here. Keep it together, soldier, said Hal, reminding me not to lose it now.

I walked into her familiar mindscape. Today she was imagining it as an empty funfair, a place of roller coasters and ghost trains, whistles and screams. Where would she place her power in this? There was nothing as obvious as a light or a reservoir.

I can't find it.

Don't look for light, look for darkness, suggested Hal. *She draws other people's lightness to her so I'm guessing hers will be the negative of that.*

Then it's all around us. I could see so much of it at the edges of the bright lights of the funfair. Some of them were winking off as the darkness came back. *And we'd better hurry. I think she's changing her mind.*

Take my power.

Will there be enough?

Well, that is the question. That was Hamlet, by the way. Shakespeare.

Cracking jokes now, soulfinder?

I learned my excellent timing from you, she who declares her love in the middle of a gun battle.

Buoyed up by his optimism, I imagined spreading his power over the funfair like a circus big top, brightly coloured to appeal to my mother's tastes. But she would need something to fill the void or she would go looking outside again. Underneath the big top, memories could now emerge, people to sit in her empty rides and play on the sideshows without fear. I put in pictures of our ancestors, the ones she had had pasted to her screen in her room, the laughing strongman, the fortune teller, the acrobats, even an invisible lady. What felt like a sinister place slowly became an idiosyncratic kind of fun. The darkness was just outside the door, but it was held at bay. *This is for you, Mum.* I left, hoping I'd done enough.

When I opened my eyes, I found my father with his arm around my mother. He was kissing the side of her neck and whispering to her, telling her what a beautiful woman she was and how he had missed her.

'How do you feel?' I asked her fearfully.

'Feel?' She pressed her fingers to her breast. 'Yes, I do feel. Me, I mean, it is me feeling. Is it me, feeling, Aidan?' She turned to my dad for reassurance.

'Yes, darling, it is you.'

She shocked us all by bursting into tears. I don't think I'd ever seen my mother weep before. 'I'm so sorry.'

My dad gathered her to his chest and ruffled her hair. 'It's not your fault, love. It never has been your fault.'

I got up. *I think that's our cue to go. Winter, want to come with Hal and me for a walk while we let them have some time alone?*

Winter followed us out. 'Thanks, Summer, but I'm going to go for stroll through Trafalgar Square on my own and enjoy the quiet. See you later.' He shook Hal's hand. 'Thanks, Hal. I look forward to getting to know you better, but for the moment, just thanks.'

We watched him walk off in the direction of the nearest underground station.

'Trafalgar Square?' asked Hal. 'For quiet?'

'Yes. He's never been able to bear places with lots of history. I guess we've opened up a whole new world of opportunities for him.'

'And for you.' Hal turned us towards Hampstead Heath. We took a path through the park that led to the top of the hill. We climbed in silence, just enjoying being together. When we reached the summit, we stood, my back to his chest, looking out over London. It looked so full of potential on this sunny late summer afternoon—church spires, rocket-shaped towers, skyscrapers, leafy parks and the gleaming white dome of a cathedral.

'I'm feeling pretty spectacular right now,' I admitted.

'You are pretty spectacular,' he agreed.

'That was an awesome thing you did.'

'That we did.' He kissed my left ear, sending shivers in a million directions. 'You realize, of course, that you don't have to stay at home now. If both your mum and Winter are stabilized and we just monitor how they are doing at regular intervals, then the world is your oyster. You can go anywhere, do anything you want.'

I leant back against him. 'I've got to finish school. I like studying.'

'I would never've guessed.'

'Huh!'

'That's my soulfinder: so eloquent. Did you know that "huh!" is the only word that appears in every human language?'

'Huh? Really? Where did you learn that?'

'I have my secrets.' He nipped my earlobe. 'And I'm very good at internet quizzes.'

I was beginning to see that we were definitely each other's lost half; he knew a whole raft of things about which I didn't have a clue. 'I think we'd be unstoppable if we entered together.'

'I like the way you're thinking.'

'So where are you going to be while I'm still studying?'

'Well, I'd say I'm going to be right where I am now, about a centimetre and no more from you.'

I laughed and turned in his arms to look up at him. 'You have a job.'

'I do. She's called Summer and she's this really cool girl who will obviously run the country at some point as she's so talented.'

I batted his chest. 'Be serious.'

He quirked his lips in his toe-tingling smile. 'That's kinda hard for me when I'm feeling so happy.'

'You'll continue to work with your brothers?'

He nodded. 'Savants need people like us. There's always a space for you on the team. You heard Scott back in Mazar. He was serious. You're savant dynamite.'

'And maybe I'll take you up on that if the right mission comes along, but for now, I just want to enjoy the feeling of having choices. I'll put in for a range of universities, if that's OK with you? London, Oxford maybe, others in the south.'

'You can pick anywhere you like. We can move our team, that's not a problem.'

'OK then, York, Durham.' I paused. 'Yale?'

265

'OK, maybe not move it *anywhere*. We are attached to the British Army.'

'Right. Somewhere in the UK then. Oh, Hal, I'm just so happy I could kiss you right now!'

'Why are you leaving it as a theoretical wish rather than trying the practical?' He framed my face in his warm hands and bent down to me. 'You are definitely educationally challenged in some key areas. Let an expert show you how it's done.'

I put my finger to his lips. 'Just warning you, I'm a very fast learner.'

'I'm counting on it, princess.'

Joss Stirling lives in Oxford and is the author of
the bestselling Savants series. She was
awarded the Romantic Novelist's Association's
Romantic Novel of the year 2015 for **Struck**.

You can visit her website at **www.jossstirling.com**.